"THIS ... ...
Man, I don't take that kind of stuff from no one."

"Now hold on there," Tom said. "I think if you checked around, you'd find that our town's barter system is as fair as any in the area. We don't squeeze blood out of anyone. . . . I know it must be tough out on those roads, but you've got to understand that we've got to survive, also."

"I don't understand, man!" The doper pulled a Mauser out and zeroed in on Tom's chest with it.

"Easy, now! No one wants to hurt you!"

"Well, maybe I want to hurt someone! You're someone, Lawman—who's going to stop me?"

"They are . . ."

It worked like a charm. The doper turned around to see who "they" were and found that everyone in the place had a shotgun or pistol aimed at him.

"Here's to the welcome arrival of an exciting new writing team. AMONG MADMEN doesn't miss a beat, though the reader's heart might skip a few."
    —George A. Romero, Director of *Creepshow*

"Nonstop action, suspense, and terror. Starts off with a bang, and keeps slamming you with shock after shock."
                                    —John A. Russo

AMONG MADMEN

by Jim Starlin and Daina Graziunas

A ROC BOOK

ROC
Published by the Penguin Group
Penguin Books USA Inc., 375 Hudson Street,
New York, New York 10014, U.S.A.
Penguin Books Ltd, 27 Wrights Lane,
London W8 5TZ, England
Penguin Books Australia Ltd, Ringwood,
Victoria, Australia
Penguin Books Canada Ltd, 2801 John Street,
Markham, Ontario, Canada L3R 1B4
Penguin Books (N.Z.) Ltd., 182–190 Wairau Road,
Auckland 10, New Zealand

Penguin Books Ltd, Registered Offices:
Harmondsworth, Middlesex, England

First published by ROC, an imprint of Penguin Books USA Inc.

First Printing, April, 1990
10 9 8 7 6 5 4 3 2 1

 ROC IS A TRADEMARK OF PENGUIN BOOKS USA INC.

Printed in the United States of America

This book is dedicated to our
own maniacal moms,
Rosemary and Henrika.

It's no small thing when we feel
how precarious is our existence.
—Vincent van Gogh

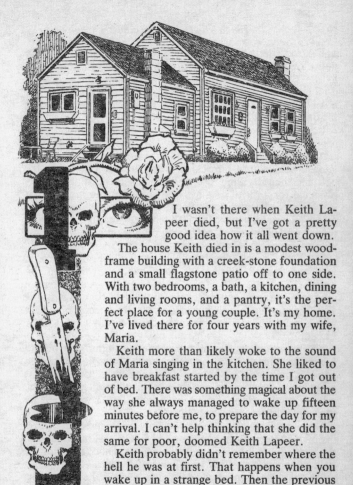

I wasn't there when Keith Lapeer died, but I've got a pretty good idea how it all went down.

The house Keith died in is a modest wood-frame building with a creek-stone foundation and a small flagstone patio off to one side. With two bedrooms, a bath, a kitchen, dining and living rooms, and a pantry, it's the perfect place for a young couple. It's my home. I've lived there for four years with my wife, Maria.

Keith more than likely woke to the sound of Maria singing in the kitchen. She liked to have breakfast started by the time I got out of bed. There was something magical about the way she always managed to wake up fifteen minutes before me, to prepare the day for my arrival. I can't help thinking that she did the same for poor, doomed Keith Lapeer.

Keith probably didn't remember where the hell he was at first. That happens when you wake up in a strange bed. Then the previous night crept back into Keith's awakening consciousness, and he smiled. It's impossible not to. I've been there, I know.

Maria probably showed up at the bedroom door about then, still in that soft and clinging silk robe I like so much, her thick black hair combed out and framing a stunningly beautiful face, her deep-blue eyes crystal-clear, with no sign of sleep in them. Keith probably felt a kind of tightness in his chest as he looked up at her in that morning light.

I expect she cheerfully ordered him out of bed and to the patio for breakfast. Keith probably tried to cajole her back to the sheets, but Maria was adamant about breakfast no doubt and remained out of reach. Keith felt disappointed, but not hurt or belligerent. Maria's smile held just a hint of future pleasures.

Keith most likely discovered his clothes wadded up by the foot of the bed. It didn't matter. His road-dirty denim-and-leather biker gear wouldn't be any worse for this experience. I can picture him starting to buckle on his cartridge belt and then deciding against it. What need could he possibly have for a pistol or a hunting knife this morning? What was there to be afraid of? Some scrambled eggs? A cup of coffee? Certainly not Maria. No, these weapons remained on top of the dresser. Keith Lapeer had gentler things on his mind.

He must have looked terribly out of place in that room with the framed Rembrandt and Delacroix prints on the walls. Off to one side of the bedroom, a large shelf held a miniature bronze reproduction of Daniel French's statue *The Spirit of the Waters,* surrounded by dozens of books whose titles and authors were probably totally alien to Mr. Lapeer.

Keith couldn't have had much trouble finding his way to breakfast, though. The house is small, only one floor; the patio is off the living room. He had to pass Maria's latest oil painting, still drying on the easel: a still life—cut flowers, a book, and a glass of wine on a table top. I wonder if he took any notice of it. Probably not.

Once outside, Keith most certainly went and checked on his bike. After all, that beat-up old BMW was his lifeline to the road. Even if he was entertaining ideas about settling in, he'd have made sure his wheels were all right.

By the time Keith finished giving his hog the once-over, Maria had breakfast ready. He strolled over to the patio and the two lovers embraced. Maria complained about Keith's three-day-old stubble, and he probably promised to scrape it off directly after breakfast. They sat down at the little metal lawn table on the flagstones. It's round and has a hole in the center for the umbrella that the wind tore to shreds long ago.

Maybe Keith started in on his eggs and then noticed he didn't have anything to cut his steak with, so Maria got up, saying she'd be right back with a knife. Over his shoulder

Keith probably told her how he couldn't believe he was really there. It must have seemed incredible to a highway bum like himself that this amazingly gorgeous creature had invited him in off the road, to bed and breakfast with her. There's a better than even chance that he carried on like some lovestruck schoolboy, right up until the moment Maria returned from the house and drove a ten-inch butcher knife into his back.

Lapeer was a big man; I doubt he died easily. He probably reared out of his seat and made a futile grab for the hilt that protruded from between his shoulder blades. But the knife was just out of reach. He'd have been losing an enormous amount of blood, and the lung, pierced by the blade, would make breathing difficult. It couldn't have taken Keith long to realize he was dying and that there was absolutely nothing he could do to prevent it.

I'm sure the thought crossed his mind about then that taking his murderess with him, on his long journey into infinity, wouldn't be such a bad idea. But Maria was already at the gate leading to the road. Perhaps she turned around to survey her handiwork. Maybe she even said goodbye to Keith. This wasn't a vicious killing. In fact, there must have been something about him she liked. She had fed him, loved him, and given him the gift of death. To Maria these were tokens of affection. These were things reserved for special people.

I'm sure Keith Lapeer could not appreciate any of this at the time. But if you must die, and it catches up with all of us eventually, isn't it better to go at the hands of someone who cares for you, even if that person is more than a little crazy?

Josh Woodward was walking down Pine Hollow Lane with a fly rod over his broad shoulder and a faint smile playing around his lips at the prospect of a fine morning. His plan was to spend it down at the Chichester Creek casting for a dinner of brown or rainbow trout. The morning was already too hot for the long-sleeved work shirt Josh had on. As soon as he was down by the water, he was going to drape it over a tree branch and let the nice hot July sun bake the weariness out of that old black frame of his.

But all those plans suddenly evaporated when he saw Maria walking across the road toward the field. As soon as he spotted her, he knew. But he didn't want to admit it. So he yelled, "Good morning," and got no response. Maybe she hadn't heard him.

Maria drifted past the collection of six rusting cars, one van, and three motorcycles that formed a bizarre gateway to the field. She headed for the hillock that rose off to the left of the acreage. Her eyes never strayed over to the ten wooden crosses that rose out of the wildly overgrown timothy grass at the far side of the field. This was all part of a ritual Josh knew by heart. Still, he couldn't quite admit it had happened again.

There was only one way to be sure. Josh says he walked through the double row of hemlock trees to the front gate and peered into the yard. Keith had finally breathed his last by then. He lay facedown on the patio, a small puddle of crimson spreading out from his body, staining the flagstones. Josh walked numbly over to him, dreading that it

might be someone he knew, and was relieved to find a stranger.

A battered old wallet gave Josh the dead man's name and informed him that Keith Lapeer was originally from Royal Oak, Michigan. Josh found it amusing that anyone still carried a driver's license. It should have been renewed three years ago. Unfortunately, there was no longer any Michigan Department of Motor Vehicles, as far as Josh knew. He stuffed the wallet back into Keith's hip pocket and headed to the garage for the pick and shovel.

Josh probably cursed Maria as he dragged Keith out to the field. It didn't matter. She couldn't hear him. She'd be off in her own little world until everything was tidied up again.

It could have been a great day for fishing. The cool water splashing around his ankles would have felt terrific. That's all it was now . . . a could-have-been. A regret. Josh's morning would be filled with gravedigging and planting. Dammit! She wasn't even his woman!

But if Josh didn't clean up this mess, Maria would stay out in that field until I came home. Josh couldn't quite remember if it was that day or the next that I was due back, so he grimly set about his task. After all, I was his best friend, and friends do for each other. Besides, Josh felt a little guilty for not keeping a close eye on Maria as he'd promised.

As he began to dig laboriously into the earth, his anger, seeking a target, turned itself rather irrationally on the biker lying on the ground beside him. "Where was your head at, man? Didn't you see the warning signs? What did you think that graveyard of cars and bikes was all about? Didn't you feel death rushing at you? This ain't the free-loving sixties and seventies. You can't trust no one . . . especially the pretty ones. You were stupid, pal, and now you're dead. You forgot that insanity is the national pastime and that paranoia is the only way to survive. So rest in peace, you poor lame jerk."

At that same moment I was traveling
down what was left of Route 28 through
the Catskill Mountains of upstate New
York with a canine partner hanging his
head out the cruiser's window. Route
28 used to be the main road connecting
the city of Kingston to the little college town of Oneonta.
The trip between the two communities had once taken about
three hours; now three days was a conservative estimate.

Fire-gutted vehicles and blasted-out sections of pavement
slowed progress to an average speed of about fifteen miles
per hour. No one dared travel at night because of the
raiders and crazies. So racing along the highway at fifty-
five to get home before the cocktail hour was the stuff of
memory.

Dirk Parker, our ham radio operator back in Shandaken,
hadn't picked up any signal from Oneonta for a couple of
weeks. So it had been proposed that a little recon patrol
might be in order. Oneonta wasn't a customer for our gas,
so it held little importance for the good folks of Shandaken.
But since it never hurts to know what's going on around
you, the matter was discussed, debated, and finally decided
upon. I volunteered to drive up and check things out. I'm
sorry I did. What a mess.

Raiders had hit that fair city and torched most of the
downtown section. The town fathers, prosperous burghers
all, were either dead or hightailing it to some safer haven.
Though a few local cops were still trying to hold it together,
it was pretty apparent that it was all over for Oneonta. It

was well on its way to joining an ever-growing list of towns and cities that once were, but are no more.

I got out of there as quickly as I could. Successful raids bring more raids on any community that's unlucky or weak enough to be marked an easy target. I didn't want to be trapped by the second wave of marauders that was sure to hit.

On my way home I got a call over the two-way radio from Phoenicia Petroleum. They asked me to accompany a couple of their boys to Margaretville for a barter session. Seems they'd had a little trouble the last time they'd been through there and wanted some extra muscle with them this trip. I agreed to help out; after all, it's my job. I'm the chief constable of Shandaken Township. Constable Tom Laker.

My traveling companion, riding shotgun on the seat beside me, was named Rex, once dubbed Rex the Wonder Dog before I really got to know him. He was a mangy little beast, sort of a cross between a cocker and a bloodhound. But when I'd seen him limping down Wittenburg Road three weeks earlier, my heart had just melted. I had to help him out and become his master. See, I hadn't had a pooch since I was a kid, and dogs have become a real rarity. I figured he might prove to be a valuabe asset at some future barter session.

He had broken his front right forepaw somehow, and it was painfully obvious that he wouldn't survive much longer out in the wild like that. So I wrapped my arms up in two blankets and put on the pair of heavy-duty lineman's gloves I carry in the trunk of the patrol car. I chased Rex down and wrestled a splint onto him. I should have known by the enthusiasm with which he bit into my protective padding that Rex would be trouble.

After I finished playing Florence Nightingale, I carried Rex over to my cruiser and left him there while I removed my "surgical gear." I came back to find that Rex had repaid my kindness by pissing all over the front seat.

Later that night, while we camped out near Arkville, Rex broke into my knapsack, devoured three days' worth of food rations, and took a leak on my sleeping bag with me still in it.

The night I brought him home, Rex immediately endeared himself to me by pretending that the left boot of my best pair of L. L. Bean's was actually a doggie rawhide toy.

Next he urinated on the sofa. The following night, I threw him out in the backyard. So he dug up Maria's flower bed and created a small lemon-colored lake on the porch for me to step in barefoot when I got up the next morning. I was seriously beginning to consider completely cutting off that animal's intake of fluids.

I didn't have much luck at trading him either. There was a man in Woodstock who offered to trade a shotgun for Rex. But he left with his shotgun and six stitches when he made the mistake of trying to pet Rex. Then another fellow in Boiceville changed his mind about offering me twenty boxes of ammo when Rex watered the poor man's shoes.

So it looked as if Rex and I were a team, whether I liked it or not. He didn't look like he was going anywhere, and no one else would tolerate him anyway. But he kept me company while I did my rounds, managed not to look too bored when I told him my old war stories, and finally stopped making a mess of the patrol car. An undeclared truce just materialized, somehow. I fed him, kept my friends from shooting him, and drove him around in the car getting fresh air. And in return he allowed me to call him my dog.

We were still about two miles north of Margaretville when I circled an overturned tractor trailer and Rex and I first spotted the smoke. It was coming from a rest area down the road. The smoke was ominous, too black and thick to be a campfire. So while Rex sampled the breeze for some data on this new development, I reached in back, pulled the shotgun out of its rack, and pumped a shell into the chamber.

I rolled up to the rest area as slowly and quietly as my patrol car, with its rotting muffler, would allow. It looked bad. The ball of flames had once been a Dodge camper. Whatever had happened, it had taken place no more than ten minutes ago, and whoever had done it hadn't passed me heading north. That meant they were either ahead of me on the highway or still there. Either way I'd soon have to deal with them.

Next to the camper lay the charred body of what I guessed had been a man. Not pretty. About fifteen feet away, another man was sitting, propped up against a boulder. But I didn't figure he was responsible for this carnage. The top of his head was missing. It looked like the work of a shotgun, at ten paces and from behind.

Off to the right about fifty feet, a small campfire still burned. I could see a can of something warming on one of the rocks ringing the flames. The woman lying by the fire must have been the cook. She didn't look too awful from where I sat. At least I couldn't see any blood. But she was lying on her side with her back to me, naked from the waist up. I figured I could live without seeing what her position hid from me. She was probably dead. I wasn't going to check.

The setup was all wrong. There was too much overgrown brush around the rest stop. A small army could be hiding in it. "Sorry, sister, but you've just become one of the hundreds of unburied dead that litter the Catskills these days," I muttered.

I nudged the cruiser's transmission into gear and prepared to drive off. But I made the mistake of taking a last glance around the site. That's when I saw the woman's leg move. Dammit! She was alive. A lot of folks would still have left her. But I just couldn't do it. Maybe that's why they gave me that badge I keep in the glove box. People with little common sense make great law enforcement officers in this brave new world of ours.

If anyone was in those bushes, I wanted to hear him. So I slammed the car back into park and cut the engine. I got out without closing the door behind me and loosened my .45 automatic in its holster. Rex decided to stay and guard the car.

I crossed the distance between the cruiser and the man with the topless head as fast and as low as I could. The dead man and I shared the protection of his boulder for a minute. No one fired at us. No one made a sound.

The woman was right out in the open. I hated that. But there was nothing to be done about it. She let out a low groan to remind me that she was still among the breathing. So I stood up and started to head over to her.

I was sure that at any moment I would hear the loud report of a gun and be only moderately surprised when my chest blew open. I saw myself falling, in slow motion, into a pool of my own blood. I could hear my heart beat its last as scavengers from the brush stripped me of my worldly possessions. This wasn't exactly how I had pictured a person's life flashing before his eyes.

But none of that happened. If the killers were in that undergrowth, they were keeping their heads down and playing it cool. Maybe the sight of Constable Laker and his shotgun had them quaking in their boots. I kind of doubted that. Either they weren't there or they were waiting for something. Waiting for what, though?

It only took me about a million years to reach the woman. I knelt beside her, keeping the rifle pointed toward the tall weeds with one hand. I touched her shoulder with my other hand. She rolled over and gleefully tried to blow my face off with a .22 caliber target pistol.

Maybe it was the ten gallons of adrenaline I had pumped into my system, or maybe it was the barely audible little giggle she couldn't quite suppress as she brought the gun up toward my face. Whatever it was, it saved me. I zigged as the bullet zagged past my right ear. Then I brought my left fist down hard, across the bridge of her nose. I felt something break.

Even over the ringing in my ears, I could hear the lady's four friends howling and bounding out of the foliage. The nearest one was firing a revolver at me. His space-time continuum, however, must have been a uniquely personal experience, maybe drug-assisted, maybe not. He wasn't even trying to aim. I guess he figured sooner or later one of those wild shots would strike home. I didn't want to take a chance on his being right, so I aimed quickly and fired. Some job—upholding truth, justice, and the law of averages.

I had a choice to make then. My next target was either the guy with the machete or the jerk who was trying to free the barrel of his shotgun from a tangle of underbrush. I chose the jerk. He flopped backward into the brush, minus his face. That choice almost proved my undoing.

The machete came at my head faster than I had expected. I barely got the barrel of my rifle up in time to deflect it. Then the big ugly brute that was attached to it slammed into me. I lost my balance and started to go over. It all became a matter of reflex action then, no carefully planned moves, only stimulus and response. I let go of the shotgun, latched onto the arm with the machete, and brought the brute down with me.

That's when I saw the fourth man. As I noticed him, he

was calmly taking a bead on me with a twelve-gauge. The only thing that saved me was that at that moment his friend, the brute, decided to stand up, pulling me up with him as he went.

I'm no lightweight, so I was exceedingly impressed by this feat. He then proceeded to further demonstrate his physical superiority by whipping me about wildly, in an effort to shake me off his arm. Let me tell you, this guy was strong. His arm was as thick as a stove pipe, and half the time I had a grip on it, my feet dangled in midair. Husky Tom Laker was nothing more than a rag doll to this monster. I held on to his arm for dear life. I liked it there.

As long as I stayed on this midway ride, his pal couldn't get a clear shot at me, and the old boy himself couldn't chop me into hamburger. All in all, it was quite an acceptable situation. But I knew it was too good to last. Sooner or later, the fact would sink into even this brute's little pea brain that it would require considerably less work to batter me into oblivion with his free hand than to continue with our current aerobic workout.

So when Man Mountain next swung me in the general direction of his buddy, I let go. Unfortunately, the time and distance of my solo flight gave him the opportunity to bring the shotgun up in front of himself for protection, so I slammed full-length into them both. It hurt like hell, and my vision filled with countless little explosions of light.

I felt myself falling and was pleased to find something squirming underneath me. My .45 was in my hand. I must have drawn it in midair. I don't remember. There was this darker section to the popping lights and for some reason it seemed as good a place as any to fire. I put two rounds into it, and it receded.

Getting to my feet seemed to be absolutely essential. So I gave it a try and found that it wasn't nearly as painful as I had expected. Somewhere on the way up, my vision cleared, so I turned around to see what the guy with the shotgun was up to. He had his own problems.

I hadn't realized until then just how puny-looking he was. He must have been around five feet ten, but he couldn't have weighed 125 pounds, soaking wet. The broken arm he was using to lift the barrel of the shotgun made him look even more vulnerable. Someone had obviously landed all wrong when we collided. I almost felt sorry for him.

But then he growled at me, and spittle ran down his chin.
I put a bullet between his eyes and turned to see what the
sound behind me was.

It was the brute trying to get to his feet. He still had his
machete in hand, but he also had two rivers of blood running down his bulging tank-top shirt. They looked too sym-
metrical to me, so I gave him a third. He fell over and that
was that.

I stumbled back over to the boulder and sat down next to
the gent who was still sunbathing his gray matter. Looking
at him, I thought how lucky I had been. Extremely lucky.
Their trick with the girl had been well conceived, and it
would have succeeded if any of them had known how to
handle firearms. They all looked as if they might have been
college kids once. Luckily they hadn't been ROTC.

The woman—make that girl—stirred. She looked to be
about eighteen or nineteen. She got up on her knees. I had
been right about something breaking when I hit her. Her
nose was sitting on her face at an odd angle, and blood ran
down her chin onto her bare breasts. She growled at me.
There seemed to be a lot of that going on.

I brought my automatic up off my knees and leveled it at
her. She threw her arms up to protect her face, as if that
was going to help her, and let out a pathetic little whine.

No way. I wasn't that far gone. I lowered my cannon and
said, "Beat it, Goldilocks. Playtime's over and your mother's calling you."

It took a few moments for it to sink in. Then she scrambled to her feet and staggered out of the rest area. I wearily
watched her disappear up the road. Maybe I should have
shot her, I don't know. Alone up in the mountains, she
wouldn't last more than a couple of days. Perhaps a bullet in
her diseased little brain pan would have been a mercy.

I sat there for a while, totally exhausted. I just couldn't
move yet. I knew mobility would return after the rush
subsided. No need to push it. There was still plenty of time
before my rendezvous with the tanker. Somewhere off in
the distance I heard a car engine start up. It didn't seem all
that important.

Rex finally decided it was safe for him to come out of the
car. Not exactly Rin Tin Tin. He hobbled over, sat down

about ten feet from me, and dispassionately surveyed the devastation.

Suddenly a big blue Buick drifted down the road and into view. It had a huge supply of provisions tied to the roof. I could see Goldilocks at the wheel. She flipped me the finger, stepped on the gas, and roared out of sight. So long, sucker. I cursed myself for not having blown her head off. The guy who observed that no good deed ever goes unpunished would certainly have plugged her. The hell with it.

My anger got me moving again. I walked over to the campfire and checked out the cuisine. Campbell's pork and beans. Good. I hadn't had breakfast yet, and mayhem has always proved to be a real appetite builder for me.

"You want some of this, Rex?" He gave me a withering look and walked over to the brute's ample dead carcass. He questioningly turned his head back toward me and licked his chops.

I felt my hand tighten around my .45. Then the tension drained out of me. *"Bon appétit,* Rex."

What the hell, it meant more pork and beans for me. Besides, it was just one of those stinking berserkers.

Wappingers Falls, New York, wasn't a bad place to grow up in. It was sort of halfway between rural and suburban. I didn't grow up suffering any of the traumas associated with big-city life, and for a while I felt kind of guilty about that. Some uncomprehending and juvenile part of me thought you had to have a rotten childhood to become a decent human being. Yes, I've managed to grow out of that ridiculous notion, thank you.

My dad worked at the Westchester General Motors stamping plant. I got my size from him and I like to think a little bit of his easygoing personality. I don't remember him ever getting really angry with anyone. I think now that it might have been because he was so big. I don't think he would ever have let anger take hold of him, because of his fear of what he might do. That was probably why I worked so hard to maintain an even strain. One hundred ninety pounds spread over six feet and three inches never exactly made me a colossus, but the couple of times I'd let myself go had proved highly destructive and terribly unnerving.

Mom was your typical housewife, meaning that she worked like a demon to keep Dad, myself, and my two brothers clean, well fed, and loved.

It was a time when the single-wage-earner family was the rule, and Mom liked it like that just fine.

I made it through high school being as average a student as anyone could be. My dad was on his way back from the Big Apple when that delivery van bounced over the guardrail and plowed into his brand-new Chevy Belvedere. He'd been down in the city picking up my graduation present. I never found out what that present was. They say he died instantly.

A dark cloud of unreality settled over me when my father was killed. I couldn't believe he was gone. He was the first person I ever knew who died. The suddenness of it made it even worse. The severity of the accident forced us to accept a closed-coffin service, so I never even got the chance to look him in the face and say goodbye. For the longest time my heart just plain refused to believe that he wouldn't be showing up at six o'clock after his shift at the plant. It didn't feel right to start dinner without him. His favorite chair looked so empty, and the evening television programs weren't nearly as entertaining without his editorial comments.

For some reason, my college applications never got filled out. So when my draft notice arrived in October, I accepted it with a certain amount of relief and, yes, even some giddy excitement. Eighteen years old and life had gone sour on me. Friends and family had become nothing more than irritating interruptions. Nothing they could say or do was interesting enough to pull me out of the shroud of self-absorption and self-pity I had wrapped myself in. Everything about me was stagnating. I had to escape from Wappingers Falls, and this was as good a way as any to do it.

Four months later I found myself in the Nam. Nothing in my quiet Catholic upbringing had prepared me for the madness I found there. It turned out that Vietnam would be my college. For eighteen months I took a crash course in soul-numbing boredom, blood-chilling fear, camaraderie, back-stabbing, power-playing, crossed purposes, futile exercises, subverted morals, dealing death, and cherishing life.

I left that place with the usual allotment of psychic scars and sweat-drenching nightmares. They made me a terribly difficult person to live with for many years.

But I have to say one thing for the Nam. It prepared me for the world that I now live in. That undeclared war cauterized a section of my soul which has made it possible for me to survive in a world where half the people you meet are insane and the other half you can't trust. A majority of the best-adjusted people I know these days are Vietnam vets. Ain't that a hoot?

I got back to the real world just in time to sit by my mother's deathbed. She had decided the lump she found in her breast wasn't worth worrying about. By the time she could no longer ignore it, it was too late; the cancer had spread throughout her body. We buried her next to father. I'm glad she didn't live long enough to see what life has become. Hers was a world of household chores, Sunday picnics, and friends she could depend on. That's all gone now.

My brothers and I were strangers by then. They'd gone off to college and didn't know what to say to the wild-eyed alien the war had turned me into. I had the feeling they suspected that I had tasted human flesh while overseas and they didn't want to take any chances of having that suspicion confirmed. Our conversations ranged from merely tedious to hair-pulling boredom. Whenever they caught me drifting onto any subject they might consider unsafe, something would come up that would require their immediate attention.

So I resettled in New York City and lived off unemployment for six months. By the end of that period I had consumed enough beer and pot, bedded enough beauties, and talked to enough other screwed-up Vietnam returnees to feel like taking a shot at working my way back into the flow of mainstream American life.

A series of odd jobs followed. I quit more than I was fired from, so I guess I wasn't doing too badly. A friend of mine finally arranged for me to take the NYPD entrance exam, and I passed it. This outrage terminated the relationship I had going at that time with this dark-haired, leggy teacher named Linda. Her liberal upbringing and her developing taste for cocaine wouldn't allow her to be associated with a fledgling pig and capitalist tool. Too bad. I liked her, but I liked the idea of being a cop more.

My first assignment was up in the South Bronx. It was inevitable. I came to the job with absolutely no political connections. Fortunately I ended up with a well-seasoned veteran for a partner. Sergeant Ralph Barr kept me from getting my head blown off more than once. After two years under his tutelage I was ready to take on anything New York City had to toss at me. Or at least that's what I thought. The future has a way of throwing you unexpected curve balls.

The department moved me around quite a bit after my tour in the Bronx ended. It was during that time that I came across my first vege. He came wandering up from a Times Square subway station, buck naked. At first I thought he might have been mugged or was stoned on something. But when I questioned him, it was as if no one was home in that slightly balding head of his. Even a person drugged up to his eyeballs will acknowledge your existence to some degree. But not this guy. He heard nothing. He said nothing. He just kept staring straight ahead at something that wasn't there. Whatever he saw had become his entire world, and nothing, but nothing, was going to tear him away from it.

Since then, I've seen veges burned by cigarettes or cut with knifes, and it doesn't register on them. Their bodies keep breathing and shuffling around, but there isn't anything going on behind their eyes.

The medical types thought it was just an extreme version of your garden-variety schizophrenia. But after extensive testing, they found that these new cases suffered from a chemical imbalance of some kind that your usual schizophrenic doesn't have. They couldn't figure out what was causing this or how to cure it. So it became a new disease for the boys and girls at the *New England Journal of Medicine* to write articles about.

At first the problem seemed to be only a big-city headache. Sociologists and other learned people would get on the tube and tell us how this new malady was being caused by the ever-growing complexities of urban life. Each claimed to be the only one who had the answer to this "future shock" dilemma, and the only cure for it was pumping millions of dollars into whatever program he or she was championing that week. Of course, this theory was shot all to hell when veges started showing up in the suburbs and rural areas.

The next guess was that it was some type of communicable virus. Plagues, you see, like the moon, wax and wane with unnerving regularity, or at least the public's perception of them do. AIDS was still with us, of course, but the fear had somehow become passé. The thrill was gone. So the new media darling, if a disease can truly be one, was crowned queen, dubbed as the "new" number-one threat and promoted daily. It was the strange set of symptoms that jointly became known as Schizophrenia X. Policies were debated. The number of people vegging out continued to grow. Finally the situation got so bad that martial law was declared.

All the veges were herded together into specially designated hospitals and quarantined. The government figured this would take care of the problem. They were wrong.

It took a while, but eventually the scientists had to admit that Schizophrenia X wasn't a communicable disease. Too few of the people who cared for veges fell victim to the disorder, while entirely too many of the people who had had absolutely no contact with any known Schizophrenia X patients were vegging out.

So no one knew why they were doing it, but the veges kept popping up. There wasn't any stopping them. It wasn't happening only in this country. All across the globe, Schizophrenia X was claiming its vacant-eyed minions. For a long time, Russia avoided confronting the problem of its citizens turning out the lights and pretending no one was home. But then some bigwig decided to vege out during the May Day celebrations in front of the international press, and our Red brothers had to come clean. No one has ever found out what became of the thousands of Schizophrenia X patients Mother Russia "never had."

Six months after the first Schizophrenia X patient was diagnosed, it was estimated that 5 percent of the world's population had fallen victim to this dread new disease. Suddenly the governments of the world had to deal with 210 million people that couldn't even go to the bathroom by themselves. There wasn't enough existing hospital space to deal with this emergency. No urban area in the world had the medical facilities to handle even a tenth of those who suddenly needed the kind of care that the veges required. The system immediately ruptured, but gamely tried to limp along.

Of course, New York City, always the trend setter, showed the world how to deal with the deplorable situation.

A fact-finding committee was formed. After weeks of researching and examining the problem, it concluded that no cure of Schizophrenia X was anywhere in sight and that there might well never be any cure. Your ordinary schizophrenia had been around for as long as anyone could remember. Science had found no cure for it. What hope was there for stopping this newer and tougher strain of the same disease?

One member of the committee went so far as to recommend immediate grand-scale euthanasia as the government's only real option. Of course, the mayor turned that idea down flat. These Schizophrenia X patients still had their civil rights to be considered. Besides, the election was coming up in six months. What politician in his right mind would want mass murder to be held up by an opponent as a major accomplishment of his administration?

But certain committee proposals were acted upon. State and local governments swiftly terminated any support or funding they had been giving to Schizophrenia X research. It had to be done. All these now nonproductive citizens, who had once been taxpayers, were no longer contributing to the public coffers. This put a big bite into the government's revenues. A certain amount of belt tightening was a necessity.

So the politicians did what they do best in these situations. They cut their losses and tried to pretend the problem had been solved. Why worry about the health and welfare of a voter who just doesn't give a damn about eating, shelter, or producing a taxable income?

Perhaps I shouldn't paint too black a picture of those elected officials. They did agree to continue to finance the vege hospitals—at their current budgets. It couldn't be helped that the number of Schizophrenia X patients was doubling every other week. There wasn't any more money to be poured down that particular drain.

Within days, the conditions in these hospitals deteriorated to a point where no sane person would even consider stepping into one of them, let alone work there. Every hospital room had at least thirty veges crammed into it. Along the walls of the corridors, countless Schizophrenia X patients squatted, staring off into space and waiting for God only knows what. Doctors had an average patient load of about two thousand. Nurses were assigned at least two hundred cases each. But I've got to hand it to some of those medicos. A lot of them stayed on even after it became obvious that their task was impossible. They were being asked to perform the labors of Hercules with the body of a ninety-eight-pound weakling. But they tenaciously hung on until they either dropped from exhaustion or joined the ranks of the undead stacked against the hallway walls.

Of course, that problem was also eventually solved. One day, this clever civil liberties lawyer who used to work for the city went to court and argued successfully that the quarantining of the Schizophrenia X patients was unconstitutional. Incarcerating them without due process was violating their civil rights. The City and the State of New York both happily went along with this decree and immediately discharged all the patients from its government-run hospitals.

Every corner of New York seemed to have a half-dozen veges wandering around. They slept and deposited their bodily wastes wherever and whenever the mood hit them. Relief centers were set up throughout the city to feed them. But the only veges that ever showed up were the ones the police rounded up out of the better sections of town and dumped there.

It was during these trying times that I took a night off, went out to relax at a cocktail party, and wound up meeting Maria Burgos. The party was at a neighbor's apartment. He was in publishing. It was kind of funny. We had never had much to do with each other before the Schizophrenia X crisis began, but had become quite friendly since then. This terrible situation started bringing people together. New Yorkers had always been a very class-conscious group. The rich had always partied with the rich and the poor had always suffered with their own kind. Cops sort of floated between the two extremes, not classy enough for the rich, distrusted by the poor. Police officers weren't exactly considered social outcasts, but it was damn close.

So when I got this invitation from my neighbor, I realized the social taboos were beginning to crumble. Folks were so scared of what was going on that they just wanted the comfort of having other people around. It no longer mattered what you did for a living. It was enough to know there were other people who could still hear what you were saying and would answer you. "A mind is a terrible thing to waste" took on a new, even more tragic meaning.

Your life and your sanity are the only two things worth a damn that make up an existence. They're all you can truly call your own. But they're also the most ephemeral entities in the universe. Any threat of their loss serves to illustrate just how pitifully vulnerable we all are. It's a demoralizing thought to contemplate.

That was probably what was bothering Maria's date. His name was Bill Hobart and he had come to the party to forget. Or more precisely, to forget just how much he was forgetting lately. He was afraid he was becoming a vegetable. So he drank too much and passed out only an hour into the party. At least it silenced his mental conversation and the accompanying fear for one night. Lots of people had trouble sleeping.

As it turned out, all of Bill's worry over his mental stability was a big waste of time. Three weeks later, while in a drunken stupor, he wandered out in front of a garbage truck and was forever relieved of all worries. It was reported as an accident, but I've always wondered. Suicide was gaining popularity as a simple, quick, permanent solution to the terror that life was rapidly becoming.

Maria was breathtakingly beautiful and seemingly alone, so I went over and fumbled my way into a conversation with her. It was embarrassing. I've never been what you'd call a successful pickup artist. Too self-conscious.

She was cool to my advances at first, but I pressed on. I don't quite know what I did or said, but finally something clicked. To this day I don't know how I managed to push the right button that convinced this gorgeous creature it was safe to let her defenses down around me. That's when I discovered the warm human being that was hidden within. The amateur pickup suddenly became so much more.

We went out for coffee after the party. The sun rose to find us with our heads together still talking, unwilling to call it a night. I dropped her off at her 86th Street apartment with a date promised for the following Friday.

That date turned into a weekend together at her apartment, which culminated with us driving over the state line to get married. I know it was crazy, but that sort of thing happens during difficult times. Why do you think there are always baby booms during, and directly after, a war?

A friend of mine from back in high school, Art Davis, got in touch with me shortly after the wedding. He was now the chief constable of a little township in upstate New York, Shandaken. Two of his deputies had vegged out on him and he was looking for replacements. Would I be interested in relocating? I jumped at the chance.

The veges had started dying on the streets faster than anyone had imagined they would. They zombie-walked into traffic, stepped off the tops of buildings, and fell down staircases faster than the paramedics could pick them up.

Most of my work days were spent hauling dead and broken bodies down to the city morgue for mass burials. Fortunately I was out of the city before they began starving to death. I wouldn't have been able to take that.

With all this confusion going on, the city's criminal classes decided it was time to put on a big push. New York had never been the safest place to live, but it now plunged into total anarchy. A state of emergency was declared and the National Guard was brought it, but it didn't help much.

Maria and I grabbed our belongings and headed for Shandaken. We knew it was running away, but we didn't care. New York was doomed, and one more cop wasn't going to save it. The crooks and psychos were claiming the city as their own. That town was finished.

As it turned out, Schizophrenia X was about to mutate. It changed into something much darker and far more dangerous. I didn't know it then, but the berserkers were coming.

The first berserkers were written off as either drug-crazed criminals or normal citizens who had gone over the edge from the pressures of what life had become. Only after a few of these crazies were taken into custody alive was it discovered that they had a chemical imbalance very similar to that of the Schizophrenia X patients. The new condition was media-christened Berserker's Syndrome.

These pop tarts could walk, talk, and almost pass for normal. But these jokers weren't going to be merely another burden to society. They proved to be walking death. This new breed of loony was weird and terrifying. They killed. That was their insanity. Butchering animals or people was all they cared about. They did it without warning or remorse.

Their motivations differed from one crazy to the next. Some of them were hallucinatory. The people they murdered were demons attacking them. Voices would tell them to kill for God. Some of the victims, according to their assailants, had allegedly begged to be put out of their miserable existences.

Uncontrolled sexual urges also played a part in some of the killings. The berserkers would get turned on, and no matter how many people they slaughtered, it was never enough. Mutilation usually played a big part in these killings.

Some of these monsters had no explanation for why they did it. It seemed like a good idea, and questions of morality simply never arose. What's more, the transformation from normal to berserker was almost instantaneous, literally as easy as stepping over a line. You might be talking about the weather with a fellow you had known for years. Then without warning he'd be at your throat or trying to bash your head in with a rock.

It might not have been so bad if these freaks had preyed upon themselves as much as they did on normal people. But a lot of them began to flock together without killing each other off. Crazies of a like bent began to form loosely organized bands. Singly they are a frightening experience. In a group they're a nightmare.

Decades of New York City's gun control laws had left its general population pretty well defenseless against this new wave of insanity. Thousands were slaughtered trying to escape the city. Those who boarded themselves up in their homes were either overrun or burned out.

The Army and National Guard did a pretty good job of protecting the important parts of New York, like the financial districts, food supply outlets, government offices, and radio and television stations. The folks who were lucky enough to work at these places set up house at their workspaces. Their families joined them, whenever possible.

But these safe havens began to disappear as members of the military began to fall victim to the same malady they were assigned to stave off. Every soldier who went berserk usually took two or three of his former friends with him before he was brought down. Some of the crazies in uniform decided the other side looked like more fun, so they took off with as much weaponry as they could carry, to help fortify their brothers in lunacy.

Up north, in the Catskill Mountains, every household had at least one firearm in the house, so the situation wasn't quite as desperate. Small hamlets, like Phoenicia and

the surrounding township of Shandaken, which got organized quickly, fared the best.

They set up local militias, which killed off or drove out the berserkers. Border patrols were instituted. Strangers were screened before being allowed into town. Instant farms sprouted up overnight. Town co-ops were organized to distribute and ration food. Population ceilings were determined and enforced. It wasn't pretty, but it worked.

I watched a good part of the decline and fall of American civilization on television. The cable system brought the evening news to the scenic vacationland of the Catskill Mountains just as always.

The latest theory the media were favoring as to why everyone was going zonkers was that some unknown agent had gotten into our air and/or our food chain. Industrial pollution was the prime suspect. But there were some murmurings about a government experiment gone out of control. Whether it was the Russian or American government depended on who was telling it.

Then one night the news brought us all the story of the Crazy General.

It seems that one fine day, some two-star Air Force bigwig's mind unraveled and he barricaded himself into a Nevada bunker, claiming he was ready to deploy America's entire stockpile of atomic missiles at the Russian menace. He was one of the folks who firmly believed the Commies were responsible for all the current problems, and he was going to show those damn Ruskies that they couldn't push us around like that.

This bunker was some place so ultra, super top-secret that no one had ever heard of it. The story was that it was a kind of doomsday installation that the military had covertly constructed in case the worst possible scenario came into being. Supposedly, the entire NORAD fail-safe system could be overridden from there. This was the place where World War III could conceivably start if the liberal in the White House decided to pussy out during some major confrontation.

I can't imagine what the conversation was like on the hot line between Moscow and Washington that night. Someone must have talked real fast and sounded awfully convincing.

For hours this lunatic general held the world at bay. He was linked up with the major television stations via telephone. Once he got on the air, he harangued America for being weak and unworthy of its grand heritage. Then he cursed the Commie hordes and said nasty things about their parentage. And all the while he did this, he claimed his thumb was poised over the one button needed to start Armageddon.

Finally, as dawn rose over Las Vegas, a Delta Force trooper took careful aim through a ventilation shaft and put an end to the general's show. I figure the old boy was just one of your usual run-of-the-mill burn-outs. A berserker wouldn't have bothered with any speeches. He would just have pushed the button.

Of course, the following day, a White House spokesman on the tube assured us that there had never been any real danger. All the talk of this bunker's being a fail-safe override center was erroneous. Everything had always been under control and would continue to be so.

Twelve hours later it was announced that Russia and America had agreed on an immediate disbanding of their nuclear stockpiles. All missiles and bombs were to be disarmed and their firing mechanisms smashed upon removal. This work was to be carried out by personnel who had no less than two armed guards per man watching them at all times.

I actually thought it was all pretty amusing. Gallows humor, I guess. Ever since the end of World War II the specter of nuclear annihilation has loomed over mankind. First there was MAD, Mutually Assured Destruction. The superpowers then tried unsuccessfully for decades to agree upon some form of arms control. But all this effort produced was staged media events, well-publicized summit meetings, and little else. Next there was Star Wars. SDI was going to be our salvation. But I read somewhere that a truckload of sand shot into space in the right orbit would knock out 90 percent of that weapons system. I couldn't understand how a setup that cost billions of dollars and could be wiped out with a little dirt was going to save squat. But what does a dumb cop like me know?

Then a maybe crazy, maybe not so crazy old man decided to pull a stunt which cost him his life. Suddenly everything looked different. For the first time in history, *everybody* realized it could actually happen. In fact, with the way people were flipping out left and right, there was virtually no way to avoid it.

All it would have taken was one berserk cruise missile technician, crossing the right wires and pushing the right buttons, to set into motion a series of events that would end what was left of mankind.

So suddenly, out of the clear blue, all the really crazy sons of bitches—the ones in charge—decided to mend their ways. I guess they didn't want to look quite as mad as the people who were now threatening to tear down everything that they represented. So the arms race unceremoniously and abruptly ground to a screeching halt.

The funny thing is, nobody much cared by then. They had other, more pressing things on their minds. Global destruction or survival was no longer a burning issue. It had all become extremely personal. The world narrowed and the concept of the "global village" died of obsolescence. No one cared about politics, ideologies, national boundaries, or any of that crap anymore. Or about anything, really, that didn't directly relate to survival.

You can't waste time worrying about what some clown in Washington might do that will affect your life when you've got to keep a close eye on the guy or gal standing next to you. It doesn't matter that he or she might be your friend or a member of your family. Anyone might try to kill you at any moment anyway. So you'd better stay on your guard. "Ever Vigilant," the old police motto, is certainly a wise rule to live by these days.

I guess they took care of all those nuclear warheads without any major foul-ups occurring. I haven't spotted any mushroom clouds on the horizon. I'd feel a whole lot better about that entire situation if I had heard a follow-up story about it on the tube. But I never did. Television transmission relays out of New York City ended abruptly one afternoon.

One of my deputies had the set on at the station house. He was livid. They had cut him off in the middle of his favorite episode of *Gilligan's Island*.

So my world has been reduced to the Catskill Mountains and my only responsibility, as constable, is to keep Shandaken Township and its five hamlets free of chaos, criminals, and crazies. At night, I pray for God to mutate whatever it is that caused the insanity into something that would drive all the lunatics into a frenzy of suicide. That's the only way I can see for this situation ever to be set right. I want life to go back to the way it was.

God hasn't gotten around to answering my prayers yet, of course. Maybe that's because this is all His doing. This might be His way of thinning out an over-populated planet. Or perhaps He decided we'd gotten too uppity with all our hydrogen bombs and space flights. Is this His way of putting us in our place? I don't know. Maybe it's all some nasty joke He's having at our expense. I can almost see Him up there in the clouds having a good chuckle over our predicament with Zeus or some other deity. Man plans, God laughs. Right?

But I guess I'd better watch that kind of thinking, shouldn't I? My line of work depends too much on luck and blind faith in certain things. Just because it looks like God's dead or has turned His back on the world doesn't mean I should go around blaspheming and antagonizing Him.

Maybe tomorrow I'll wake up to find that this had all been a bad dream and none of the killing or dying had really happened. But I've awakened from many a night's fitful sleep during this endless nightmare, and the detail of the horror is too clear for me to really have much hope.

I'd go on . . . because suicide doesn't hold any appeal for me and I'm fresh out of other alternatives. It's not much of a life, but it's the only one I've got.

I hate berserkers more than anything else in the world. Everybody hates them—because they're what we may all become.

4

I drove past Margaretville and found the fuel truck already waiting for me at the abandoned gas station outside of town, where we had arranged to meet. Bernie Leonard and Dan Wrightson lounged near the dead gas pumps. The two of them looked unmistakably like the cousins they are. Both are medium-height, rawboned, wiry dishwater blonds in their midtwenties. Their personalities, on the other hand, are as different as day is from night. Bernie emanates an easygoing friendliness; Dan's a tightly wound skeptic. They complement each other perfectly and make a great team. I hid the cruiser behind the station, leaving Rex in the car to sleep off breakfast.

Dan and Bernie watched my every move as I came up to them. You always have to keep your guard up when anyone approaches you these days, even a friend. I didn't resent their caution. After all, they hadn't seen me in almost a week. I could easily have turned berserker in that time. I figured because there were two of them that they were still okay. But I kept my eyes open and a little distance between us until we chatted a bit.

"Hi, guys. Sorry I'm late."

"No sweat, man. Bernie and I just got here ourselves. How you doing?"

"Getting by," I replied as I watched Bernie check out my soiled trousers and the split shoulder seam of my shirt. My apache dance with the berserkers hadn't exactly left me in top form for *Gentlemen's Quarterly*.

Bernie loosened the revolver in his holster as he observed, "You look a little the worse for wear."

"Had some trouble up the road. Five crazies ambushed me. They were pretty inept as bushwackers, so I got some new hardware out of it. Shotgun, pistol, some ammo, and a machete," I said as casually as I could. Bad move. I immediately saw that I had handled it wrong. I wanted to allay any suspicions they might have had about my appearance, but the off-the-cuff way I'd explained it had set alarms going off in their heads instead. Sometimes it's not all that easy to convince folks you're not bonkers.

"Where's your dog?" Dan asked.

I smiled broadly. At last that damn animal was going to prove useful. "He's napping back in the car. Why don't you go back and say hello. I'm sure he'd be glad to see you."

So Dan did just that. Bernie remained behind, glancing uneasily at me and nervously fingering his gun. I was sort of afraid he was going to shoot his foot off. Suddenly I heard Rex growl ferociously, and Dan let out a lusty yell. A moment later Mr. Wrightson came scurrying around the side of the building holding his right arm.

He looked at me sheepishly and said, "The little shit nipped me! I just wanted to make sure he wasn't dead."

"I told you he was napping. He hates to have his beauty rest disturbed. Did he break the skin?"

"No, but I don't understand how you tolerate that nasty, flea-ridden cur, Tom. He's a monster." Sanity certified.

I owed Rex one, so I came to his defense as best I could. "He's got his good points—not many, I'll grant you, but a few. Shall we get going? I'd like to get back to town before dark."

Dan jumped behind the wheel. Bernie grabbed the shotgun position. I climbed up onto the tanker and parked myself behind an ice cooler than was centrally located and bolted to the top of the rig.

Bernie leaned out his window and yelled, "Catch!" as he tossed the switch and wiring up to me.

I caught it on the first try, plugged it into the small junction box that was welded to the side of the cooler, and called back, "All set! Let's hit it."

Dan slipped the big semi into creeper gear and we were on our way to Margaretville.

*   *   *

There hadn't been any oil exploration in the Catskill Mountains for nearly half a century. The geologists knew there was black gold here, but the low cost of foreign crude made pumping oil out of these mountains economically unfeasible. So for decades the Catskills lay untapped and unspoiled.

But about a year before anyone had ever heard of Schizophrenia X, the OPEC nations finally got their act together, stopped trying to shaft each other, and decided to start in again on the western nations. They cut back production, and the cost of oil went through the roof. The prices at the pump and for home heating oil tripled. The late 1970s were here again.

So a new, domestic outfit called CATEX set up a small refinery halfway between Hunter and Phoenicia. New York City didn't like this, because it claimed the refinery threatened the groundwater that ran down to the Ashokan Reservoir. This reservoir was the source of nearly half the city's drinking water. But the demand for black gold was greater than any ecological considerations. So after CATEX installed a few extra safety devices it got the green light from the state and federal boys to start pumping and producing.

They sank a half-dozen wells around Ulster and Greene counties. It looked like they were going to make a nice little business out of it. Unfortunately, Schizophrenia X and the Berserker Syndrome hit and effectively put an end to their little entrepreneurial dream.

Most of the plant's staff were outsiders who headed for more familiar territory when things started getting bad. But fortunately, two locals had been working there.

Warren Green had been an assistant foreman in the refinery. Johnny Morelli had worked the wells. They got together with the Shandaken town board and convinced them that taking over the plant was not only a great idea but the only way to keep the town alive.

You see, Shandaken does not have a lot of bottomland. The cultivable acreage is limited because of the mountainous terrain. These rocky slopes and valleys make it easy to defend the town, but make it difficult to grow food. We could produce enough to feed our current population, but everyone knew that our ranks were going to grow. We'd need more people to strengthen the militia and replace the folks who were going to vege or berserk out on us as time went by.

So we annexed the refinery. The folks in Hunter didn't like this move at first. But we pointed out three things to them that settled the disagreement before it ever got out of hand:

1. They had more flat land available to them for food production and were already set up for that kind of enterprise.

2. We had a couple of men who knew how to get this operation going again and keep it going. No one from Hunter had worked at the plant, so the best they could probably manage was to blow the place up with themselves inside it.

3. We had more guns than they did.

After about four days of haggling, we granted Hunter preferred-customer status and agreed to refine the oil from the one well in Hunter. We cut the same deal with the town of Fleischmann, which had two wells. Ever since then, things have worked out fine between our three little communities.

Trouble is, not all the towns in the area are as well organized or as endowed with marketable resources as we are. Margaretville's a good example. Before the crash, Margaretville got by on lumber and tourism. But all of the towns in the Catskills have at least one lumber mill, so there's no local market for Margaretville's wood. And the tourists—well, the big-city people stopped coming up here a long time ago. Margaretville does have more farmable land than Shandaken, but it also has more people. They've always been kind of lax about enforcing population quotas.

We try to be as fair as we can with them. We've worked out a couple of deals where they could send down work crews in exchange for gasoline and oil. We've had the gangs do road work and some construction on our town's fortifications. But there's only so much of that kind of thing we can use. Our oil business is our survival. If Margaretville can't come up with the barter that we ask for our petrol, some other town will.

That's the crazy part about the way things have worked out. Inside the townships, socialism has become the rule. It's the only way to handle the situation. Everything is shared equally. Everybody has a job to do, and in return everybody gets a fair share of food, fuel, and whatever luxury items we can procure.

But when it comes to towns dealing with other towns, it's hardcore capitalism with no holds barred. No one gets something for nothing. The marketplace sets the worth of an item or service, and that commodity doesn't leave town until something of equal value is exchanged for it. Most folks in Margaretville understand this.

Unfortunately, Margaretville has never been very good about separating the workers from the shirkers—or trouble-makers, for that matter. There's a sizable group of men there who haven't adjusted too well to the new order of things. They're the type who always seem to have some kind of a medical problem whenever there's work to be done, but when they get boozed up and feeling mean, they seem to have no trouble at all picking on someone half their size. A couple of these characters are former residents of Phoenicia. We had to ask them to leave. We were real nice, but firm about it. They never forgave us, though, for failing to appreciate what they had contributed to our little community.

One of these layabouts was Luke Chesterman. He was the first person I saw as we pulled into Margaretville. The word "trouble" stood out all over him, like a road sign. He was taking a hit off a pint bottle of apricot-flavored brandy when I spotted him. He stuffed the bottle into his hip pocket and sullenly followed us down the road to the gas station. Mayor Dunderson was waiting there for us.

Dan and Bernie hopped out of the cab and walked over to the mayor. I stayed on top of the tanker with my cooler and switch. My job was to keep an eye on the crowd that was already forming around the fuel station. But I kept half an ear on how Bernie was doing with Dunderson.

Mayor Dunderson is a heavyset man in his early fifties; he looks like his food ration is a wee bit larger than anyone else's in Margaretville. He's a fascinating relic, a leftover government official from the town's pre-berserker days. He keeps the community running smoothly and is obviously smart enough and tough enough to keep at least one step ahead of the rougher and meaner elements in town, who might just covet his job. He beamed his best politician's smile at Bernie. "How was the trip up, boys? No trouble, I hope."

Bernie was busy looking into the cartons that were piled up by the gas pumps. He didn't bother turning around to reply to the mayor. "Uneventful. You know, Dunderson, this doesn't look anything like what we talked about on the radio. You're short again."

Dunderson carefully arranged his face into an impassive mask, then forged ahead with his obviously prepared statement. "Well, lads, things haven't been going as well as we had hoped of late. We've had too much rain this summer and trouble with borers in the corn." It was all part of the game to Dunderson. He loved the bartering and was a champ at it. His slow and cartoony manner was designed to give the impression that he'd invited you into a friendly little game of checkers. But the truth was that his "fumbling excuses" were a very respectable opening gambit.

"Yeah. We noticed that when we examined the last load. I'm to check every ear this time before I accept delivery."

"Of course, but as you can see we've got more loaves of bread than we agreed on, and I hope you'll accept them in lieu of the short fall in corn."

Finishing his tabulations, Bernie turned back to the mayor. "You're also short on eggs and canned goods. I'm not going to be able to accept this in exchange for the petrol." Good defensive move. This match could possibly go on for quite some time.

I turned my attention back to the crowd. Bernie would be able to handle the mayor without any help from me. The problem I suspected I was going to have to deal with myself was presently forming over on the sidewalk. Chesterman was gathering a crowd around him, a crowd both noisy and restless but too far off for me to catch what they were saying. They were all big beefy gents, like Luke himself, except for one pimply-faced kid of about nineteen or twenty. He was as tall as the rest of them, but didn't have the kind of meat on his bones that his companions did. Chesterman was sharing his brandy with this kid and seemed to be lacing it with a lot of attention. I had the feeling ol' Luke was priming his young friend for something nasty.

Across the street from Chesterman and his pals stood Margaretville's chief constable, Ben Ferris. He was nervously watching the goings-on. The rumor mill had it that Chesterman had worked the constable over pretty badly last month. Ferris was in his mid-fifties and not exactly up to this line of work anymore. But he was a second cousin or something to Mayor Dunderson, so he kept his job and did the best he could.

Ferris looked like a man who was trying to figure something out. I was hoping that something might be how to help us if Chesterman decided to cause trouble. But that hope dimmed as the constable limped his way down the street, then over to the old department store and out of sight.

Bernie was on the radio, calling Phoenicia to find out whether Mayor Dunderson's latest proposal would fly with our own mayor and her councilman. They always stayed near the town's com center whenever a load of petrol was scheduled to arrive in Margaretville. Mayor Dunderson's short counts were an accepted and expected part of the negotiation.

Chesterman's crowd started getting louder. The good ol' boys were all slapping Pimples on the back and yelling, "Go tell them, Ken!" and "Don't take no shit from them, boy!" Ken pushed his way through the crowd and began strutting over toward the tanker. His companions spread out a bit. It didn't look good. I was ready to start putting my wagons in a circle.

Dan saw the kid coming and came around to head him off. "You know the rules. No one but the mayor comes near the tanker while delivery is taking place."

Young Ken halted his advance and glared at Dan. When that didn't produce any noticeable result, he looked back toward his mentor for obviously much-needed spiritual guidance. Chesterman screwed up his face and nodded his approval and support.

Thus fortified, the youngster turned back to Dan, puffed up his chest, and squared his shoulders. "I want to know how you sleep at night after coming up here and bleeding us dry of all the things we need to survive," he demanded.

Dan grinned and answered, "I sleep just fine, sonny. Don't trouble yourself about it. Now why don't you just go back over to the sidewalk. We don't want no trouble now, do we?"

I was surprised when Ken turned and looked like he was about to heed Dan's advice. But after only a few steps he turned again, pointed at Dan, and in his best Jimmy Stewart voice yelled, "Did you hear what he said, people of Margaretville? He has no trouble sleeping at night after he strips us of our food and clothing in exchange for his gasoline!"

I listened to Ken's oration, amazed. What we had here was a genuine dyed-in-the-wool crusader. I realized that this kid was 100 percent sincere in his outrage. In his mind's eye, he was adorned in white garments and rallying the citizenry to rise up against the dark-garbed agents of the evil Catskill oil cartel.

From the smirk of Chesterman's face I could tell that he had helped fan the flame of this young man's passions with approval, promises of support, and apricot brandy. I wasn't at all sure what Luke Chesterman was up to, but I was damn well going to be ready for it. I shifted the switch to my left mitt to free up my gun hand.

"Why do we put up with this exploitation? Why don't we rid ourselves of these greedy scavengers?" he bellowed. Ken was really warming up to his subject now. He was getting kind of poetic and swaying a bit. Too much brandy. But then he went too far. "Why don't we liberate this oil from these devils? Haven't we paid for it a dozen times over, already?"

Dan pumped a shell into the chamber of his shotgun. This gesture caught the young orator's attention. He shut up. Then Dan took a couple quick steps forward, grabbed Ken by his shirt collar, and hauled him back toward the tanker.

"You want to know why you're not going to be taking anything away from us devils today, punk?" Dan bellowed into the face of his captive. "You try anything stupid, kid, and we'll blow your fucking town off the fucking map!"

Wrightson gestured toward me and continued, "You see that man up there on the fuel truck, punk? You see what he's got in his hand? That's a dead man's switch! See that cooler the wires of the switch lead to? Well, that ice chest is full of plastique explosive! We've got twenty pounds of that shit in there!"

Dan shoved the young rabble rouser away. Ken lost his balance and landed rather heavily on his rear end. He was down but not for the count. From this undignified position he drunkenly demanded, "What the hell are you talking about?"

"That's something your pals didn't bother to tell you about, did they? You see, as long as my friend up there keeps hold of that switch, everything's just fine. But if he should let the terminals of that switch separate for any reason, those twenty pounds of plastique are going to blow.

They're going to explode right above several thousand gallons of very volatile gasoline and fuel oil. Do you have any idea of what that would do to your precious little town and its citizenry? It would instantly char-broil all of downtown Margaretville, that's what!"

Dan's little speech unpleasantly reminded me of how vulnerable I was sitting on top of this liquid bomb. This rig was one of three tractor trailers Shandaken township possessed. Two of those rigs were modern aluminum-bodied tankers. A bullet going through one of those fuel tanks would do no more than cause a leak. I wasn't sitting atop one of those fuel trucks. The tanker I was trapped on was affectionately called Ol' Faithful. It was nearly fifteen years old, held about four thousand gallons of fuel, and was very vulnerable to stray bullets.

I suddenly noticed that ol' Luke had been inching forward during this exchange. Suddenly it hit me what he was up to. The crazy bastard. I quickly checked out the position of Chesterman's men, and my fears were confirmed.

They were all lined up so they could take out Bernie and Dan without worrying about hitting the fuel truck. I wasn't to be a target. My guess was their plan called for them talking me down from the tanker after the slaughter. They probably figured that with my two friends dead, they could convince me that my only hope was to show them how to defuse the plastique. I wouldn't sacrifice my life just for a load of gasoline now, would I? They'd promise me my life and put a bullet into me once I made everything safe for them.

Well, I saw the game plane, but I had no idea how to counter it. I didn't want to instigate a shoot-out while sitting on top of this tanker, and yelling a warning would only start the fireworks that much sooner. I was stuck. We'd really botched it this time.

On all other occasions, our strategy had been to let a town's own sense of self-preservation work for us. The crazies on the roads, we knew, we'd have to fight. Townies we figured we could bluff into behaving. It never occurred to us that anyone who wasn't a berserker would be crazy enough to start a firefight around this much gasoline. We hadn't counted on Luke Chesterman. But I wasn't going to see him survive this fiasco. To hell with it. If I was going to die, there was no reason to put if off any longer. I reached for my gun.

Chesterman saw me make my move and grabbed for his shoulder holster. But before either of us had his gun clear, I heard the dull crack of a small-caliber pistol. Ol' Luke jerked a little bit and looked rather confused. Then another and similar report sounded and Chesterman fell over on his face.

Suddenly the streets were filled with gunfire. I had my own gun out by then. But every time I took a bead on one of Chesterman's cronies, he'd spout little crimson fountains of blood and fall to the ground before I could fire. I took a quick look down at Dan and saw that he was having the same problem.

Then, as suddenly as it started, it was all over. Like the finale in a Fourth of July fireworks display, its abrupt ending was eerie. All that could still be heard was the low moans of the wounded survivors of Luke Chesterman's doomed expedition. I looked around and did a quick body count. By my calculations there were five dead, another likely morgue candidate, and two who might just survive this encounter with a little medical aid.

Mayor Dunderson casually walked up to the prone figure of Luke Chesterman and fired another round into him. Luke didn't look like he really needed it. The Helwan 9mm looked awfully small, but quite at home in the mayor's meaty fist.

He then strolled over to Ken, who was still sitting on the pavement. Ken's pimply face looked horribly confused, scared, and sober. He stared up at Mayor Dunderson with the look of a person who knew he wasn't going to like the answer to the question he wanted to ask.

"I trust you've learned a valuable lesson today, young man. From now on, I hope you pick your friends with a little more care." Dunderson slipped his Helwan back into its shoulder holster under the lapel of his sports coat, turned, and dismissed Ken: "Now head on home and tell your mother I'll be a little late for supper, tonight. I've some work to do at the office."

The mayor then threw back his head, cupped his hands, and loudly announced, "It's all over, boys! You can come down now."

I looked up to see who he was speaking to. There on top of the department store roof was Constable Ferris. He had a scooped hunting rifle in his hands. I spotted two of his deputies on other buildings before they turned to leave. They were similarly armed.

The mayor sauntered over to Bernie with a big grin on his face. "I apologize for all this fuss, my boy. We've had this problem, you see, that we've been meaning to take care of, and this seemed the only way to handle it."

Bernie kept rubbing his hands together and shaking his head. "Seems to me, Mayor, it was a mighty dangerous way to clean up your trash. If one stray slug had hit our tanker . . . well, I don't even want to think about it."

Dan, always the pragmatist, said, "Couldn't you have handled this in a more discreet manner?"

The mayor shook his head. "No. As much as I would have liked to have someone sneak up on each of those thugs and slit his throat while he slept, it couldn't be done. The citizens of Margaretville still labor under the misapprehension that this is a civilized little town. They'd never stand for their mayor going around having people assassinated. It had to be done this way to show we still really have control of the town."

I felt my two cents' worth of fury spring to my lips. "Your honor, you took a damn big chance in not informing us of what was going down. In our ignorance, we might have started shooting everyone in sight—yourself included!"

This pronouncement took Dunderson by surprise. He stared at me for a moment or so before answering. "Take it easy, Tom. We only got wind of their scheme to hijack your truck the other night. We sent two men to clue you in, but I guess they must have missed you somehow."

"Were they supposed to meet me or the tanker?" The question was only a formality. I already knew the sad answer.

"You. We'd heard over the radio that you were on your way back from Oneonta."

"Were they in a Dodge camper?"

"That's right. Did you see them?"

"Yeah, but not until after a pack of berserkers got done with them. I'm sorry. I took care of the crazies. It was all I could do."

Dunderson pulled a handkerchief out of his hip pocket and mopped at his forehead. He stood there quietly for a moment, lost in thought. "Well, thank you for that at least. I must be going now. I've got to let the families of those men know what's happened. I take it the terms of our exchange have been settled?"

Bernie nodded agreement and asked, "So where's this case of scotch that's supposed to make up for the food shortages?"

"Inside the gas station door. Help yourself," Dunderson said as he turned to go. "I think you'll enjoy it—it has a marvelous bouquet. My cousin, Waldo, makes it."

I watched the old boy hustle on down the street. What a piece of work he is. I suddenly knew, without a doubt, that feisty ol' Mayor Dunderson was the only thing that was holding this town together. When he died, Margaretville would also. There couldn't be two of him in this burg.

Of course, I shouldn't have been surprised. I'd heard of some of his past victories. But this one topped them all. In less than an hour he had eliminated what must have been a very dangerous element in his town, laid the trouble between his community and ours to rest, and set his son back on the straight and narrow as he saw it. Plus he managed to do it all without creating any political ill will within his little domain.

It took us less than an hour to transfer the contents of our dual-compartment tanker to the station's holding tanks. The food was loaded on top of the tanker, covered with a tarp, and tied down. We left Margaretville without any further excitement. The trip down Route 28 was also "uneventful," as Bernie liked to say.

Rex was sitting out in front of the gas station as we pulled in. When we came to a stop, Dan tossed up his keys to me and said, "How about a few cans of plastique?" I selected the right key and removed the padlock that kept the cooler closed to prying eyes. Of course, I found no plastique to chuck down to Dan and Bernie, but I figured one of those cold Millers would do just as well. Much more thirst-quenching, too.

I chugged down several long, ice-cold, satisfying swallows from my beer and sat back. Suddenly I was very tired. The day had been too long, humid, and nerve-racking. I wanted to get home and take a nice hot bath. I wanted some food that hadn't come out of a can. But most of all I wanted to hold Maria in my arms and have her tell me it was all going to be okay.

It was a little before seven o'clock when we pulled into Shandaken that evening. The trip back to town went without incident; our early arrival pleased me, because it meant I had about two hours of daylight left. I love long July days. And there was still some business I wanted to attend to before heading home.

I followed Dan and Bernie onto Route 214 and watched the tanker head out of town to the refinery. I'd told them to inform Warren Green, their supervisor, about what had happened in Margaretville, but no one else. The fact that our tankers had no doomsday charges in their coolers was a secret entrusted only to the few who needed to know this—the drivers, the top brass at the refinery, the mayor, and the constabulary. That charade, however, suddenly seemed terribly foolish and dangerous.

I'm sure Dan and Bernie realized by now that they had almost been taken out today. I hadn't driven back in the cab with them, so I had no idea how they were reacting. Not well, I imagined. They were both invited to the emergency meeting I was calling for tomorrow. I knew I'd hear about all their fears and anxieties then.

I pulled the cruiser into the stationhouse parking lot. Even after several years, the place still looks more

like the restaurant and bar it used to be than the police
station it has become. The town hall, sheriff's department,
and constables' offices had all shared a small building out on
Route 28 until the trouble with the berserkers started. Then
it was decided that everyone would feel much better having
a police presence right in town. So we were given an out-of-
business restaurant as our headquarters. It's the only station
house I've ever been in that has a huge, ornate wooden bar
in the middle of its squad room. Of course, we'd emptied it
of all the alcohol and filled its shelves with files, maps,
ammo, and extra firearms. Still, it looks pretty unusual, and
newcomers looking for the police station always think they've
wandered into the wrong place.

The town government has taken over the top floor of the
Hotel Phoenicia, a block away. It was a bit of a tight fit
squeezing all its files and desks into the little rooms above
the hotel's bar. But after the constable's office moved into
town the city fathers suddenly realized how vulnerable they
were, sitting all alone out there on Route 28. They immediately hightailed it into town. Official functions and trials are
now held below in the bar, just like in the old west. All
things considered, it's worked out pretty well.

I left Rex sniffing and poking around in back of the
station house. He was persona non grata inside. But that
was okay with him. He was more than happy to stay out-
doors, where there were acres and acres of virgin territory
behind the building that he hadn't had a chance to explore
and befoul yet.

Ricky Skeats greeted me as I walked in the door. He was
one of my new officers. He looked like he was going to
work out just fine, after all. I noticed a report lying half-
finished on his desk. Paperwork was the one part of police
work Rick seemed to be having trouble with. I suspected my
return was a welcome respite for him.

"Anything of interest happen while I was gone, Rick?"

"Nope, it's been pretty quiet. Had a gang of about fifteen
bikers pass through town, day before last. But they weren't
any trouble."

"You almost sound disappointed. Not getting bored with
this job already, are you?"

"No, Tom, you know it ain't that. It's just that I've been
wondering about when I might get a chance to get some

road work in. Something like a fuel run, maybe? Patrolling the city limits does get a bit monotonous."

"You may not feel so hot about doing any fuel runs after tomorrow. I'm calling an emergency strategy meeting for ten in the morning. It'll be here in the squad room. I want all constables that are not on road patrol to be here. That goes for you too, Hollaster."

Ben Hollaster, the only other one of my officers present, finally pulled his nose out of the old magazine he had it buried in. For a second I thought he was going to say something. But he just grunted, which I took to mean he'd be there. Benny—as most folks around here knew him—and I seldom if ever talked. There was a good reason for that. We hated each other.

Benny had always been a problem around town. He drank too much, and liked to fight and break things. When he got properly juiced up, he made it a habit to run his car into other people's property. I would have run him out of town years ago, but he was too damn useful. When it came to getting a group of men together for any dangerous purpose, Benny Hollaster was always the first to volunteer.

It didn't matter to him whether it was tracking down a berserker or facing a gang of road raiders. Benny was ready and willing, and damn good at dealing with any situation that called for guts and brutality. He feared no man, sane or insane. In fact, he never requested backup unless the odds against him were at least five to one.

Benny was a local boy. He'd spent nearly his entire life in these mountains. The only thing that had ever torn him away from his roots was a friendly letter from Uncle Sam back in 1968. Like me, he'd won an all-expenses-paid vacation in the Nam. Unlike me, he'd finished his time in the army cooling his heels in a guardhouse. Benny busted up a Saigon hooker two weeks before he was due to ship home. He broke her back. The only thing that saved him from some hard time was his record in the field. The Rangers had taught Benny a useful trade, fighting and killing. He was well suited to the work and would have had a home for life in the Army. But his rotten disposition screwed it up for him. He returned to Shandaken with a dishonorable discharge and no future.

Back in the pre-berserker world, his criminal record alone would have been enough to keep him out of any police force. But the days of judging an individual by what's written down about him are long gone. Now a person is measured by his actions, size, and skills. How you feel about a man's personality doesn't enter into it anymore. If he can do the job, he's got it. At least that's how I felt when I hired Hollaster. Benny was an animal, but I felt if I got him on my side at least he'd be easier to control. An opening came up in the department and I asked Benny to fill it. He worked out all right for the first six months or so. But then the idea of how much power he had as a constable began to go to his head.

I started to pick up rumblings about Benny, but no one would come forward to actually accuse him of anything. I could hardly blame folks. Benny stood about six feet four and had about thirty pounds on me. He was built like a professional wrestler. And strong—good God, yes. Some part of me was hoping nothing would ever come of those rumors. It they did, I knew it meant Benny and I would have to have some kind of showdown. There was something about the blackness behind Benny's eyes that made me want to postpone that confrontation as long as I possibly could. I admit it. He scared me. A lot of people do. For lots of different reasons. Benny was way up near the top of that list, though.

But then one night, he finally pushed it too far. I stopped back unexpectedly at the station house that evening; I'd left the book I was reading behind. I wanted to finish it that night. I wasn't even aware he was on duty, let alone what he was up to.

Joyce McKern had been one of our elementary-school teachers. Everyone in town liked her. She was a lovely, warm person, always ready to lend a hand with a problem. If a woman's husband berserked out or was killed, you knew Mrs. McKern would be there within the hour with food and comfort. She was just good people. That's why it seemed so outrageously unfair when Joyce McKern herself vegged out at age thirty-five. She had so much life ahead of her and so much still to give. She wasn't dead, of course, but the results were pretty much the same as far as most folks were concerned. Her husband, Terry, didn't see it that way, though.

A lot of men and women leave their mates out on the road when they go vegetable. Other folks put their former

loved ones out of their misery with a bullet. Since no one's
ever come back from that state, they figure why put off the
funeral until the body dies. There are no longer any laws on
my books about euthanasia. It's a family matter now. There
are still a few hard-line "right to lifers" who curse me for
this decision. But I manage to live with myself and sleep
okay at night, so screw 'em.

But there are a number of good people who figure that
the ones they love are still in there somewhere, behind
those vacant eyes, and they continue to treat them lovingly.
It's not an easy job taking care of people who can't feed or
clothe themselves or go to the bathroom alone. And veges
have a bad habit of walking off into dangerous situations, so
you've either got to watch them constantly or tie them
down. They only sleep when they feel like it, so you've got
to be on the alert twenty-four hours a day. It's a road less
traveled. The folks who choose this way have my respect.

Well, Joyce McKern slipped out on Terry somehow. He
might have dozed off or perhaps just turned his back on her
for a few too many minutes and she was gone. It happens,
no matter how careful you are. Benny must have come upon
her during his rounds. He'd more than once said what a
good-looking woman he thought she was. I guess I shouldn't
have been too surprised when I found the two of them
together at the station house.

But I was, and I was appalled. I stood there for a moment
and stared at them. Benny, looking embarrassed, was trying
to get his pants back on as quickly as he could. He kept
mumbling something, but I can't recall if I even heard what
it was.

Everything had been pushed to one end of the desk,
forming a pillow of sorts for Joyce's head. Her long bare legs
dangled off the other end. She quietly stared up at the
ceiling. There was no expression on her face. There hadn't
been for nearly a year. Her skirt and shredded panties lay
on the floor. I'd never seen anything so pathetic in my
entire life.

I wasn't quite sure if it was rape or not. I figure there has to
be a victim for there to be a rape. Joyce McKern was way
past feeling victimized, or feeling anything else for that
matter. But it seemed to me even that empty shell should be
allowed a little dignity. I was trying to put it all together in
my head when Benny stepped back into my field of vision.

He was still attempting to explain this all away. Suddenly all
the moral and mental gymnastics I was going through seemed
like a monumental waste of time, so I decided, instead, to
hit Benny as fast and as hard as I could.

Unfortunately it wasn't quite fast or hard enough. He
came back at me like a runaway train. I was told later that
the fight lasted close to twenty minutes. When it was over, I
had three cracked ribs, two broken metacarpals in my left
hand, and not one square inch of body that didn't hurt.
Benny was unconscious for thirty-two hours and needed to
have an arm set and his jaw wired. Neither one of us was
worth a damn for almost a month, and I don't think it really
settled anything.

Benny Hollaster still worked for me, because I needed
him. Neither of us talked to the other unless absolutely
necessary. Benny behaved moderately well otherwise, be-

cause he'd developed a certain amount of respect for my authority and right hook. I was sure he was still misbehaving behind my back, because it was his nature. But I hadn't followed up on my suspicions, because the next time Benny and I crossed swords, one of us was surely going to end up dead.

Benny's woman came down to the village a little more bruised and stooped each trip. One week it was a black eye. The next it was another chipped tooth. Someday she'd stop coming to pick up the groceries altogether. Then I'd have to go up to Benny's backwoods mobile home and get the answers to some tough questions. There are some things in life you just can't avoid. I figured killing or being killed by Benny Hollaster was one of them.

I spent a few minutes reading through the last week's reports in the log book. Ricky had given it to me straight. Shandaken had gotten along fine without me for a whole week. I was crushed. There was a note sitting on my desk from Dirk Parker saying he wanted to talk about some strange radio transmissions he'd picked up on the scanner. Another note asked me to contact Mayor Hayden when I got back. This didn't bode well. Mayor Hayden only contacts me when there's trouble. We're not exactly on a come-on-over-and-have-a-drink basis. I said my goodbyes and strolled down 214 to Main Street.

The sun had disappeared behind Mount Sheridan, and twilight wove its magic spell upon the town. Blue shadows lengthened and details became soft and diffused. Most people were home having dinner at this hour, so Main Street had a deserted feel about it. I checked to make sure everything was exactly where I had left it before my trip to Oneonta. It was.

The lookout tower, with its fire siren, still guarded the town's northwest entrance over the little cement bridge. Sandbag bunkers still sat on either side of the crossing, waiting for the next band of bike bums or raiders who were stupid enough to think they could cause trouble in our town. I glanced up at the similar stations set up on the roof of the pharmacy and the boardinghouse across the street. The mountains still loomed above the town in every direction. Nothing had changed.

I peered down Main Street's two-block-long business section. Everything was closed except for the three bars in town, Ricardella's, the Hotel Phoenicia, and the Sportsman's. Beyond the last buildings, which now housed the food depots, lay Tent Town. This is where Phoenicia's newest citizens live. We're trying to get them all into houses eventually. But it takes time.

Looking at it in midsummer, it's hard to imagine how tough it gets for the citizens of Tent Town once the winter hits. If I walked by now, I knew I'd see families barbecuing and eating at crudely made picnic tables. Folks would be drinking homemade wine or beer, and someone would be playing a guitar. It would all look like a jolly summer camping trip. But come February, it's a different story. In these mountains, the temperature has been known to drop as far as thirty-five degrees below zero. We've had a few people freeze to death.

There are a number of private houses past Tent Town, and beyond them the fortifications. More than a few folks live outside them. But if trouble comes, they head into Phoenicia, the town closes up behind them, and no one else gets in. On one side of the road, Mount Tremper rises almost straight up at a 90-degree angle. The Esopus Creek butts up against the other edge of the highway. It's a really crazy place to try to assault the town from. But people have tried it and people have died there.

I wandered into Ricardella's to find the mayor. Mayor Hayden was at her usual table. Dinner at Ricardella's was her favorite ritual. If you have an idea or a problem you want to talk to the mayor about, you go there. She's never to be found in her office across the street, at least not during the day.

Shandaken Township couldn't survive with a mayor who liked to sit down a lot. Her honor's day always starts with the sunrise. She claims, "As long as there's light, there's work to be done." Nothing ever happens in Shandaken Township that Mayor Ruth Hayden doesn't know about and hasn't inspected at least three times, personally.

But come six o'clock, Mayor Hayden immediately heads for her favorite eatery and watering hole. Dinner and sitting in state usually lasts until nine, and then she heads over to her office to do paperwork until some early-morning hour. Her husband held the office before her. She'd been his assistant, until he berserked out. Ruth soon proved she could do a better job than he ever did. She has more imagination and guts.

My trip to Ricardella's netted me a bonus. Warren Green was having dinner with the mayor. They made quite a pair. Ruth is short, round, and slowly graying. There's always a smile on her face. Warren's a little over six feet tall and is as close to skeletal as a living being can get. He almost never smiles.

Appearances can be deceiving. I seldom manage to get through a meeting with Mayor Hayden without a shouting match starting, while as far as I can remember, Warren and I have never had even one argument. Which is remarkable, because Warren is frank with his opinions and cares little for other people's feelings. He's not mean-spirited. Warren just doesn't feel it's worth his while trying to pussyfoot around other folk's sensibilities.

I like Warren. He seems to know a little bit about more diverse subjects than any human being I've ever met. When I first met him, I suspected he was conning me, so I checked up on some of these "expert" statements and bits of advice he's in the habit of tossing off the top of his head. Turned out he was right on the money, every time. So whenever I need any kind of information about anything, I come to Warren. If he doesn't have the answer in his head, he'll find it within a couple of days, unless there's no answer to be had.

He loves to share all the wondrous things that are floating around in his brain, especially after he's had a couple of drinks. This makes him Shandaken's most valuable and popular citizen. I've spent more than one night sitting at a table at the back of the Sportsman's Bar, tilting back boilermakers and listening to Warren's stories. He's far better than television ever was. The only thing he's close-mouthed about is what he did before he came to town, fifteen years ago. I suspect it was some kind of government work, but I've never pressed it.

He always greets me like some long-lost relative. "Well, what is this my tired old eyes behold? Will you look at that, my dear mayor. Can it be true? It is! Constable Tom Laker has returned from the wilds. Let there be celebration. Barkeep, a magnum of your best champagne!"

I pulled up a chair between the two of them. "Hold it

down, you old reprobate, or I'll be forced to run you in for disturbing the peace. Is this bum troubling you, madam?"

"Not half as much as you do, Mr. Laker." I know I'm in trouble when it's Mr. Laker and not Tom. "I understand you were involved in a shooting earlier today in Margaretville. I don't like my constables going off to other towns and shooting up the citizenry. Those towns have their own lawmen to do that kind of work."

"My, bad news travels fast around here . . . but not very accurately."

Warren poured me a glass of wine and with a twinkle in his eye beat Mayor Hayden to the punch by asking, "Well, won't you set the record straight then for us mere mortals?"

"My gunfight took place before I ever reached Margaretville. Crazies on Route 28. The shootout at the Margaretville Corral, on the other hand, was strictly local talent, but it brought to light something disturbing that we've got to talk about tomorrow. There's an emergency meeting in my office at ten."

Ruth leaned forward and asked, "Don't you think you ought to let your mayor in on what happened? Hmmm?"

"It'll hold until tomorrow. I'm exhausted. I need some serious bathtime."

"I can tell that from here. But how about giving me the short form in case there's anything I should consider overnight."

"Okay, here it is in a nutshell. Our plastique-in-the-cooler bluff almost got called today. Some crazies, non-berserkers, nearly succeeded in offing my drivers, leaving me with a phony detonator and some cans of beer to defend the fuel truck with. It was scary."

Warren whistled at the news, then drifted off into his own little world to consider what he'd just learned. That left Mayor Hayden and me to get down to basics. "Yes, I'm sure it was terrifying, but what can we do about it?"

"Set up real dead-man charges."

"Isn't that a little drastic?"

"You wouldn't think so if you had been with me today. Besides, I think it's the only option we have open to us."

"Why do you say that? Did anyone actually see that we had no explosives in the ice chest?"

"No, but they made a run at taking away our gas today and came damn close to succeeding. The story's going to get around. People are going to think about it. Someone's going to refine that plan and try it again. Maybe the next guy will blow it too—and the guy after him. But sooner or later, someone's going to succeed. That'll mean the end of us as a town."

"In other words, you think that unless we blow up a few of our trucks, people, and customers, no one's going to take us seriously."

"What I'm saying is that if someone takes one of those loads away from us and it doesn't blow up, everyone's going to know we're nothing but bluff. Every biker and raider in New York State will flock here to take a bite out of Shandaken. It'll be the end."

"He's right, of course. That's the way life is these days. Natural selection, only the strong and mean survive." Warren returned to this world just in time to help me defend my position. "But what will the drivers think of this?"

"I suspect they won't like it any more than I do. But after Dan and Bernie tell their story, everybody will have to go along with the program."

"Don't like the idea of an instantaneous trigger, though. It's been fine on our imaginary charge but wouldn't leave much room for error in a real-life situation."

"Well, those are details we can work out tomorrow. I'm heading home. Maria will be holding supper for me."

I bit my tongue as soon as I said it. Mayor Hayden visibly stiffened at Maria's name. She looked up at me and asked, "How is that wife of yours these days?"

"Just fine, Ruth."

"That wasn't a making-polite-conversation question, Tom. I expect more than just a polite answer."

"Okay, no change. Satisfied? Now, if you'll excuse me." I got up and split before Mayor Hayden and I drifted into stage two of our continuous debate over my wife. I was in no mood for it tonight.

As soon as I hit the street I felt better. Nightfall hadn't cooled the day enough to be indoors yet. The early-evening breeze felt so pleasant that I was tempted to walk home. It was only a little over a mile. But the sun would have set by the time I got there. No reason to give Maria a heart attack. Someone stumbling his way up to your house in the dark usually means trouble. I decided to take the car home.

I was almost to the station house when I heard my name called. I turned around. It was Josh Woodward. My danger alerts went off. There was something odd about the way he was approaching me. I stood so I'd have to turn my head to the left to look at him. This somewhat covered my right hand drifting lazily to the gun butt.

But Josh noticed anyway and smiled. "At ease, Constable. I haven't turned berserker on you, yet. I am the bearer of bad news, not bad times."

He sounded like his normal self. But I was relieved when he diplomatically stopped a few feet away from me.

"What kind of bad news?"

"You've got a new motorcycle in that auto boneyard out in front of your place."

"Maria?"

"She's all right. Don't sweat it. I cleaned up. She's back home and probably fixing your dinner right now."

"Thanks, Josh. What happened?"

"I'll tell you all about it some other time. Why don't you head on home. You look dead on your feet."

"I am, so I will."

And I did.

Maria heard me pull the patrol car into the garage, next to my old Camaro, and came to the door to greet me. Then she decided she couldn't wait for me to reach the house, so she dashed across the grass and threw herself into my arms. She smelled great. I picked her up and carried her into the house. Rex looked on with more than a little disapproval. I was heading for the bedroom when I got sidetracked. "What is that wonderful aroma wafting from the kitchen? It smells almost as good as you do."

I set Maria back on her feet. "It's half a wild turkey, you big oaf. Josh shot it the other day. It's your dinner. Come sit down." I obeyed the little lady's command. My belly and my head also demanded that food come before Maria. Within minutes I was digging into some of the best chow my mouth could ever remember savoring.

"How did you ever get one of those stringy old birds to taste so good?"

"It's my secret marinade. Although I suspect that your eating out of cans for the last week has a bit to do with it."

"Nonsense, this is a meal fit for a king. Wilds't thou not join me, wench?"

"No, I got tired of waiting for you and ate earlier. I will join you for some wine, though." I liked the lascivious grin she flashed me.

"Anything interesting happen while I was on the road?" I cautiously asked between bites.

"Yes, I spotted two deer on the lawn the other day . . . it

was near dusk. They were so beautiful, Tom. Remember how they used to come around here all the time?"

"I sure do. Now they stay pretty high up in the mountains, afraid of the hunters."

"Damn hunters! I hate them."

I didn't bother trying to explain that those hunters weren't the beer-bellied buffoons we used to get around here every November, before things got really bad up this way. These deer hunters were our friends and neighbors, who were simply trying to put enough food on the table to keep their families alive. I had learned that such fine distinctions were more than Maria could comprehend. The line between before and after the advent of the berserkers was blurred and confused for her.

"How'd you like to do me a tremendous favor and run a bath for me?"

"Of course. You didn't really think I was going to let you anywhere near my bed without sanitizing you first, did you?" She collected a candle to take into the bathroom. The electricity didn't make it this far out of town anymore. We had a little gas-powered generator, but it was only used on the water pump and kitchen lights.

"Sorry, love. I see, or rather smell, your point. It's just that it was so hairy up by Oneonta that I didn't want to risk being separated from my gun for even the few minutes it would have taken to bathe in a stream."

"Was it really bad?"

I was kind of taken aback by Maria's asking such a question. Usually anything that happened past our front gate held no interest for her. "Yeah . . . I'm afraid it was. Oneonta's finished."

"I'll be back in a second," she said and disappeared through the kitchen door. A few moments later, I heard the bathtub start to fill. When she didn't return, I finished my turkey and potatoes and got up to see where Maria had gone.

She was in the living room. Maria was staring out beyond the patio doors, watching the darkness deepen. I came up behind her and put my arms around her. She looked up at me, smiled, and said, "We've got a good life here. Nothing's ever going to change that, is it?"

I didn't know what to say, so I turned her around and kissed her. She responded as if her life depended on it. In

some way it probably did. There was a desperation about
her embrace that scared me, but slowly the tension began to
drain away. Before I knew it, the old Maria Burgos was
back, feeling warm, alive, and tempting. She must have
read my mind.

"Your bath's going to overflow," she warned as she pushed
me down the hall. I did a little striptease for her on my way
to the bathroom. She loved it. The water was a mite cool for
my taste, so I shut down the cold tap and cranked the hot
wide open. A couple minutes later, I was lowering myself
into that steamy potion and feeling my entire nervous system shorting out from the sheer delight of it. What bliss!

Maria brought me another glass of wine. We sat together
in silence for a long time. I didn't like it. Something was
wrong, but I was afraid to probe for the trouble. The silence
was finally shattered by the sound of a loud and heart-felt
yawn. It wasn't mine. Maria had let loose with that rafter
shaker. She looked quite shocked by it and daintily covered
her mouth much too late to keep it from escaping.

"I'm sorry about that. I haven't been sleeping too well
lately. I've been having bad dreams. Maybe it's because
you've been gone."

"Well, I'm back now. Is there anything I can do to help?"

"Maybe. I'll give it some thought." She smiled as she
gathered our empty wineglasses and closed the bathroom
door behind her. I let the tub start to empty, stood up, and
grabbed a towel. Dreams? What kind of dreams? I'd have
to ask her about them tomorrow.

The rest of the house was dark by the time I'd shaved and
brushed my teeth. I slowly pushed the bedroom door open
and saw the two flickering candles, one on each side of the
bed. Everything was just as I expected. The candlelight gave
the room a nice friendly glow. Maria lay on her side in the
middle of the queen-size bed. She wore the silky blue-and-
white robe I'd given her for Christmas last year. I knew she
had nothing on underneath it. One well-formed leg rested
outside the robe's gently caressing folds. It looked quite inviting. So did Maria's smile. In the dim light, her pale skin
looked china-white.

I sat next to her, bent down, and kissed her. Her arms
slowly snaked around my neck and her tongue found the
inside of my mouth. I lost my towel as I twisted around to

lie beside her. She pressed herself against me. I reached between us and pulled her robe open. She was very quickly disappearing into that state of wild abandon she had brushed against earlier. But this time she didn't put a halt to her passion's soaring flight, because she could feel that I was following, right behind her.

I barely felt Maria slide out of bed that morning. She had managed to slip out from under my arm undetected. But the slight shifting of the bed springs was enough to awaken me instantly. You'd be surprised how lightly you can sleep when your life depends on doing so. It was time to pay for my pleasures.

As soon as Maria drifted down the hall, I bounded out of bed and positioned myself behind the bedroom door. Maria's Other Mind, as I liked to call it, had taken a while to sort me out from the rest of her victims. I now held a place of honor in its black little heart. I was the one who kept getting away. I was the one who had to be treated differently. So the Other Mind slowly changed the rules of the game, especially to entrap me. A sort of left-handed compliment, I suppose.

I could hear Maria finally returning from the kitchen. I peeked between the door and the frame. Good, she only had one knife with her. I let her come through the doorway, grabbed her wrist, and twisted. The blade dropped to the floor. I quickly gathered her up in my arms, before her clouded brain registered that she'd been duped again. A few steps brought me to the hall closet. In she went.

Nothing had been kept in that closet since the second attack. It became the Quiet Room. I had padded it as best I could with old clothes and large sheets of thick black plastic. Fortunately Maria kept her nails short, because they got in the way of her piano playing. I'd fixed the closet door so it only opened from the outside.

I dressed and headed to the kitchen to make my own breakfast. Maria always skipped breakfast on these mornings. But she kept me company by thrashing against the door and screaming obscenities.

The Other Mind didn't like me. I'd survived dozens of its attacks. It stopped making me breakfast long ago. That became a privilege only the less troublesome were blessed with. Its strategy for dealing with me slowly changed as the months went by. Luckily it was so slow-witted that I was able to stay several jumps ahead of it, without even trying. I imagined its next permutation in this escalation of hostilities would be a twin-blade attack. I wasn't worried. I'd be able to handle it.

As I fried my eggs, I remembered the first time Maria tried to kill me. It was right after breakfast, which was her usual pattern. I turned around at the last moment to ask her something, saw what was coming, and escaped with only a small gash on my left trapezius. It wasn't hard to twist the knife out of her hand and pin her to the floor.

Of course, I knew what had happened, but I didn't want to believe it. My wife had gone berserk. She had tried to murder me. It was all over. She'd have to be either killed or driven out of town. This couldn't be. I screamed at Maria that it was all a mistake. My tears fell onto her snarling face. She bit at my hands. I sat on top of her for about an hour. I couldn't figure out anything else to do.

This was Maria. This was the woman I'd sworn I'd comfort, protect and honor. I was going to spend the rest of my life with her. We had made plans, talked about having kids. This was our kitchen that we were wrestling in.

Slowly her gyrations began to lessen. She started to go limp on me. At first I thought it was a trick, but I was wrong. Maria's collapse was quite real. I think this scared me more than the attack had. I thought she might be dying. Was this what happened to berserkers who didn't get to shed blood?

When she was completely out, I took her to our room and put her to bed. I called in on the patrol car's radio. I wasn't coming in today; Maria was ill and I wanted to stay home and take care of her. No, it was nothing serious. I could handle it.

Three hours later, Maria woke up to greet the day. She was surprised to see me. The fact that it was nearly noon escaped her. She headed for the kitchen to make us a second breakfast. I had dumped the first one while she slept. The morning had never happened as far as Maria was concerned. She had never tried to kill me. I hadn't twisted any bloody knife out of her hand. The day was like any other. Only my throbbing trapezius kept me from believing the lie.

I kept a close eye on her and stayed some distance from her for several days. I slept on an easy chair that shared the bedroom with us and never turned my back to her. Every time she came close I felt my stomach tighten and my fists clench.

That other morning began to take on an unreal quality. Maria continued to be her sane and normal self. She fed and pampered me as always. She was even understanding about the odd way I was acting toward her. Was I coming down with something?

Then one night I woke up to find Maria standing above me. She was draping a blanket over me. You see, she didn't want me to catch a cold, sleeping in that old easy chair. It had to be me who was crazy. Maria had never tried to kill me. I crawled into bed with her and slept like a rock. I awoke the next morning completely rested and as suspicious as ever. My eyes never left Maria as she prepared breakfast.

The eggs and bacon were delicious, and at no time during the meal did Maria try to jam any of the kitchen cutlery into my body. I was completely befuddled. What had set her off the other day? It hadn't been breakfast or any of the pointed

objects she used to make the meal. We had just repeated that ritual and Maria was still her lovable old self. It wasn't just sleeping together that did it, either. Was it something I'd said that morning? I was wearing the same plaid work shirt and blue jeans I'd had on that day. It had occurred to me that color might be the stimulus that had gotten her going. I had to check everything.

The most glaringly obvious reason for the attack was the one I least wanted it to be. I was determined to test every other possibility I could think of before I was forced to follow that train of thought to its inevitable conclusion. But I eventually exhausted my other options. I had to face the truth. There was only one difference between the two mornings, and that was afterglow. The night before Maria tried to stab me, we had made love. Sex had to be the trigger. There was only one way to test this theory.

I felt very awkward that night. The purpose of our lovemaking kept popping into my head as we did the deed. I muddled an orgasm out of Maria and then faked one of my own. I'd never heard of a man resorting to that before and felt pretty silly doing so. There was no way, however, I was going to produce the real thing that night. I could get the soldier to stand up, but he wasn't going to fire his weapon.

Maria soon drifted off. I stared at the unseen ceiling through that entire night and into the dawn. I closed my eyes only when I felt Maria begin to stir. She slipped out of bed at her usual time and soon began puttering in the kitchen. Her singing was my signal to get up, so I did just that.

I dressed in silence and sat at the kitchen table. I positioned myself facing away from Maria. The sharply angled morning light streamed in through the kitchen window and onto my back. By looking over to my left, I could see a clear silhouette of Maria on the refrigerator, every time she stepped up behind me.

She placed eggs and steak down in front of me. Nothing

for her, thank you. She was watching her girlish figure. Normally that would have made two of us, but just now I had other things on my mind. "Oh look! I forgot to bring you anything to cut your steak with. I'll get you a knife," she said and turned away. I could hear her opening a drawer and selecting the proper blade. I could also hear that she wasn't anywhere near the silverware. The cutlery drawer, however, is right next to the stove. So was Maria. Her shadow confirmed this for me, so we soon ended up with me sitting on top of her again. I had figured it out, all right— and survived. Success! My keen deductive mind had solved the problem. Great! Then why did I feel so wretched?

Sex was obviously the killing stimulus. Well, this was a dandy turn of events, I thought. But as I sat there and wrestled with this new situation, I suddenly saw everything in a different light and cheered up. It wasn't as bad as I'd feared it might be.

I assumed, you see, that this current state of affairs made me the only possible victim of Maria's bloodlust. It could be handled. I'd have to be very careful, of course. But I could swing it and no one would ever know that Maria was a berserker. Apparently not even Maria. I guess we all know what we make of *you* and *me* when we *assume*. Well, I won't make that mistake again. Ever.

Two weeks later, I had to go out on a fuel escort. When I got back, Maria was out in the field rocking back and forth. There was an old Chevy El Camino parked out in front of the shrubbery. Inside the kitchen lay a young man with dark hair, black leather clothes, and a knife sticking out of his back. I cleaned up the place, buried the stranger, and brought Maria back to the house. Within the hour she was her normal self again. When I gently questioned her, she vaguely remembered a young man driving past the house the day before. She drew a blank on the rest of it.

All my plans for keeping Maria's problem a secret collapsed then and there. I was outraged. I had accepted it when Maria had tried to kill me. It was the disease. She couldn't help herself. But this was different. That man Maria had killed had spent the night here. She had cheated on me. Murder was one thing. Infidelity was another.

It took me most of the day to get this stupid idea out of my head. Maria wasn't being unfaithful to me. I had kept her mania from reaching its desired goal, by not letting Maria kill me. So this was the first of many rule changes the Other Mind would make. The force within Maria that wanted to bestow death had decided that a little roll with someone who didn't know all her tricks was the only way it was going to get any serious bloodletting done.

I had to let the folks in town know what had happened. It was embarrassing and difficult. A number of people I talked to wanted to know why I wasn't shooting Maria or driving her out of town, as I did all the other berserkers. I patiently explained that Maria wasn't like any of the others. She wasn't a threat to anyone she didn't have sex with. As long as no one let Maria seduce him, he was safe.

Unfortunately, the sexual aspect of Maria's berserkerism didn't seem to quiet anyone's fears about her, as I had hoped. In fact, the volatile mix of "immorality" and murder made Maria loom like more of a monster in some people's imaginations.

Thank God, most folks understood our trouble and accepted it. Those who didn't I told to shove off. Being chief constable does have its benefits. One of them is being better armed than anyone else. I made it clear that if anyone got the idea to do something about Constable Laker's berserk wife, then that someone was going to get his or her ass blown off. Mayor Hayden was one of the folks I had to inform of this fact. She thought the head lawman of Shandaken Township, like Caesar's wife, should be above reproach. I didn't like the simile and didn't want to hear any more about it. I did my job. That was all this town could reasonably expect from me. If the mayor had someone in mind who could handle the position better, I'd gladly turn in my badge.

But no one was going to touch my wife or tell me how to handle her. Maria was my problem. I'd deal with it. The town folks had been properly warned off. So I started the auto graveyard in front of the house to scare off strangers. Maybe I should have done more. I don't know. I thought about putting up warning signs. "Beware of Wife!" "Danger, Mad Brunette!" They wouldn't have worked. Passersby would have thought them a joke and Maria, when rational, would have thought them an outrage. So I was finally forced to hope that word-of-mouth advertising would do the trick.

As Maria's body count got higher, her reputation spread.

It had been four months between the death of the nameless man in the camper and that of Keith Lapeer. Having Josh warn folks away, whenever he spotted them in the area, had also helped. Maybe it would be six months before the next fool came through that bedroom door.

I finished breakfast, did the dishes, and went to check on Maria. About half an hour of frustration was all the Other Mind could handle these days. Maria was sleeping at the bottom of the closet. I picked her up and gently carried her to bed. I knew she'd be up and about by the time I came home for lunch. You see, the game was all worked out so life could go on in a grim parody of normalcy.

Part of Maria had to kill. But another and more dominant part of her still loved me and our life. The deceits were complex. They had to be, because the opposing desires could not be denied. Maria wanted to live, so she built a house of lies for protection against the truth. I loved Maria, more than anything in the world, so I moved into that house with her. Of course I constantly had to watch what I said and did. Maria's reality was a fragile affair.

But the end result was worth it. When the horrors of the world invaded my sleep and I awoke drenched in my own fear, Maria was there. The terror soon faded. When she smiled at me, all the problems in the world disappeared and there were only the two of us. The madness would surely have engulfed me long before if it hadn't been for my lovely wife. She was my lifeline.

I kissed Maria's cheek and tucked her in. It was time to go to work. Time to go play that other game I had going with death. The roads awaited me. The berserkers were calling my name. How far could I push my luck today?

As I walked out the door, I wondered if Maria was really the only crazy person in our house.

The strategy meeting went more smoothly than I expected. Everyone had his two bits to contribute to the discussion, but within the hour a solution was produced. Live charges would be placed on all tankers. But they'd have a 120-second delayed trigger. That way if someone screwed up, he'd have two minutes to unlock the cooler and defuse the charge. Two minutes wouldn't allow any bad guys to do the same. The key to the ice chest was to be hidden in a prearranged spot under the dashboard, and the cooler would be booby-trapped to explode instantly if forced open.

Warren Green was put in charge of the project. He assured everyone that the charges would be in place by the end of next week, though he'd have to use dynamite at first because that was the only kind of explosive he could get his hands on. Warren didn't like dynamite. In hot weather it becomes unstable. Dry ice would be a temporary remedy. But he urged the barter committee to immediately begin a cautious search for possible sources of plastique. It would be tough to find, but Warren was sure it was out there somewhere. If they looked hard enough, they'd come across some former GI who would be more than happy

to exchange some C-4 charges for something Shandaken Township had to offer.

So the meeting adjourned and everyone headed back to work. Everyone, that is, except Warren. He decided he didn't feel like earning his daily bread today and would hang around with me instead. Being the town genius, Mr. Green could get away with behavior like that. He wasn't even slightly deterred when I told him I was doing a perimeter patrol that morning. He just checked to see if his old Colt .380 was loaded and hopped into the patrol car beside me.

As we headed down Main Street, a naked vege strolled into traffic. Geoffrey Austin, the town mime, danced feverishly about, signaling traffic to slow for the catatonic stroller. His black-and-white grease-painted face grinned broadly. Geoffrey enjoyed his work. I reached over for the car's two-way radio transmitter while I waited for Geoffrey and the vege to clear out of my way. "Big Chief to Home Base. Come in."

Greta Evans, our day-shift radio dispatcher, answered in her usual wry fashion. "What's up, Tom? You just left here. You're not in trouble already, are you?"

"No, Greta, I've still got it under control. What I'd like you to do, though, is have someone stop by and tell Mrs. Tower that Walter is out roaming again. This time without clothes. Remind her I've warned her about this before and tell her she can find him near Brio's. Over and out."

"Catch you later, Tom."

I returned the mike to its hook and lowered the two-way's volume. Warren looked over at me and smiled. "She's not much on radio procedure, is she?"

"I guess not, but she gets the job done and never plays hooky like some people I know."

"We're kind of testy this morning, aren't we? Wake up on the wrong side of the bed, as they say?"

"Had to jump out of bed so I wouldn't be skewered. It's enough to ruin anyone's disposition." Warren and Josh were the only people I felt comfortable talking about Maria with.

Warren understood, lit up his pipe, and asked, "Any change?"

"She says she's having nightmares. I didn't get much of a chance to talk to her about them. I'll probably do it tonight. Think it means anything?"

"Probably. Dreams are the only way for the subconscious

mind to let us know what's going on in there. The subconscious is usually pretty coy and oblique about what it's trying to say, so any message from it generally has to be decoded. That's not always the easiest thing to do."

"Well, when I get the message I'll come to you for an interpretation."

"You may not need my help for that, Tom. I imagine Maria's subconscious is a real snake pit these days. Her dreams are probably very painful and dreadfully obvious."

Good old straight-talking Warren. I was suddenly sorry I had let him come along. Sometimes he's too painfully honest. Warren saw that his words had had the desired effect and let his attention drift out to the passing scenery. I kept my eyes on the road, but my mind locked on Warren's ominous prediction.

A short while later we passed a weary but wary-looking man on a horse that was slowly clip-clopping its way toward town. The noble steed had made a triumphant comeback since the berserker's debut. Horses aren't fast-traveling, but they don't require expensive gasoline and don't need new parts every other month. They're not limited to traveling the highways, either. And there was a lot less berserker and non-berserker trouble to run afoul of in the woods than on the road.

I came to a stop at the Wittenburg Road–Route 212 cutoff. We'd had some serious trouble along 212 over the last six months. People had disappeared while traveling this roadway between Woodstock and Phoenicia without a trace. Some joker had started the rumor that there was a monster or demon lurking along that road. Children were warned that if the 212 Spook got you, he'd roast you over an open flame and devour you whole, bones and all. 212 had become our local Bermuda Triangle, so I decided I'd patrol it later, without Warren tagging along.

It had been a while since I'd scouted Wittenburg Road. Things were usually pretty quiet over that way. Boiceville and Woodstock didn't let a lot of strangers pass through without carefully checking them out, so I seldom expected trouble from that direction. Still, it never hurts to be sure.

Warren decided the silence I had drifted into wasn't going to put him off. "I know you didn't want to hear what I said about Maria. But I had to speak my mind. You're my friend, Tom, and I feel that friends deserve the truth, whether they want it or not."

"I know. I know. It's just that I seem to be getting more truth than I can handle these days, Warren. I'm afraid I may be burning out."

"If any man has a right to, it's you. But I kind of doubt if that's really what's happening. You're overtired, that's for sure. It seems to me you should let your deputies handle more of the work load. That would mean extra time for you to spend with Maria. You don't know how much of that you've got left."

"What the hell do you mean by that crack?"

"Take it easy, big fella. Don't take my head off. No one knows how much time he has on this earth with the ones he loves. In Maria's case that uncertainty is doubled by her condition."

"Sorry. See what I mean? I've got the jitters. Maybe some time off wouldn't be a bad idea."

"That's the ticket, Tom. Help Maria plant some flowers. Catch up on your reading. Maybe you can try your hand at some landscape painting. I'm sure Maria would let you use her oils."

"I've already tried that. I wanted to do a painting of Gormley's horse. It ended up looking like a dog made out of mud."

"Well, I'm sure you could find something to do with a week off."

"Yeah, I suppose so. Say, Warren, you said Maria's condition doubles the uncertainty about the time we have together. You don't think it will shorten her lifespan, do you?"

"I don't see a direct correlation, Tom. No, I imagine that physically Maria's as sound as ever . . . for now. But from what you've told me, I understand that Maria's illness is not a constant. The only constant about it is change. And mental illness often has the uncanny ability of triggering a suddenly descending spiral of physical decline. That's what I meant by the uncertainty. The daily living, with a heightened sense of a much larger expanse of the unknown. Haven't you ever considered the consequences of some of the many existing possibilities?"

"Of course, but I've always felt I could maintain Maria's current status and keep things going the way they are."

"If wishes were horses . . ."

"What?"

"Tom, your fool's paradise is going to come crashing down on you."

"Even for you, that's being brutally frank. Thanks a lot, Warren. You've really made my day."

"Mr. Laker, you're one of the toughest and cleverest people I know. But everybody has his blind spots. Maria's yours. I'm just shining a little light where you should be looking. I imagine you're pretty fed up with me by now. So you can turn around and drop me back off in town, whenever you feel like it."

He was absolutely right. I had seen enough of this territory and had heard more than enough of Mr. Warren M. Green. I pulled into the driveway of a burned-out house, backed out again abruptly, and headed back to Phoenicia. We traveled in the uncomfortable silence that falls when one steps into a friend's out-of-bounds acreage. We both knew that within a few days the relationship would heal. But it didn't make it any easier till then.

I caught the faint mention of my call sign over the radio's speaker. Good. I needed something to focus my thoughts on. Something to silence the mental monsters that were screeching for attention. I twisted up the volume control and called in, "Big Chief here. What's up?"

"Got a report of an out-of-town-customer problem over at Brio's. Possible berserker," Greta's voice answered, distorted and scratchy with static.

"I'm fifteen minutes out of town. Can a lid be kept on it until I return?"

The silence stretched over a good thirty seconds. Finally Greta came back on the air. "Can do, Boss. The problem's eating lunch and is probably manageable through dessert. Benny and Deputy Burton have got the place covered."

"Have them stay outside and keep a low profile. Let's see if we can handle this without getting anyone killed."

I made it back to town in ten minutes. Traveling forty-five miles per hour, on roads that are dangerous at twenty-five, is a real cobweb-clearer. Warren didn't look like he enjoyed the trip much at all. The passenger, in these circumstances, never does. Too bad. Who'd asked him to come along in the first place?

*　　*　　*

Randolph Burton was waiting for me at the service station across from Brio's. His car was parked right next to the pump and he was leaning up against it, staring over at the restaurant. Geoffrey, the mime, was with him. I pulled my unmarked patrol car up next to them. Burton was the only deputy I had who went to the trouble of keeping his uniform in a recognizable state. The rest of us very seldom even wore badges. I dug mine out of the glove box and pinned it on.

Then I went around to the trunk and deposited my cartridge belt into it. It took a while for me to find the cigar box that held my .22 caliber double-barreled derringer. It was buried way at the bottom of the mess I stored back there. Cleaning out my trunk was one of those high-priority tasks that never seem to get done. I checked the tiny weapon's load and jammed it into my back pocket. I was hoping a nonconfrontational approach might make dealing with the troublemaker in Brio's easier. The derringer was in case that approach failed.

Officer Burton had brought out his shotgun while my back was turned. The mime was dancing about him, pantomiming someone firing a machine gun.

I walked over to my constable and asked, "This your idea of keeping a low profile, Burton? Why didn't you just shoot the restaurant's windows out to let him know you're here?"

"I . . . I just thought a strong police presence might calm the—"

"Never mind. What's the story here?"

"Bike bum. He came in about forty minutes ago. Apparently he thinks that Brio's prices are too high. Complained about it awhile, then finally settled for a sandwich and some soup. Then he went to the bathroom and came back, surlier than ever. He demanded more food. When the cook asked what he was planning on paying for the additional eats with, the biker threw a sugar dispenser at him and pulled a gun. One of the waitresses snuck out the back and ran over to report it."

"Many customers in there?"

"The regular lunch-hour crowd."

"Great. I'm going on in. You move your car down the street and out of sight. Take Geoffrey with you. Then take up a position over by the food depot. Where's Benny?"

"I'm not sure, boss. We came together. He must be here

somewhere. I guess he took what you said about keeping a low profile to heart."

"From one extreme to the other. Terrific. Well, get your ass moving!"

I waited until Burton was in position before I headed across to the diner. Benny was nowhere in sight, but I knew he was around. He'd come through if trouble started. He didn't like me, but he wouldn't let me get gunned down in front of the whole town. The good people of Shandaken would string him up if he did. Besides, Benny liked shooting people.

There was a beat-up 1950s Harley parked in front of Brio's. That had to be his. I wondered where he'd got such an old monster. It was a real road machine from the days of the interstate highways and rock and roll. Marlon Brando in *The Wild Ones* came to mind. I doubted if there'd be any similarities. I was right. There were none.

Brio's usual early lunch-hour crowd was indeed in residence. Old Mrs. Peabody and her friend Mr. McElwaine were at the front table. Next to them sat the Baxter brothers, chowing down on burgers and home fries. There was a hollow-chested and vacant-eyed stranger sitting at one of the center tables. Mike Ricardella, Brio's owner and co-owner of Ricardella's restaurant, sat way in the back. He glowered at me as I came in. He didn't like crazies disturbing his customers. "Where have you been?" was written all over his face. I couldn't begrudge him his anger. For a town Shandaken's size, a fifteen-minute response time was pretty lame.

I looked over at the counter. Another stranger sat near the back. He was a big man in road gear. I could see a nasty-looking automatic, probably a 9mm, hanging from his belt. But he didn't look especially like trouble. I was hoping, mostly because of his size, that he wasn't.

The rest of the counter was filled with familiar faces. There was Gene Roper, the mechanic from across the street, two lumberjacks whose names escaped me, and Doc Rogers. Behind the counter stood John Pearson, the cook. He still had some sugar in his hair and didn't look happy about it. He nodded toward the stranger at the table.

So this was the irate customer. At first glance he didn't appear to be very menacing. He looked to be about five feet ten, 160 pounds, dirty and road-worn. But a closer examination changed my mind about the not very menacing part. This guy was not only dangerous, he was ready for me. Next to his plate lay a cloth napkin. I could just make out the shape of the pistol underneath it. His hand rested inches away from it.

What disturbed me even more about this character was his ominous looks. His dark hair was matted with dirt and sweat. There was something terribly pinched about his features. He wore a heavy fur vest and a sleeveless baggy shirt, which I was sure concealed a multitude of weapons. It must have been sweltering inside that outfit in the July heat we were experiencing. His bare arms rippled with tensed, stringy muscles. Everything about him shrieked that he was primed and ready to go off. I had this feeling, though, that I was still missing something important . . . but what? Then I got a look at his eyes and everything fell into place, with a dull thud.

I'd seen dead eyes like those when I worked in New York City. They were doper's eyes. This guy was flying. Coke? Crack? Junk?

It was crazy. I couldn't believe it. Half the world had lost their minds and the other half were afraid the same thing was going to happen to them. So what did this bozo do to deal with the situation? He baked his brains on chemicals. It sure as hell didn't make him any less dangerous.

At least I knew that a berserker would try to kill me. This doper, on the other hand, was completely unpredictable, and that made it rough. I had to go on the assumption that he was going to try to do me in, also. But I really didn't want to have to blow him away if I could avoid it. There was more than enough killing going on already. I knew a junkie was only a notch better than a berserker, but I decided that running him out of town was the way I was going to play it.

I strolled slowly over to his table with a big oafish grin on my face. Doper Dan stared up at me with a confused look. That smile always got them. "Mind if I sit down, buddy?"

The mean and suspicious look returned. He cautiously slid his fingers under the edge of the napkin. Then he cracked a twisted sort of half-smile and said, "Sure, Officer, pull up a seat."

I did so, all the while watching his hand calmly close around the covered gun. I had to get his mind off that weapon. "I understand you had some trouble here earlier. You want to tell me about it?"

"Yeah. This dive tried to gouge me. Man, I don't take that kind of shit from no one."

It was time, I realized, to lay on my best chamber of commerce rhetoric. So I said, "Now hold on there, son. I think that if you checked around, you'd find that our town's barter system is as fair as any in the area. We don't squeeze blood out of anyone. I know it must be tough out on those roads, but you've got to understand that we've got to survive also. To do that, we have to charge a fair price for what we provide."

I knew my routine would never make the big time when he shouted, "I don't have to understand shit, man!" The gun, a battered old broom-handle Mauser, came flying out from under the napkin and zeroed in on my chest.

"Easy, now! No one wants to hurt you!"

"Well, maybe I want to hurt someone! You're someone, lawman. Who's going to stop me?"

"They are."

"Hunh?"

It worked like a charm. He just had to turn around to see who "they" were. Of course, "they" were everybody in the place. John Pearson had the sawed-off shotgun out from under the counter and leveled at my dining companion. Everyone else, meanwhile, had pulled out his pistol and had it trained on the doper. Even the stranger at the end of the counter had gotten into the act. The only imperfection in this tableaux was that dear old nearsighted Mrs. Peabody was pointing her derringer at me. So it was imperative that no shooting start.

Timing is everything, you know. I made a quick grab at my tablemate's pistol. He was so shocked by the turn of events he didn't even notice the gun leaving his hand. His eyes widened as he turned back to me and mumbled something I couldn't quite understand. Then his jaw tightened and he spun around again to have it out with the rest of the restaurant. He was all ready to go down in a blaze of gunfire and glory. Only trouble was his hand was empty. He pulled a trigger that was no longer there. Nothing happened. He squinted at his hand, looked back at me, focused, and in a blurred voice said, "Think yer pretty clever, don't ya? Well, I think yer a smartass!"

"Okay, I'm a smartass. But I'm a live smartass, and if you take it easy, pal, you just might leave this town in the same condition." I popped the ammo clip out of his old Mauser and emptied its firing chamber.

"It's always the same, no matter where I go. Smartasses! Everyone's a smartass."

"I guess you can see it that way if you want. I don't care. But if you've got any sense left in that foggy brain of yours, you'd better listen real carefully."

He didn't say a word. He just glared at me. I wasn't sure if this was going to work or not. He looked pretty far gone, past caring. I couldn't tell if there was enough of him left in there to make the difference between living and dying matter anymore. So I blindly plunged on.

"Now you're going to get up, go outside, get on your bike, and leave town. If you ever come back, we'll kill you. It's as simple as that. Do you understand?"

"Sure, lawman. This ain't the first dump I've been kicked out of. There's always some bigshot who wants to push ya around. If ya push back, they get tough. Okay, I got the message. I'm going."

He got unsteadily to his feet. It looked good. I was that close to buying it. But there had been just a slight bit of resistance when I yanked the gun out of his hand. He had grasped the situation in a flash. If he had made his move then, all he would have succeeded in doing was getting himself killed. Oh, suicide was his desire, all right, but this junkie wanted company on his ultimate trip. He stumbled toward the front door. I followed, reaching behind me and palming my derringer.

Once outside, he turned to me and asked, "You ain't going to set me on the road without my piece, are you?"

I handed him his empty Mauser.

"What about my bullets and clip? It ain't much good without bullets."

"We'll be keeping your ammo. Consider it a fine for disturbing the peace."

He stared down at the empty slot where his pistol's ammo cartridge should be, shrugged his shoulders, and tossed away the useless gun. It landed by my feet. "Got no more bullets for it. You keep it."

I could see his elbow bending as he turned toward his bike. I raised the derringer to chest level. He swung full

circle, past the motorcycle, to face me. I caught a glimpse of the snub-nosed .32 before I fired. I always hit where I aim. He caught the little .22 bullet in the right shoulder. It was enough to make him drop the gun.

But he wasn't going to have it that way. He started to dive for the fallen pistol. I cocked back the second hammer on the derringer and aimed for his head. I flinched at the shotgun's blast. The doper's head and chest exploded. It rocked him back on his feet, but he still stood there for a couple of seconds. It hadn't registered yet that he was dead. Then he made a gurgling noise and fell over.

Benny Hollaster, with his trusty shotgun still at the ready, came out from behind the restaurant's sidewalk shrubbery. He kicked the fallen .32 out of reach and gave the doper's bloody cadaver a good boot. The dead body didn't respond. Benny looked a little disappointed.

Doc Rogers came out of Brio's holstering his revolver beneath his sport coat. "Get away from him, Benny. That's no way to find out if a person's dead or not . . . though there seems to be very little doubt about this youngster's condition. But we've got to do this the official way. It helps maintain some dignity in death, even under the existing circumstances."

Geoffrey, the mime, walked over to the scene, crossed himself, and began a silent prayer. I couldn't decide if his solemn ritual was sincere or merely more street theatrics.

The doctor squatted, his friendly, round bulk oddly incongruous next to the body, and grasped the biker's wrist for a pulse. When he was satisfied, he dropped the hand, looked at his watch, and pulled a small notebook together with a pencil out of his breast pocket. "Eleven thirty-four A.M. Cause of death: shotgun wound to the head and upper body, sustained while resisting arrest. Does he have any identification on him, Benny? I'll need it for the town records."

Benny went through the doper's pockets and came up empty. The motorcycle's saddlebags didn't provide a name either, only some old clothes and a couple of sketch books. Doc Rogers scowled. "Another John Doe. No one carries ID anymore. He's the sixteenth, or is he the seventeenth, we've had this year. Well, I guess I can look through last month's records and come up with a proper number for him. You boys want to take him over to the undertaker's?"

The two nameless lumberjacks picked up the town's newest John Doe. Benny hopped onto the Harley and over his shoulder said, "I'm going to take this ol' darling for a little spin before I drop her off at the motor pool. Any objections?"

"Don't break your neck."

"Don't sweat it, Chief. We both know wishful thinkin' when we hear it."

Constable Burton picked up the dead man's sketch books and thumbed through them. After a while he pronounced his verdict. "Not bad. Okay if I keep them?"

"Sure, just keep them out of my sight."

I wandered back into the diner and asked John for a cup of coffee. I had a bad taste in my mouth, just as after every non-berserker killing. I should have hardened to it, but I couldn't be blasé about death. It always hit me too hard.

The bloodstains on the street were visible from my counter stool, so I moved to a table and nursed my java. If only I hadn't seen those sketch books.

Everyone's a smartass.

It happens to them sometimes. The road and the loneliness get to them. They're the ones who don't fit it. The ones no one wants around. So they ride their roaring steel coffins down the ribbons of concrete, until the quiet hours eat away the last of their humanity and they decide it's time to die. They usually head for a town—they need witnesses to the brilliance of their destruction. One brief, shining flash and they become one with the flame. Besides, they know we'll provide the service they require. Ours is an unforgiving culture. In a world of chaos, harmony is a diamond that must be carefully and brutally guarded. It can't be any other way.

But I can't help feeling sorry for those poor doomed misfits who can't make it in this law and orderly society and sanctuary of the sane. We've had a few of them here. They weren't trouble making bums, like Luke Chesterman. They were simply people who couldn't live in a world where their own individuality didn't mean much anymore. When you live in a town, nowadays, the town is everything and everything you do must be for the benefit of the group. I know it, it seems vaguely un-American . . . but self-indulgence and going it alone have no place in a community during this era of the berserker. Everyone has to work together to stave off the darkness.

You can't consider these folks, who can't or don't "fit" into the new order, deliberately arbitrary or traitorous. They're just different . . . and that in itself is a dangerous concept. They belong to a world, you see, that doesn't exist anymore. They hear the music that we can't. It's sad, but a lot of these misfits that I've known were artists and writers . . . dreamers. I'm not at all certain what's going to become of us if all the dreamers disappear. I know for now it has to be this way, but still I'm sometimes afraid for us. Maybe somewhere . . . in the future perhaps, a place can be found for the non-productive visionary and artisan. Lord knows, we can't afford them now. But I hope a few of them last out there on the road, long enough to come back someday, and remind us that there was once something more to life than just surviving.

But now the siren call of the killing highways speak to them in a louder and clearer voice than do the towns. Some of them get forced out onto the roads . . . Most of them merely drift out to the life. I can feel its pull sometimes.

Out there, all you have to do is exist. There are no responsibilities on the road. You don't have to worry about moral issues or what anyone thinks of you. You don't have to feel or care. You owe no one anything. It's freedom of a sort. "Freedom's just another word for nothing left to lose . . ." Eloquent fragments of an old song, sung by a lady who flashed briefly but brightly before she became a part of the flame.

Maybe that's why I do so many patrols. Perhaps that's why Mayor Hayden is always harping at me to stay in town and become a supervisor. I think she can see the hunger in my eyes. That's probably why she's never yet taken a tough stand on Maria. Yes, I think she knows . . .

Maria is my only anchor in this sea of madness. She's the safe harbor I can escape to after I've done my killing for the precious township of Shandaken. She's the calm eye of my hurricane. Without her, I would blow away and never be seen again. That's why I don't want to hear any of Warren Green's truths. My days among the friendly people of Shandaken are numbered. I know it. Warren doesn't . . . no one does for sure. I couldn't go on, as I must, if anybody had an inkling of the darkness inside me.

*   *   *

The light pressure of a hand on my shoulder drew me back from my dark musings. It was Wendy Loomis, one of the waitresses at Brio's. I was kind of surprised by the look of concern that clouded her pretty face. "You okay, Tom?"

"Yeah, fine. How you doing?"

"I'm all right. John made me split when that loony started acting up. I was across the street at the gas station. I saw the whole thing."

"I wish it had worked out differently. The poor dumb bastard just wouldn't let it go."

"Go easy on yourself, Tom. There was nothing you could have done for him. He was on a death trip. You should have seen him in here earlier. He was just asking for it. I was real surprised when John didn't blast him with that twelve-gauge he has stashed away."

"That's because I've read John the riot act about blowing away his customers. Troublemakers are police business. We're supposed to handle these situations without getting too many people killed."

Wendy contemplated this for a moment while she played with a curl of her blond hair. "I suppose you're right. John's scattergun would have probably taken out poor Mr. McElwaine along with that crazy."

"And that would have ruined Mr. McElwaine's lunch, wouldn't it?"

That got a big grin out of Wendy. She had a great smile. Over her shoulder I could see the large stranger, with the automatic on his hip, get up from the counter and pay John for his lunch. He nodded to us as he went by and disappeared out the front door.

"Wendy, you know that guy?"

"Sure, his name's Frank. Bike bum, I guess. Blew into town while you were away. He's okay. He don't cause no trouble and he's polite. He ain't like your regular road hog. I kind of like him."

"He got business in town?"

"I don't think so. He's sort of been hanging around, talking with folks. He's real friendly. John D. checked him out. Say, why're you so interested in him?"

"Don't know. There's something about him that hits me wrong."

She sucked on her lower lip as she reevaluated Frank. I could see it was hard work for her. After a few moments she reached her conclusion. "I wouldn't worry about Frank none. He seems to have plenty of barter chits and he's nice to have around. So don't you go rousting him. Hear?"

"Sounds like someone's caught Wendy's eye."

"Around here, a gal's got to keep an eye open for outside talent. All the good townies, like you, are spoken for."

I gulped down the last of my coffee and stood up. "Well, happy hunting, Wendy. I got to get back to work. See you later."

Frank had disappeared by the time I got out on the street. He had managed to set off my little cop alarm. I always heed that warning signal. It's kept me alive more than once. Something wasn't right about that stranger. I wasn't sure what. I knew I'd seen it; it just hadn't worked itself up to my consciousness yet.

I wanted to know more about this Frank. Wendy said he had lots of barter chits. That meant my next stop was the town's trading post.

Geoffrey, still doing his sidewalk act, followed me down to the trading post. He fell in behind me and started up on his impression of how I walk. Being a little bowlegged, I never found Geoffrey's act all that amusing. Anyway, I don't like mimes. Who does? In fact, I might have done Geoffrey some serious violence a long time ago if he hadn't been such a good mechanic. Out of his white-and-black pancake makeup he could tune an engine so it almost sang.

I've no notion why Geoffrey did his mime routine. He offered no explanation. A lot of people got somewhat eccentric when the berserker crisis started. I guess everyone was thrown a little off balance—nothing was the way it used to be. Old values gave way to new.

Money, for instance, was a pretty useless commodity,

probably only worth its weight in toilet paper. Then again, perhaps toilet paper was more valuable. After the advent of the berserkers, the governments of the world crumbled and their currencies lost their symbolic power. Paper money once represented the gold in the possession of its printer. If, however, no government remains to back up their paper with all that glitters, then there's no value to that currency. That's what happened to Confederate money after the Civil War. Somewhere in an old family stamp album, I remember a three million mark stamp from post war Germany. A grim reminder of what a government bellying up does to an economy. That's what the berserkers had caused throughout the entire world.

Gold itself was still as precious as ever. Coins had the value of the metals within them, which isn't much. Most coins had been melted down for other uses. Stocks and bonds weren't much good for anything except papering walls and covering windows to keep out drafts. They made lousy toilet paper. Too scratchy.

But commerce had to continue. At first, straight forward barter was the rule, but this arrangement had its drawbacks. Suppose someone wanted a loaf of bread, but all they had to trade was a Cadillac. The trick was to set up a system that would allow a business transaction between the car owner and the man with the loaf and the gun he had handy so his bread didn't get stolen.

So towns set up their own monetary structures. In Shandaken it was modeled after the old dollar system. But instead of dollars we use chits. We have one, five, ten, twenty, fifty and one hundred point chits. A one point chit is the same as a dollar bill. We've even gone as far as issuing half point chits. The market place, itself, sets the point value on any object. If an item or service is in demand or rare it naturally brings a good price. If it's an easily acquired commodity, it's priced accordingly. Like I said before, capitalism is alive and well in this world of madness.

There are two ways of legally getting chits. One is to work for or perform a service for the Township of Shandaken. Every citizen in town has a job to do, so everybody gets paid something. A few get paid better than most, either because they do highly skilled jobs that no one else can, or as in my case, exceptionally dangerous work that no one else wants.

We've got a few people on the dole . . . they're the

elderly and the disabled. A person really has to prove his or her neediness before they can become a ward of the town, though. Those who make the list are truly unable to do any work. We've got no welfare cheats in Shandaken, but we don't abandon our unfortunates, either. There's even a small stipend allotted to families that have Schizophrenia X patients in their households.

The other way chit points can be obtained is by barter. The town has a central trading post. If anyone has an item of value to trade, they go to the post and that object or service will be exchanged for point chits. These chits are accepted throughout town for anything from ammo to hookers.

Some of the neighboring towns that we do business with will even honor our chits. They use them when they purchase our petrol. There's been some talk of setting up a uniform money system for the entire Catskill Mountain range, but certain municipalities have refused to join in, so nothing's come of it so far.

The trading post in Phoenicia used to be the local Trailways bus stop. The buses stopped running, so we put the building to better use. It's stacked to the ceiling with firearms, ammo, fur pelts, camping equipment, clothing—the works. The post has an annex across the street in what used to be an artist's studio. Behind the annex is the town's car pool. That was where John Doe's chopper was headed. It's also where any vehicle that the trading post takes in barter ends up. The town keeps most of these cars, trucks, and bikes for its own use. But we'll trade off some of our stock if the right offer comes along.

When I entered the trading post I found Josh Woodward playing chess with Sid Douglas, the post's proprietor. They didn't bother to look up from their game when I walked in. "Hi, guys. Who's winning?"

Sid ran his hand through his thin white hair without taking his eyes off the board and said, "Hard to say just yet. How'd your contest of skill and wits go?"

"Cops one, doped-up crazies zero. I'm surprised you two were even aware of what was going on. How long's this game been going on?"

Josh made his move and took over the question answering duties, "A couple of hours now. Little Nicky Oliver ran in a while ago and informed us of the impending gun battle."

"I want to take this opportunity to thank you both for your timely assistance."

"Can the sarcasm, Tom. I did come out and spotted Benny Hollaster hiding in the bushes, salivating over the prospect of blowing yet another human being to kingdom come. I decided you had all the help you needed and came back to finish the game. I've seen Benny do his act before. Didn't like what I saw, so I skipped this performance."

"Can't blame you, I guess. That man sure does like to kill. It is pretty revolting."

"Natural-born berserker, if you ask me."

Sid shifted one of his bishops to a position on the board that got a groan out of Josh. Satisfied, he got up and headed to the back of his shop. On the way he offered Josh and me some lemonade. Josh accepted the offer. I declined. A few moments later, Sid returned with a couple of frosty glasses, set them down, and resumed his station at the board. "You looking for anything in particular, Tom, or just killing time?"

"Looking. I could use some info on a customer you might've had last week. He goes by the name of Frank. Six feet four, almost one-ninety pounds, beefy, short blond hair, blue eyes, dressed like a biker. Remember him?"

"Of course. What do you want to know about him?"

"He seems to be well off. Did he get rich here?"

"Sure did. He brought in a nice load of pelts. Fox, coyote, and bear. High-quality stuff. He traded in a hunting rifle, also."

I looked up at Sid's overstuffed rifle rack and asked, "Which one?"

"None of those. Wait here, I'll show you."

Sid hopped up and darted into his back room again. He returned a short while later with a grin on his long face and a hunting rifle in his hands. "Take a look at this beauty."

He was right. It was one fine piece of work. A scoped Yardly clip-fed .30–06. This was a Rolls-Royce of a firearm. It didn't make much sense. "He traded you this?"

"That's right. I don't think he knew what a terrific piece of workmanship he had there. He claimed he got it and the pelts off a dead trapper he came across up in Arkville."

"Did you happen to ask him if the trapper was dead before or after he came across him?"

"Nope, none of my business. Besides, he's too big to ask a question like that. Why're you so interested in him, anyway? Did he murder that trapper?"

"Don't know. Don't care. What happens up in Arkville is Arkville's business. I'm just curious about him. I can't exactly say why. There's something about him that doesn't ring right."

"Well, I've seen him around quite a bit since he brought that stuff in. He seems a decent enough sort. He's friendly and he's not looking for trouble."

"That's what I keep hearing. Maybe I'm being paranoid. He'll probably drift off in a few days, when his money runs out, and we'll never hear of him ever again."

Josh finally made his move and grinned up at his opponent. Sid's only comment was a low grunt of acknowledgment as he reassessed the situation. Josh stretched out some of the stiffness in his neck, turned to me, and said, "Maybe you ain't as paranoid as you think. There is something definitely out of kilter with that Frank character."

"How so?"

"That's going to take some explaining. Let's take a walk. I'll be back in a few, Sid."

Sid grunted again as Josh and I headed out to the street and toward Tent Town. Josh waited until we were safely out of anyone's earshot.

"Well, as you know, I wasn't exactly what you might describe as a saint when I was younger . . . growing up in New York City . . . "

"Yeah, you ran with a street gang and pushed a bit of grass. So what? You've told me all this before. What's that got to do with this Frank?"

"Gimme a chance, will you? I'm getting to that. When I was pushing dope, I got real good at reading dudes. You had to learn to do that or you could easily end up dead or busted. I got to where I could pretty well size up what a person was by the way he moved and talked."

"So? I learned the same skills in law enforcement. Maybe that's what's bothering me about this guy. He doesn't move or act like any of the bike bums I've ever met. I can't put a finger on him."

"Have you figured out what he might have done before the berserkers came?"

"No, and that's kind of unusual. Even after all this time, most folks carry all the earmarks of what they used to be like flags. Former executives and politicians continue to strut. Physical laborers still have the forward-leaning walk. Mechanics' hands all have those thick stubby fingers. Hell, there are a thousand different ways to tell what a person used to do or does now. But I'm drawing a blank on this Frank, and it worries me."

"Maybe that's because you're looking for things that are different about him."

"What do you mean?"

"I mean that I see him from a different vantage point than you do. You're too close . . . so you can't even see that he's a brother."

"Brother?"

"That's right, my man. I don't know what ol' Frank does now for a living. But I'm willing to bet my life that he was a cop once."

Maria couldn't believe it either, when I mentioned it that night. "He's a policeman?" she sputtered in surprise and amusement.

"*Was* a policeman, of some sort," I corrected. "At least that's what Josh figures."

We were sitting on the living room's shag rug with our backs to the couch. Nightfall had brought no relief from the day's heat. The thermometer outside the kitchen door still read in the mid-eighties. Maria and I had abandoned our clothes for the cooling comfort of nudity as soon as I had returned home from work. It had been too hot and sticky for dinner, so we lazed around the house and read until the sun went down. I was making my way through Umberto Eco's *The Name of the Rose*. It was a book Maria had forced on me. I couldn't imagine how a story about twelfth-century monks could be interesting, so I was pleasantly surprised to find out it was a murder mystery. I'd made a pretty good dent in it by the time my stomach started rumbling. Maria brought out some white vine, vegetables, and dip to remedy the situation.

"What do you suppose Frank's doing here?" Maria asked as she nibbled on a piece of raw cauliflower.

"Maybe he's passing through, as claimed. Maybe he's looking for a place to settle down. Who knows?"

"You don't think he's after your job, do you?"

"If he is, he can have it."

"Be serious, Tom. What if that's what he wants?"

"That doesn't seem very likely. If it's work he's looking for, I think he would have come and talked to me before this. That would be the only way he could get my job—start at the bottom and work his way up. He'd know that, even if you don't. I know you hold my line of work in low regard. But the truth is that it isn't always the strongest and loudest ape that gets to be boss. Leadership has to be earned."

Maria poked me in the ribs and gave me a nasty grin. "You're really being an awful shit tonight. Straighten up and fly right, mister, or I'll have to get tough with you."

"I love it when you slip into a disciplinary mood."

"Some more wine, swine?"

"Sure. Thanks, babe. And that's Mr. Swine to you."

Maria poured the homemade brew into the somewhat tarnished silver-plated goblets that she used to call our love chalices. I always got a big kick out of watching her. She moved with a grace I found enchanting. There was something almost deerlike about the way she crossed a room. Those strong lean legs stepped lightly and cautiously, always sure of their footing, but ready to change course at a moment's notice. I think that feeling of imminent flight was one of the first things that attracted me to Maria. She was a challenge. Tread carefully around this woman, her movements said, or she'll disappear the first time you blink.

I had that same feeling as she returned with our freshened drinks. But there was nothing appealing about that quality right now. In fact, it left me rather uneasy. I wanted to find out about the dreams, but was afraid to. I had put it off all evening. I hoped the alcohol had sedated her enough for me to ask my questions and receive an answer or two. As she plopped down beside me, I dived in, headlong. "Those dreams you mentioned yesterday—you want to talk about them?"

She froze instantly and stared off at something out of this realm. The distance I suddenly felt reminded me of when we first met. The walls were going up. Damn! It wasn't going to work. But then Maria surprised me. She always had that knack. She shook her head a little, turned to me, and said, "No, I don't want to talk about them at all, but I will. They've been really bothering me lately. I think a little psychic airing might be beneficial."

"Is it always the same dream?"

"There are occasionally some variations, but basically it's always the same story."

She fell silent. I could tell from the look on her face that the dreams were rerunning in her head. There was no reason for me to say anything. I knew she'd get around to talking again when the replay ended, so I just sat patiently, sipping my wine.

Maria began very quietly. So quietly, in fact, I had to lean closer to hear. "I'm always alone at the beginning of the dream. I don't know where you are. I never even wonder about that. You have nothing to do with these dreams. You don't exist in them. Only I do . . . and my loneliness.

"I don't know where the dream takes place, either. There seems to be a lot of mist and bright light from somewhere above and off to one side. Everything I see is either deep in shadow or bleached out by the intense glare. There's furniture in my dream, but it only seems to show up when I need it, then it fades away again. Like props in a surreal stage production."

"What happens in the dream?" I asked.

"I'm crying. I don't know why. Maybe it's because of what's happened to the world. Sometimes I feel it's because my parents are dead. The reason's not important. I'm alone . . . lonely, with a bottomless hole in my stomach. My life has dropped down that hole. And there's no way I can retrieve it. It's lost. I'm lost.

"Not long after that the stranger shows up. He's heard my sobbing and has come to find out what's wrong. He has a featureless face—no eyes, nose, or mouth. He sees nothing. He says nothing. But he understands my sorrow. He strokes my hair and tells me that everything will be all right. I hear him even though he can't speak. I hear his words in my mind. For some reason that telepathy seems quite normal. I don't question its existence at all.

"I put my arms around the stranger's neck and ask him to hold me tightly and never let the world touch me ever again. He lifts me in his arms and promises to do just that. We end up in bed, of course. The dream always turns terribly erotic at this point. It's not always the same. This is where the scenario changes from one dream to the next. Sometimes the stranger is very gentle. At other times he roughs me up. Once he climaxed before I did and I had to . . . get him hard again so he could finish the job. At that point, I'm not sure why it's so necessary for me to come. I just know that it's essential that I be completely satisfied.

"Finally I lie there, warm and drowsy in my afterglow. The stranger is beside me, asleep. There's a smile on his featureless face. I lie there sleepless and watch him for a while. But I can't quite understand what I saw in him earlier and I'm annoyed at myself for having slept with him. I'm not ashamed, just annoyed. It's very odd.

"I get up and stand next to the bed, look down upon my slumbering lover, and stretch. As I do this I feel fur sprouting from my arms and legs. Then the metamorphosis quickens. My face extends forward to form a muzzle of my nose and mouth. My gums hurt as the canines push out and come to points. I can feel my eyes become almond-shaped and change from hazel on white to black on yellow. Then my ears push their way to the top of my head and fan forward. My nails lengthen and harden. Finally, my breasts fade into my torso and suddenly I'm completely covered with silky smooth black fur. My tail twitches in pleasure.

"I'm standing on my haunches now. My lover has slept through my entire metamorphosis. I purr out his name to wake him, even though I don't know who he is. I want him to see the wonderful change in me. I tickle one of his ears with a whisker and call his name again. His eyes flutter open, shut, and open again. He looks at me but doesn't really see me yet. He's not quite awake, and so I press a sharp claw against the back of his hand. I draw a trickle of blood. The pain snaps him completely awake. He stares at me. His eyes widen. His mouth drops open. There's no pleasure in his face. He doesn't like the new me.

"So I rake my claws very quickly and deeply across his

midsection. He just stands there with a shocked and puzzled look on his face, asking why. All of his organs fall out onto the floor then. He looks down at them, then tries to gather them up into himself again. Of course he can't do it. I hear him whining about the mess I've made, as I pad out, nails clicking rhythmically, on my way to the field.

"The moon's high in the sky. It floods the grassy knoll with an unreal, diffused light. I look about the clearing to see if I am alone. I'm not. Other great cats, like myself, have come to worship the lunar god. We growl out our prayers in unison. It's like thunder. For there are thousands of us. My claws dig deeply into the grass and I feel my frenzy going out of control. My coat crackles with electricity. My roars become louder and shriller. As my voice cracks, I suddenly realize I'm not growling any longer. I'm laughing and I can't stop. It's a terrible and frenzied laugh. That's when I wake up.

"Most of the time I'm right here in bed. But sometimes I find that I've been sleepwalking. I wake up in that field across from the house, Tom. I don't know how I've gotten there. All I remember is the dream."

It took me a moment to realize she'd finished her narration. I was numb. She had told her entire story in a monotone. At no point did any emotion flicker across her face or in her voice as she spoke of the dream. It was as if some disembodied spirit had taken possession of Maria but didn't quite have control of the face and voice. There was a distinctly occult quality about it all that scared the shit out of me.

Damn you, Warren Green! Why did you have to be so right about Maria's painful dreams? And you had to be right about how it wouldn't be hard at all to interpret Maria's little subconscious drama. I consider a mankilling catwoman as her subconsciousness's way of being quite up-front about the whole affair. I had only one question. What was I to do? Maria looked over at me, waiting for some comment. What was I going to say?

Well, Maria, it's like this. You're a homicidal maniac and the dreams are your subconscious mind trying to tell you that you've taken up hating men and sticking knives through their hearts in your spare time. Of course, you've been carefully hiding all this from yourself, because your conscious mind can't handle the horror of the situation. So it writes off the killings as just another dream. You also filter it a bit through symbolism to take the edge off even further. The feline bit is actually quite a nice touch. But I think the time has come for you to face this "little problem" and either solve it or berserk out completely.

No, that wasn't the way to handle this. I decided to check out the lay of the land before I committed myself to any set approach. "I don't know what to say about that, Maria," I offered tentatively.

"I'm not sure there is anything to say. It's just that I haven't had a week go by in the last six months without being haunted by that dream. Lately the dream's been re-curring two or three times a week. It frightens me, Tom. I don't know what to do about it. I thought talking about it might help."

"Yeah, that sometimes takes the edge off."

"Not this time, I'm afraid. Now that I've talked about it, my fear of that dream seems to make more sense than ever. But I don't know why."

"Maybe it's because I haven't found the proper magic incantation to make your fears instantly vanish."

"Yes, maybe that's it. You've always done that for me, haven't you? You found me at that ludicrous party in Man-hattan doing my best urban sophisticate number and saw right through it. But you recognized it as a shield rather than an affectation. You were so nice. Just talking to you made me feel safer. I nearly forgot all about the pain and suffering that was going on out in the streets while I was with you. You were quite a serendipity, Mr. Laker."

"I felt pretty lucky that night myself."

"No, I was the one who made out like a bandit on the bargain we sealed that evening. You were looking for a gentle ear to tell your troubles to and some warm compan-ionship. I was more than willing to trade those items for the protection you had to offer."

"You make it all sound rather sordid, my dear."

Maria smiled and snuggled close to me.

"You and I both know it wasn't at all that cut-and-dried, but certainly that unspoken bargain was the basis, the foun-dation you might say, of why we got together. Yes, and we've both stood by that deal. I have shared your days and given you what comfort I could. I've loved you . . . and loved being loved by you. I've tried to be as much a part of your life as you'd let me be. I've done the best job I could at being your woman, Tom."

"You're aces at it, doll."

"Well, you've done a bang-up job yourself, fella . . . you've helped me through the worst time in my whole life. I know everyone's scared by what's happening to this world. But it's only my own personal terror that matters to me. You've eased that fear for me, Tom. There's a planet of madmen just outside that door, but I feel safe sitting here next to you. I know if anyone can protect me from them, it's you. I've always known that, and I know it will never change."

"Where are you going with this, Maria?"

"I don't know, Tom. But I wanted you to know how much I love you and how much you've helped me. I'm not saying that the outside world holds no fear for me anymore. It's still a pretty scary place out there. But you've taught me how to fire a gun and how to watch out for trouble. Those were real confidence-builders, believe me. I guess what I'm trying to say is that I know you've done all a person can do . . . and I thank you."

She stared down into her wine with a puzzled look on her face. Finally she turned back to me and said, "You know, it seems I've got nothing left to say, but what I've said also seems so inadequate. I wanted to tell you somehow that no matter what happens, I know you did the best you could and I love you for it. But that sounds so melodramatic, as if tragedy were right around the corner. Anyway, I know it's something I've got to say, even though I don't know why. It's like a compulsion. Sometimes I think I'm going crazy."

The tears started rolling down her cheeks. I pulled her even closer to me and held her tightly. I couldn't do anything else. There was a secret devil rampaging inside her. She could dimly hear his foul curses, but couldn't quite make out the words. The demon jabbed her heart with his pitchfork and seared her soul with his evil flame. He was having a great time and Maria was suffering a brutal agony without knowing why.

I could feel my tears joining and mixing with Maria's as I tried to kiss hers away. I gathered her up in my arms and carried her toward the bedroom. The french doors leading to the patio made the living room seem too exposed suddenly. There was something out there that wanted my lover.

I'd never let it get her. She had anointed me her knight. Her safety was my mission and my honor. The bedroom's darkness would enfold us both. Once inside, we could give ourselves over to the oblivion of our joined bodies. For only the unthinking are safe from the monster of truth that sits outside the door, whispering of the ephemeral nature of mortality.

Fifteen minutes later, I lay spent across the coverless bed. I was drenched in sweat. Maria had already slipped into the realm of Morpheus, curled peacefully in the crook of my arm. I could hear my heartbeat slowly receding from the cannonade level it had been at moments ago. I smiled to myself in the darkness.

I had everything back under control again. I had doubted myself and panicked. But that was over. Once again I could feel my confidence returning. Okay, so Maria had had a bad day. But she didn't know what was going on, so everything was still manageable. It would work out as long as I held the world on course.

A soothing breeze blew through the window, brushing across my skin. It felt exquisite. I had been awaiting its arrival all day. It drained off whatever tension remained. The cooling wind sounded a little like a whisper as it wafted through the trees outside. But I decided I didn't want to think of whispers. I didn't want to think of anything. I closed my eyes and let little waves of sleep wash over me. The darkness behind my closed eyelids muffled me. All sound receded from the universe. I was falling weightlessly into the safety net of slumber.

I was mildly surprised when the mushroom cloud of smoke and flames rose out of the ground beside me. But that's the sort of thing that happens in hell. Surprisingly I didn't feel any particular emotion when I realized where I was. It was a fact I immediately accepted, but didn't get worked up over. I guess those nuns back in Catholic grade school hadn't pounded the fear of damnation far enough into my soul. In fact, I found walking around in Hades nowhere near as horrible as I had been led to believe.

I had to admit that it was loud, though. With all the fiery geysers and volcanoes erupting, you could hardly hear the vege chorus singing the Chiquita Banana song. "I'm Chiquita

Banana and I'm here to say, you must treat a banana in a special way!" They kept singing that one verse over and over again, as they stumbled amid and occasionally into the towering columns of fire.

Above the flames sat a gigantic Mephisto in a gargantuan throne made of human skulls. His finger tapped out the time for the veges' tune and he whistled along with them. This devil seemed like a nice enough chap. I felt he was very pleased that hell finally had its very own choir. The veges had lovely singing voices, even though they somewhat lacked passion.

Those beautiful voices echoed on even after the berserkers sprang out from behind the rocks and began to tear the veges to shreds. The steamy rocks hissed as they became spattered with blood. The killers tore arms off their victims and used them as cudgels. The veges continued their ode to the banana even with ripped-out throats. I walked amid this carnage, unmolested and untouched. I wasn't singing. I was safe. I left the massacre behind and walked out along a wide ledge which overlooked pockets of flame in the canyon below. The ledge drifted away from the cliff face and turned into a ribbon of stone which floated above the flaming valley.

I began walking along the rock strip with a purpose I didn't understand. I knew, however, that I felt better with every step that took me away from the crazies. But the farther along I walked, the narrower the ribbon became. I soon found myself balancing on a six-inch-wide beam of stone. A few more steps and the width of the walkway diminished to four inches. Another step and it shrank to three inches. Its length disappeared into darkness.

It was a pitch-blackness like nothing I'd ever seen before. I balanced on my precarious perch and examined it. It was like a dark mist that began only inches from my nose and trailed away. But this mist didn't drift anywhere. It hung in the air as if it were nailed to the spot. That's when the little wordless voice inside me began to speak.

The voice told me how wonderful it was on the other side of the darkness. It told me of the peace and happiness that I would find once I made it beyond the black boundary. I believed the voice. There was a sincerity to it that I couldn't doubt or resist. It told of instant nirvana waiting beyond that dark veil, and I believed it.

It was quite apparent to me that I wasn't going to tightrope-walk my way into paradise. I was barely able to maintain my balance on the two inches of path I was currently enjoying. The strip showed no signs of widening. I knew I had only one chance and I knew it was a crazy decision. But I didn't care. It didn't seem to matter. This was a dream, right? I could do whatever I felt like. What was to stop me?

Utopia waited for me in the darkness. I had to reach its unseen border. I took one quick step and lurched forward into the void. The nothingness embraced me. I began falling. My hands flailed about in front of me, grasping, but came away with nothing. I twisted around quickly, hoping to make a grab for the path I had just vacated. But my movements only managed to send me into a slow rolling tumble which disoriented me completely. The ground was coming up fast and I knew I was going to meet it with bone-pulverizing impact, even though I couldn't see it. I squeezed my eyes shut and brought my arms up to protect my head. My speed began to build. A tightness seized my chest. I screamed out a banshee-wail greeting to death and woke up in my own bed.

My head ached and I was covered from head to toe with sweat. I rubbed my forehead with a shaky hand. Boy, that was one hell of a coded message from my subconscious. I rolled over to Maria to see if my trip through Hades had disturbed her sleep. The empty sheets were still warm. There was a movement behind me.

I shot my hand out toward the sound and by some miracle managed to grab Maria's incoming wrist. The butcher knife's point stopped inches from my neck. Then suddenly Maria sprang forward, bringing her full weight down onto the hilt of the knife. I wrenched my head to the left and the blade flashed past my neck and into my pillow. As I rolled aside I laid my right hand along the side of Maria's head. She dropped like a sack of grain, leaving a trail of goose feathers in her wake. I bounded out of bed and got her in a hammer-lock. Thirty seconds later I had Maria in the Quiet Room. I slumped in front of the door and began to shake.

It was still dark! I couldn't believe it. The next step was supposed to be two knifes, not a night attack! She always waited till morning! How had this happened? Maria screamed and beat at the door above my head. "Shut the fuck up!" I yelled.

I got up, walked to the kitchen, and lit a couple of candles. The battery-powered clock said it was three thirty-five. The night stretched on before me into infinity. I wanted to scream, but I wouldn't let myself. I knew if I started, I wouldn't stop. They'd find Maria and me on different sides of the closet door shrieking our love and hate for each other. I didn't want it to end like that. Somehow I'd hold it together. Somehow.

I escaped from the house even before dawn broke over our mountainous horizon. The walls had begun to close in on me. The car would only have made that feeling worse. So early that morning I walked through the woods to town. I had deposited Maria back into bed before I left and disposed of the pillow she had thoroughly gutted. When she awoke in a few hours, there would be no sign of my close call. There'd be nothing there to upset the delicate mental balance she was maintaining. She'd be okay. But what about me? What was I to do?

It didn't take long for the woods to work their magic on me. Wandering along the narrow deerpath, which skirted the edge of Mount Tremper, was just what Doctor Tom had ordered for himself. The forest was alive with early-morning activity. Every ten or so strides would bring another scurrying chipmunk into view. They all seemed to be gathering up foodstuffs and rushing back to their burrows with such intensity that one might have been led to believe that winter was only hours away. I knew better, so I was merely amused by this furious display of the work ethic.

A couple of deer crossed my path over by Crosley's Pond. There was a flurry of motion followed by a few seconds of branch-breaking flight and then they were gone. It was as if they'd never truly been there. I knew I'd find their tracks less than a half-dozen feet off the hard-packed trail. But I wasn't about to look. I liked the idea that they might not have been real. The rising sun slanting through the trees added to the wood's mystical quality. Anything that contributed to that illusion was all right by me. There was no room in my fantasy for crazy wives and berserkers. They simply didn't exist.

The frogs at Crosley's Pond didn't know what to make of me at first and fell silent. I gave them a few of my best ersatz ribbits. They bought the act and soon the air was once again filled with their morning chorus. I sat there for a while and listened. My nerves began to lose their violin-string tightness. Sunlight and the woods do that for me. The light shows me the possibilities I'd forgotten about in the darkness. Once again I was beginning to feel I'd be able to make it all work somehow.

After a time I tired of the frogs' Sunday-morning symphony, got up, and wandered into the hamlet of Phoenicia. The village looked almost as devoid of humanity as the woods. I spotted a couple of cats sneaking their way across the narrow blacktop roads to some nameless but highly important rendezvous. But none of my fellow *Homo sapiens* were present on the streets at this odd hour. The only assurance I had that the entire town hadn't mysteriously emptied during the night was the sound of heavenwardly raised voices drifting from the Baptist church's early-morning service.

I spotted a lawn chair under a weeping willow. It was directly across the street from the church. Seemed like as good a spot as any to wait for Brio's to open for business. I leaned back, closed my eyes, and let the churchgoers' musical praise of God envelop me. They sounded pretty good. I marveled that anyone could work up so much spirit this early in the morning. The sleepless night had taken its toll on me. I may have actually dozed out for a second or two. I didn't hear any running feet until after the shattered window wrenched me back to full consciousness.

From between the drooping branches of my retreat, I could see small bits of the church's stained-glass window still falling out of its huge circular frame. I sprang from my seat and sprinted after the footfalls I heard growing fainter down

Romer Street. As soon as I rounded the corner I spotted and recognized my quarry. I called to him. "Johnny Benson, I see you! You'd better stop right there!"

To my surprise, the fleeing teenager obeyed my order. He came to a stop next to a huge maple and turned around to face me. It was only then that I realized he had something slung on his back. It was a quiver of arrows. He reached over his shoulder and coolly pulled one of these barbed shafts out. This didn't worry me much. Johnny had no bow and I had at least eighty pounds on the skinny fourteen-year-old. I slowed as I got about twenty yards from him and warned, "Now don't try anything silly, John. We can talk this out."

That's when he reached behind the tree he was standing next to and pulled out a very businesslike bow. He kept a nasty smile on his face as he notched, aimed, and fired that arrow at me. I veered to the left, far enough for the steel-tipped shaft to zip harmlessly past my head.

Johnny reached back for another arrow. I turned on the juice and closed the gap between us as quickly as my adrenaline-powered legs could carry me. He was bringing up the shaft and bow to his shoulder when I slammed into him.

I connected with my full weight. Johnny flew gracelessly through about eight feet of air, then bounced onto a nearby lawn. The shaft ricocheted off the roadway and disappeared into some shrubs. I couldn't halt my momentum and ended up running about ten feet beyond Johnny's fallen form. By the time I turned around, the kid was scrambling to retrieve his dropped bow, ready to take another crack at me. I beat him to it and glared down at him. He smiled up at me and said, "Hi, Constable Tom." Then he tried to stab me in the foot with a loose arrow.

I cuffed him behind the ear to quiet him down and emptied the rest of his quiver onto the lawn. He brought a roundhouse right up from the ground. If it had connected, it would have easily rattled a few of my teeth loose. Fortunately young John had telegraphed its arrival, so I simply sidestepped and grabbed him by the collar as he went by. I gave him a few good shakes and shoved him up against the tree. "What the hell's wrong with you, Johnny?"

A hate-filled glare was the only response I got. That look made my skin crawl. The whole situation was completely

haywire. I'd known Johnny Benson for the last three years. He was a good-natured kid and an excellent student. I'd seen him around town almost every day, and he always had a smile and a wave for me. He didn't go around breaking windows and shooting arrows at policemen. His father had been a cop. It couldn't be happening to him. Not like his brother. "C'mon, Johnny, we're heading back to the church to see if you hurt anyone."

The hymns had started again. We could hear them much more clearly with the stained-glass window removed. Bert Jullian, the head usher, stood out on the church steps. He had something I couldn't identify at this distance hanging from his hand. When we drew nearer, the object came into focus and I finally recognized it: Mrs. Wagner's tuxedo cat, Freddie. The poor cat must have really suffered to have twisted itself into such an unnatural posture. The arrow still protruded through its midsection. Bert pointed the rapidly stiffening animal at Johnny and asked, "This his handiwork?"

"Looks that way. I'm sorry I didn't spot him before the damage was done. Anyone hurt?"

"No. It gave everyone a bad start, of course. I picked up the poor dead thing and brought it outside. The service started up again as soon as I left. We've all seen too much death over the last few years to let something like this put us off for too long."

"I guess so. Why don't you give me that and head back in. I'll take care of it."

"Thanks, Tom. May God go with you." Bert handed him his grisly charge and disappeared back into the large white building. I stood there for a moment and listened to the gentle hymn the parishioners were filling the air with. I knew what I had to do now, and I hoped Bert had meant what he said about God going with me. I was going to need a Supreme Being by my side. Johnny and I turned and slowly headed down the street toward his house.

Rachel T. Benson didn't answer when I knocked on her front door, so I walked Johnny around the house to the fenced-in backyard. I found Johnny's mother on the screened back porch. She was eating a breakfast of scrambled eggs and sausage. She stared out into space as she chewed her food. Her left eye was nearly swollen shut and already darkening. "Mrs. Benson?"

She turned her head and stared vacantly at me. I raised the cat up for her to see. "We've got to talk, Rachel."

"Come in, Tom. But please leave that outside, will you?"

I tossed the dead tuxedo cat with the bloody red bib onto the grass. I heard a stirring to my left and looked over to see Charlie Benson crawling out of his quarters. Charlie was Johnny's twelve-year-old brother. He lived in the backyard. His lodgings were constructed of found boards and sheet metal. The structure looked like a badly slapped-together chicken coop. Charlie wore a metal collar. A length of chain ran from the collar into the darkness of Charlie's ramshackle home. He looked over at me and growled; spit at me and missed. I ignored him the best I could and pushed Johnny through the porch door.

"Coffee, Tom?"

"No thanks. We've got a big problem here, Rachel, something we've got to talk about."

Rachel looked down at her eggs, shook her head, shrugged, and said, "So? The boy killed a cat. It's no big deal, Tom. Kids sometimes kill things. They've got to learn about death, too. It's all part of growing up. It's a stage."

"He also tried to put an arrow into me."

Johnny grinned broadly at the charge, but it didn't seem to elicit much of a response from Rachel, so I tried another tact.

"That was after he threw the dead cat through the window of the Baptist church."

"Oh, sweet Jesus!" Rachel spun around to glare at Johnny so quickly and savagely that the boy flinched, thinking he was about to be hit. But no blow came. Rachel's angry scowl softened. The strange smile slowly reappeared on the boy's features. It wasn't a pretty sight. "How could you do such a thing? What am I going to do with you?" demanded Rachel angrily.

"Did he also do your eye?" I asked.

"That's family business, Tom Laker."

"Don't give me any of that 'family business' crap, Rachel. Johnny's berserking out on you, isn't he?"

"No! It's adolescence! All kids get a little wild when they reach his age!"

I glanced over at Johnny and saw the brave lie in her words. It was that look again. The hair-raising one. I guess I hadn't wanted to admit it at first either. The truth. But by now the magic of my woodland stroll had been completely banished from my mind and spirit. Welcome back, Tom Laker, to the real world. Welcome back to a place where teenage boys go mad and their mothers have to lie about it.

Charlie Benson had berserked out about nine months earlier. He had tried to strangle his mother. Fortunately Rachel was a strong and healthy, thirty-six-year-old woman. Charlie, on the other hand, had always liked his sweets and never took to physical activities or sports. She wrestled him to the ground and tied him up, with Johnny's help. They made the tethered collar and had him housed in their backyard before I ever got wind of anything.

I don't usually let berserkers stay in town. It's the one rule I thought I'd never bend. Of course, I was wrong. I've broken it twice. First when I discovered Maria was a berserker. I did it again for Charlie. Rachel Benson wasn't going to see her little boy sent out onto those killing roads. She'd seen him through bad tonsils, chicken pox, the mumps, and several different viruses. Just because he'd gone crazy didn't make him any less precious to his mother. I suppose I could have had my deputies rip Charlie from his mother's chain-linked embrace and force him into exile. I could have lived with it. I'm a pretty hard character. It didn't matter to me that Rachel's husband had been one of my deputies and that he had died by my side fighting raiders. I could have booted Charlie out of town.

But the truth was that it wasn't necessary. Charlie was a roly-poly little teenage lunatic who was securely chained to his mother's backyard instead of her apron strings. He wasn't a threat. So I let him stay. It was a mistake. Time had slimmed and hardened Charlie. A dangerous-looking young man had replaced pudgy Charlie Benson. Rachel now had a wild animal tethered in her backyard.

Rachel had changed, too. I hadn't noticed before how the life had been draining out of her over the last few months. There was a hopelessness in those eyes. I couldn't believe the weight loss. She was almost skeletal. On the table next to her sat an overflowing ashtray. I took a long look at the woman I once knew. My uneducated guess was that the cancer would get her within the next six months. That sure made my job a lot easier. Now it wasn't just a mother I was going to have to separate from her children. It was a dying woman I had to do this to.

"They've got to go, Rachel. You're not going to be able to control them both. I'll come over here one day and find you dead. They'll have killed you. I can't have that."

"They're my babies, Tom. What do you want me to do?"

"You've got to let them go, Rachel. Your babies are gone. They died and all that's left of them is these shells."

"If only it were that easy, Tom. Sometimes I talk to Charlie. He has his lucid moments, you know. He's my ol' Charlie then. He's my son. He's the baby I carried inside my body for nine months. When Charlie's like that he doesn't understand what's happened to him. He's not a killer at those times. He's just a scared little boy who doesn't understand the cards fate has dealt him. It's so heartbreaking." She fumbled in the pocket of her robe and retrieved a silver cigarette case. Out of it she pulled a hand-rolled cigarette. She lipped it and struck a match to light it.

She blew out the smoky death and watched it slowly rise into the air and fade. "I can't send them away."

"And I can't let them stay in town. Johnny's nearly a man. He's too dangerous."

"Then I'll go with them."

I didn't know what to say. I had no doubt of the sincerity of her intentions. But could I allow it? She wouldn't last a day out there with her two psycho sons. They'd tear her to pieces. I had to talk her out of this mad plan. But she shot me down before I even got started. She simply turned to me and said, "I've no choice, Tom. I'm their mother."

Such a basic and unshakable stand. I took her frail hand into mine and stared into those sad but determined eyes. A half-dozen sentences died stillborn in my throat. Finally the only thing that came out was, "I'll miss you, Rachel. You and Johnny Senior were the first close friends Maria and I made when we came to this godforsaken town."

The tears started to roll down her hollow cheeks. "Yes, those were good times. We had a lot of laughs back then, despite the terrible things that were going on all around us. I guess we figured they'd never happen to us. We were invulnerable to the tragedy. Nothing would touch us. We were such fools."

"No, Rachel, we were typically human. We all see ourselves as the heroes or heroines of our own stories. We want our stories to have happy endings. We never realize that only fairy tales end with 'and they lived happily ever after.' True stories always end in death."

"I guess so. It's all over for us. John's gone. The kids are as good as gone. So am I, for that matter. Poor Tom, going to be all alone now. No one to play with Tommy. Even Maria's gone away."

"Not completely."

Rachel stared silently at me for a long time. Somewhere from inside that ravaged exterior, my old friend Rachel looked understandingly out at me.

"You don't get it, do you? You can't love death, Tom. I've tried. It's claimed me as one of its own. It'll do the same to you."

"Maybe it will. Maybe it won't. You've got a pistol, don't you?"

The dead woman that had once been Rachel didn't answer at first. She merely stared at me with those tearful dark eyes that knew more than I wanted to hear. Finally she nodded and answered, "Yes, but I could use a couple pairs of handcuffs."

"I'll have someone bring them over. I think leg shackles might be a good idea too."

"Only if they can be removed with a key. I want my boys to have a chance after . . . I'm gone."

"Sure, I understand," I said. Of course I didn't. I stood up and placed a kiss on her forehead. She didn't bother to look up.

"Goodbye, Rachel."

"Goodbye, Tom. Have a good life."

I turned back for one last look before I closed the porch door. Johnny had taken the plate off his mother's lap and was stuffing scrambled eggs into his face. Rachel blew smoke into the air and saw death and the future in the twisting snakelike shapes. But she no longer saw me. I realized that Rachel had turned into a memory before my very eyes. Charlie growled goodbye, and I walked out of the yard thinking about love and other deforming maladies.

I decided I should write up the incident at the Baptist church in the station-house log book. Constable John D. Maxwell looked up from the papers on his desk as I walked in. He had a surprised expression on his face. "What the hell you doing here? Forget it's your day off? Moore's in charge of today's shift."

I filled John D. in on what had happened with the Benson boy and my conversation with his mother afterward. When I finished, he shook his head sadly, got up, and fetched us each a cup of coffee. Constable Maxwell's a towering giant of a man, in his mid-fifties; he is more than competent in his own slow, methodical way. I knew the trip to the coffee mess was his way of gaining time to digest the new information I'd just laid on him.

When he returned he said, "When Rick comes on duty, I'll have him run the shackles and cuffs over to her. Nasty business, but you must have known it'd come to this someday."

I looked over at John D., wondering if that was an "I told you so." He'd been with the constable's office ten long years before I came along. Under normal circumstances he would have inherited the job of chief constable because of his seniority. Before the berserker outbreak, the position was a fairly easy job, not requiring an extensive background in police work. Back in the old days the chief constable had to worry more about the political front than he did about heavy criminal activity. Shandaken, like most towns in the Catskills, was a community fairly free of serious crime. Things changed. That was why I'd been given the top job, instead of John D. He always claimed that he thought it had been the right decision, but I wondered sometimes. A little paranoia always comes along with command.

I decided I was too exhausted to pursue the matter just then. I glanced around the squad room to see if I could spot something that would give me a chance to change the subject. That's when I noticed the lights on in the little room, at the back of the station, we call the com center.

I got up and walked over to the door. Several of the radios and scanners were on. I turned back to John D. and asked, "You been trying to reach someone?"

John D. shook his head as he walked over. "No, Parker's been here all night monitoring some radio activity he picked up. He was going to stop by your place later today to talk to you about it. I think you ought to stick around until he gets back. He may have something this time."

"Where'd he go?"

The noisy plumbing of the station house answered that question before John D. got the chance. A few moments later, Dirk Parker wandered out of the men's room. Ol' Dirk's a pistol, about five feet ten and a little overweight— which he refers to as "undertall." When that doesn't work he blames it on too many doughnuts munched "in the line of duty" at the com center. Dirk also blames his poor eyesight on his work. His spectacles are the closest I've ever seen to *really* looking like the bottoms of Coke bottles, despite the popular saying.

He flashed me a big grin when he spotted me, but it quickly faded when he remembered why he wanted to talk to me. Without even a hello, he grabbed my elbow and ushered me into his domain. "Boy, am I glad to see you. I think we may have some Grade A trouble on our hands. Didn't want to bother you until I had more info, but I don't think I can wait that long anymore."

John D. remained by the door, casually listening in. He had the look of a man who had heard it all before but was willing to sit through it twice, to make sure he hadn't missed anything the first time. That's John D.'s style.

Dirk began to rewind a tape on a nearby reel-to-reel. He slipped on a set of earphones, unplugged a couple of leads from the rewinding tape recorder, and replugged them into another nearby machine, which he immediately flipped on to record. But the recorder just sat there. Dirk noticed my perplexed look and said, "Sound-activated. Won't start recording until there's traffic on the channel I'm monitoring."

I nodded my appreciation of the basic concept, trying to fake an understanding I didn't really feel. It's always been like that for me, watching Parker tinker with his precious monitoring equipment. Even though Dirk Parker's com center is officially a department of the constable's office, I've really never had much of an idea what he does back there. All I know is he manages to keep us in contact with the rest of the world. He does that with an assortment of equipment so arcane it looks like it came off the set of a Frankenstein movie. He understands the setup, though, and even managed to teach Greta Evans enough so she can handle police calls. But her working knowledge of the other equipment jammed into the tiny room is sketchy at best.

Too impatient to wait graciously for Parker to stop his tinkering, I asked, "What sort of trouble, Dirk?"

Dirk pulled his earphones down around his neck and stared intently at an illuminated meter on one of the sets. I wasn't sure if he had heard me, so I was about to ask again when he softly said, "I think we're about to be hit by raiders."

Needless to say, this got my attention. "When? From where?"

"When? Oh, I'd say sometime in the next three days. From where? I've got no answer for you there."

I looked over at John D. to see if he shared my opinion of this little bombshell of Parker's. He shook his head and said, "Dirk, I think you'd better tell Tom the whole story from the beginning. Less confusing that way."

Parker blushed some, rubbed his eyes, and said, "Of course, sorry. I was running a monitor scan over the different frequencies I can pick up. I like to do that a couple times a week. Always know what's going on around you, that's my motto. Well, anyway, three days ago I came across some transmissions on a frequency the military used back in the old days. At first all I get are garbled bits and pieces, so I don't think much about it. The source of the transmissions is too far away. I figure it's maybe an old GI mobile unit traveling down the New York Thruway.

"But I check back on it over the next twelve hours. During that time the transmissions get stronger. I'm picking up two separate parties trying to contact a third party that's apparently not yet in range. But what's interesting is that these two parties seem to be talking in code, a sort of quasi-military lingo. This gets me to wondering.

"So I've kept a close ear on this frequency ever since then. The third party finally came on line early yesterday morning, complaining about the mountains screwing up his reception. This got party number three a thorough tongue-lashing from party number one about radio security. Kind of funny, no? Some people out there don't want anyone to know they're transmitting from inside the Catskills, even though any numbskull would know we wouldn't be picking them up on this frequency unless they were inside this mountain range.

"Would you like to hear the tape I've made of their communications? It only comes down to about ten minutes of conversation. I used a sound-actuated pickup system, so there's no dead air."

I nodded assent, and Dirk flipped on the recorder. At first all that came out of the speakers was garbled nonsense. Occasionally I recognized a voice heavily overlain with static, but nothing was decipherable. Dirk noted my irritation and assured me the show would get better.

In a few moments the transmissions became clearer. Only a few words came through distinctly to begin with, but within sixty seconds I was able to catch everything being said. And what I heard chilled my blood. I recognized the jargon and most of the nomenclature, unmistakably military in nature. Suddenly I was back in the Nam, listening to a field radio screech out orders and requests.

I listened intently to the rest of the tape. The transmissions continued to get clearer as it went along. When Dirk's recording came to an end, he flipped off the machine and turned to me. "Well, what do you think?"

"I think I want to hear what you make of this. You've had some time to digest it all."

Parker got up, wandered out of the com center, and headed for the coffee maker. I followed. Dirk Parker's penchant for dramatic pauses has always annoyed me. He chose not to answer until he'd poured himself a fresh cup of java.

"What I think we have here are three bands of travelers converging on one spot. They refer to their destination as Cornucopia, but by the way all three transmissions continue to clarify evenly as they draw nearer, I'd say Shandaken is Cornucopia.

"This group sounds military, so my guess is that they're well armed. From what I've been able to gather from their communications, they're only vaguely familiar with this area. There's only one way a band of armed men survive any distance from their home base. They raid. These guys sound like they must be from New York City. They're probably supply raiders for some community down along the Hudson."

I stepped over to a desk and pulled out an old dogeared map of the county. "But where are these raiders coming from? Surely we'd have gotten some reports from neighboring communities if they'd been spotted passing through their territories."

John D. stared down at the unfolded map. "I've been giving that a lot of thought since Parker told me about these transmissions. Wonder if these raiders didn't come up together? Suppose they traveled in groups of twos and threes, only meeting up at some prearranged staging area? Who would have taken any notice of them? We've got heavily armed men passing through all the time."

I began to catch John D.'s drift. "Yes, they'd rendezvous in the woods, out of sight. Someplace no one would stumble across them. They probably sent out a forward scout to map out the area for them weeks, maybe months, in advance."

Parker came up behind us. "But wouldn't someone spot them once they started heading toward us?" John D. and I smiled at each other. Dirk was a whiz in his com center, but we were now entering the real world, an area in which guys like John D. and me shine.

"They're not coming along the roads, Dirk. These raiders are coming through the woods, through the mountains. John, have we still got that topographical map around here somewhere?"

John D. started rummaging through another desk and finally came up with the desired article. He spread it out on top of the bar. The three of us crowded around. The first step was to eliminate any valley that had a highway through it. Roads meant houses, and houses meant a good chance of being spotted before they'd reach their destination. These guys, if they're any good, wouldn't take needless risks.

That left three possible routes: though Woodland Valley, across the park in Chichester, or down the old rangers' trail from the fire tower on Mount Tremper. Parker had picked up three separate transmissions. This all began to make a terrible sort of sense. Each route was impassable by car, but could be managed by foot or all-terrain vehicle. I went over and sat down at my desk.

"Of course, it's all conjecture at this point. We might just be imagining monsters at the door."

"You don't really believe that's the case, though, do you?" John D. said grimly as he proceeded to lace all three of our coffees with a pint of rum I didn't know he had hidden in his desk.

"No, I think we're going to be hit. But the only way to find out where and when, exactly, is to send some scouts of our own up into the hills."

I started jotting down names on a sheet of paper. When I finished, I handed it to John, and he nodded in agreement. "They're the best for the job. Every one of them's a good hunter and knows those mountains."

"Have Ricky round them up. Can you brief them, John? Fill them in on the whole story and set them up with hand radios. Tell them to call in as soon as they spot anything."

"Can do. What are you going to do?"

"Take the rest of the day off, exactly as planned. The way Dirk's got it figured, we probably have at least a couple days before trouble starts. I'm going to get some rest while I still can. If anything comes up, I'm only a radio call away."

John D. rubbed the back of his neck, looked up at the ceiling and back at me, then spit it out. I could tell it wasn't easy for him. "Maybe your taking the day off isn't such a good idea."

"What do you mean? We've had raiders make runs at the town before. Everyone knows the drill, forward and backward. What we have here is maybe two dozen men planning on hitting the food depot. It's bad news but not a major disaster. You and Gary can handle it. I'll be back on duty long before anything heats up."

John D. glanced over at Parker and said, "It's not that, Tom. How about we talk outside."

*   *   *

He didn't wait for an answer, so I followed him out the front door and over to the park bench across the street. When he got himself comfortably settled, he stared back across the road and said quietly, "Mayor Hayden stopped by last night to talk to me."

"Oh, great. What'd she want?"

"She wants me to take over your job."

John D. turned and gave me a hard stare so I'd know he wasn't kidding. He needn't have bothered. I'd been half expecting this move for some time, but it still hit me like a physical blow. Damn that woman! When I didn't say anything, John D. looked away again and muttered, "She'd just found out about that new grave up at your place. Said eleven killings is eleven killings too many."

"You agree with her?"

"Have to say I do. I like you, Tom. You've been a good man to work for. But the situation with your wife is completely out of control. Even though she don't come to town no more, she's still got everyone spooked."

"What's Hayden planning to do?"

"The mayor's called a town council meeting for tomorrow. She's going to demand a vote on having you and your wife posted from Shandaken."

"Have us posted? I don't understand."

"That means they're going to pass an ordinance saying you and your old lady are a menace to public safety and shouldn't be allowed in town any longer. They used to do that in the old west. It was a way of keeping troublemakers out of the community."

"Oh, yeah, now I remember."

"So you see what I mean about taking the day off. With a crisis going on, it might not look so good."

I got up from the bench and wearily stretched. "John, I've been on the road for a week. I had a couple of shootouts during that time and another one just yesterday. Not only do I deserve a day off, I'm in desperate need of one. If Mayor Hayden plans to put this proposal to the council, then it means she's fairly sure it's going to pass. And in that case I don't see where it's going to matter what I do." The words came out sounding glib and unconcerned enough. I doubt they fooled John D. for a second, though. In the

Orient this maneuver is called saving face. I was in trouble, and we both knew it.

John D. pulled out a half-smoked cigar and relit it. "Yeah, maybe you're right."

"Under the circumstances, it might be best if we hold off informing Mayor Hayden about the possibility of raiders. She might think I'm only manufacturing a convenient emergency. Let's wait until we've got more proof to back up our theory."

John D. got up, smiling and shaking his head. "Okay. But this raider trouble couldn't have come at a better time for you. The town council is not going to want to change horses in the middle of such troubled waters."

"Maybe, but they've got short memories. As soon as the danger's past, they'll be after my scalp again."

"Yeah, you may have a point there."

"John, are you going to back Mayor Hayden's play for my job?"

"No, but I won't oppose it either. Ruth said that if I don't take the job, it goes to Benny Hollaster."

I whistled. "Boy, that Ruth. For a sweet old lady she really knows how to go for the groin."

As I turned to walk off, I said over my shoulder, "I'll be at Brio's for the next hour or so, if anything comes up. After that you can reach me at home. See you later, J. D. Thanks for the storm warning."

John D. may have said goodbye. I don't remember. My mind was on my stomach. This latest development and the station-house coffee were conspiring to eat a hole in my intestinal lining. Breakfast had become an urgent priority. The last thing I needed was an ulcer on top of all my other problems.

Breakfast was rather tasteless. It wasn't the restaurant's fault. My mind just didn't have enough unoccupied work space left to deal with anything as mundane as registering gustatory sensation. I'm just not one of those folks who sublimates with food when my entire life comes crashing down around my ears. For me self-pity requires every bit of energy I can muster. It leaves me with very little appreciation for anything else.

I was finishing my second cup of coffee and last bite of toast when Josh wandered into Brio's. He looked bleary-eyed and unsteady, having obviously tested some of his own bootleg hootch the previous night. I guess it isn't actually bootleg. Josh isn't a moonshiner; he's Shandaken Township's leading bottler of alcoholic beverages, since there are no tax men left to make the distinction between bootleggers and "purveyors of fine liquors."

His recreational poison is produced from the old jerry-built stills behind his place. It's become his business rather than just a hobby. I try to avoid his firewater. So does Josh, usually. It's really not fit for human consumption. Admittedly, it has one hell of a kick and gets the job done. The trouble is that when you wake up the next morning you feel like a zombie from *Night of the Living Dead.*

Josh spotted me and staggered over to my table. He made a valiant but vain attempt at smiling, gave it up, and settled for saying, "Morning."

"Morning yourself. I'm surprised to see you up and about this early."

"Never been to bed. Smitty and Kermit Grover stopped over last night for a couple of bottles. We got to jawing and tilting a few back. The next thing I knew, it's morning and the two of them are passed out in my hammock, together. Well, they're no fun anymore and my stomach started to rumble so I decided to come into town for breakfast."

"It must have been a rough walk in your condition."

"Walk? Are you kidding? I'm still too drunk to walk. I drove into town."

"Terrific."

Wendy, recognizing Josh's condition, rushed him a cup of caffeine and a shot of her own special medical advice. "Josh, you look just terrible. You've been hitting that rotgut again, haven't you? You should be ashamed of yourself. That stuff will eat your liver clean away."

"You're absolutely right, Wendy my love. It's an awful thing I've been doing to this temple of a body of mine. It won't happen again, I promise. At least not until next time."

"Very funny! You men, I swear." Wendy turned her back to our laughter and hurried off to tend to more deserving customers.

Josh turned to me and sized up my condition through bloodshot eyes. "You look like you had quite a night yourself."

I filled him in on what happened. I told him everything from Maria's late-night assault to John D.'s warning. I knew he wasn't going to force-feed me any unwanted doses of reality concerning Maria, as Warren would have. I was looking for sympathy and knew Josh would provide it. He didn't let me down.

"Heavy trip, man. You got yourself one hell of a set of problems there. Guess the only thing to do is deal with them as they come at you."

I leaned back in my chair, feeling better now that I'd had a chance to voice these worries. Hearing them out loud made them more manageable. "Well, the way I see it, the town's either going to survive this raid or it won't. We've got an early enough warning of its coming to be ready by the time the fireworks start. It's a waste of time for me to worry about it. Whatever's going to happen will happen, and there isn't a thing I can do about it.

"The same goes for Rachel Benson and her kids. I feel rotten about it, but they're history.

"My only real problem is Maria. I haven't the slightest notion what to do about either her or Mayor Hayden. Maria's getting worse, and there's no telling what she'll do next. Perhaps Ruth's right. Maybe it's time Maria and I thought about moving on. We've outstayed our welcome here."

"What the hell are you talking about? Living on the highway? You won't find another town to take you in, and you know Maria won't be able to hack it on the road. She ain't put together for that kind of life."

"I'm not going to have much of a choice in the matter if Ruth manages to get us posted, now am I?"

"Think that'll happen?"

"Not if I can get John D. to back me. The trouble is, John's a bit naive about the way things really run around here these days. Guess I'll have to give him a little crash course in reality. I'm not sure how he'll take it."

Josh slowly shook his head. "You and that Mrs. Benson are sure between a rock and a hard place. I don't know what to say."

"There ain't anything to say, Josh. Rachel and I both, deep in our hearts, know what's coming. We've both lived with our respective situations too long not to recognize the inevitable when we see it. I guess today's the day we've both had to face up to the truth. I've been fighting that. It's not easy to give up on someone you love."

"You know, if you need help with anything, all you have to do is ask."

"Thanks. I guess I could use some advice. Hell, maybe it's not exactly advice. 'Reassurance' is a better word for it. I've got to ask you something, Josh. I know I probably shouldn't, but I'm going to anyhow, because I need to know the answer."

I could see from Josh's face that he knew what was coming, but he said, quietly, evenly, "Go ahead. Ask it."

"I know how much you loved your wife and kid, Josh. I watched you hurting when they died. But you put it all together again and got on with your life. What I want to know is . . . how did you do it, Josh? How'd you manage to hold it together after they were gone? How'd you stop yourself from going off the deep end and blowing your brains out?"

Josh didn't say anything. He stared into his coffee cup. The seconds of silence stretched on uncomfortably into what seemed like years. I started to regret having asked Josh the question. Did I really expect an answer that would help me in the least? I certainly didn't think Josh would have some secret insight into life that would put everything back in order for me. I knew no one had those answers, but somehow I couldn't stop myself from asking. No intestinal fortitude I guess.

It was beginning to look like Josh was never going to come out of that silent inspection of his java. So I took to studying Josh. I remembered his telling me about moving up from New York City. He had grown up on Harlem's unforgiving streets. As a teenager, he had run with a street gang and done all the things he felt he had to do to survive in that asphalt jungle. But Josh had more on the ball than his brutal friends did. He began to realize the outlaw existence he was living wasn't leading anywhere but to an early grave. This suspicion was confirmed soon after, when a close friend of his met an especially grisly death at the hands of a rival gang.

Josh split from his compatriots, went back to high school, and graduated. Along the way, he met Jennifer Isley. They fell in love, married, and soon had a child on the way. Jennifer's unexpected pregnancy derailed a lot of Josh's plans for the future. College was out. But that was all okay. Josh was going to be a writer. You didn't necessarily need a college degree to be a good writer. You could learn on your own.

What did bother Josh was that he was going to be bringing his son or daughter into the same hostile environment that he had grown up in. He wanted something more for his kid. He wanted fresh air and grass for his child to play in. He didn't want the streets that his kid would have to walk through to school to be infested with junkies, hookers, pimps, and other assorted hustlers. So Josh and Jennifer packed their bags and moved out of New York City. They left without a backward glance.

They weren't the first black family to move into the Catskill Mountains, but that didn't make it any easier. Everywhere they went, they were greeted by the same curious and measuring stares. It wasn't as bad as Josh had feared. No one burned a cross on his lawn. But then again, no one went out of his way to be friendly, either.

Josh took odd jobs to earn a living for his family and eventually got into construction and landscaping. Construction workers up in the mountains weren't unionized, so his skin tone didn't get in the way. He hooked up with Chet Houston's outfit. Chet was color-blind. If you did an honest day's work for him, he couldn't care less if you were polka-dotted.

Josh kept at his writing; short stories mostly. He'd do it at night, after putting in a long hard day on the job. He let me read a few of them once. They were quite good, all about growing up in Harlem. Some of the stories were heartwarming. Others were chilling, and still others were hilarious. They were all very interesting and quite readable. But the editors Josh sent those stories to invariably returned his manuscripts with polite little letters telling him his work wasn't "commercial enough" or "exactly what we're looking for." Not one of those marvelous stories ever saw print.

Poor Josh. He never had much luck at creating anything that was both worthwhile and lasting. His stories remain unpublished, his gin is only good as a paint remover, and his son, well . . .

It was a warm evening in August when Jennifer and Josh had their little boy. They named him Marvin after Jennifer's favorite crooner. By the time the kid was ten, Josh had started a landscaping business of his own and was doing quite well at it. Marv was twelve when Schizophrenia X began mutating into Berserker's Syndrome. He was only thirteen when the tragedy struck.

I had been in town less than a year at that point. But I was already the chief constable. Art Davis, my predecessor, had been killed only a month before. A berserker in a pickup truck ran him down and continued to drive back and forth over him, until another constable put a bullet through the truck's windshield and the driver's head. Poor Art. He

hardly had a body worth burying by the time that crazy got done with him.

Josh had done a little work on our house when Maria and I first moved to town and we'd played a few games of chess down at the trading post. We got along all right, but I wouldn't have called him a friend yet. We were working at it, but not quite there. Then one day, I got that berserker call over the patrol car's radio. I recognized the address as Josh's.

I found him sitting on a rock out in front of his house. He had a shotgun resting on his lap and a river of tears flowing down his face. I kept my gun trained on him as I approached. He didn't even notice my arrival until I yanked his shotgun away. Then he slowly came out of his sorrow enough to tell me what had happened.

He wasn't the berserker. His son was. Marvin had stabbed his mother to death with a kitchen knife and then tried to do the same to Josh. Josh had fought his son off and grabbed the gun. He knew what had to be done. But he just couldn't do it. So he called in the berserker report on his CB.

Josh looked up at me, hoping I wasn't going to make him ask. I didn't. I walked into the house, found Marvin, and shot him.

I helped Josh bury his family and then had him come stay with Maria and me for a couple days. He didn't say much during that stay. He spent much of that time out in our yard. Sometimes he'd cry. Other times he'd sit there for hours like some tragic ebony statue. Then, on the third morning of his bereavement, he came and thanked us for our hospitality and said it was time he went home and started living again. And that's exactly what he did.

Josh never talked about his loss. Oh, Jennifer and Marvin sometimes come up in his conversation. But it's always in a warm remembering way. Always positive. Never sorrowful or bitter. I couldn't understand how he had managed to cope so well. Maybe that was why I had asked him that stupid question. I wanted to know the secret of surviving after all you've ever loved has died. I wanted a nice simple answer to the hardest problem anyone ever has to face. I was hoping Josh could supply it.

Finally Josh pulled himself from his coffee reverie. He didn't look up, but his voice slowly cut through the terrible silence. "I thought about killing myself at first. It was all too horrible to live with. I still feel that way when I'm tired and lonely."

"Then how do you get past it?"

"By remembering Jenny and the kid. They wouldn't want me to go and murder myself. They'd be ashamed of me. I always told them never to give up hope. They'd expect me to do the same."

"Do you think about them often?"

"Not anymore. Sometimes I can go through almost an entire day without them coming to mind. Then all of a sudden, I'll hear a joke I'm sure Jenny would get a kick out of. Or I'll read something that seems like a good thing for a growing boy to know. But when I get home at night, there's no one to tell these things to."

"I'm sorry I asked you this, Josh."

"Don't be. I know exactly what you're going through. But I also realize that you're looking to me for a painless way to solve your troubles. I'm sorry, my friend. There's no easy out on this one. There's only a lot of hurting and tears. You can't get around that. Either you're going to have to learn to live with it or you'll wind up putting that big ol' .45 automatic in your mouth and pulling the trigger."

Wendy dropped off Josh's usual breakfast without saying a word. I imagine the looks on our faces proclaimed the seriousness of our conversation and Wendy decided she wanted no part of it. As she hurried away from our table, the wiggle of her shapely rear end distracted us both. The mood broke. My friend poked at his sausage and eggs and smiled wisely.

"I guess the trick is to remember the past, but not allow yourself to be chained to it. There's a whole planet out there full of people who have lost, not only people they love, but the nice safe world they once called home. I know it doesn't really help to know that everyone's in the same boat as you. But you've got to keep that in mind for perspective. If everybody takes the suicide out, there won't be anyone left to help and teach the children. Someone's got to take that responsibility. Whether you're here or not, tomorrow's going to come. I still have some faith left in me. So I think mankind's going to weather this berserker business, and I want to be able to help the kids put it back together after the shooting and the killing end. Someone's got to be here to tell them how it used to be and how it can be again."

"I never realized what a philosopher you are, Josh."

"Ain't philosophy. It's pragmatism. I figure if I help reform society after the berserker problem gets settled, society will take care of me in my old age. If I make it to old age, that is."

"Why shouldn't you? Warren Green's made it."

"Yeah, that certainly is amazing. You'd think with all that I-calls-'em-as-I-sees-'em honesty of his, someone would have shot him a long time ago."

"Say, why don't you eat up and I'll drive you home—I walked in myself. I'll even help you wake up and get rid of your house guests."

"Yeah, we can stop by your place and pick up Rex. He can piss on them.'

"Not funny, Josh.

Josh finished his breakfast and managed to keep it down without too much difficulty. His color got a little strange at one point, but he forced down another cup of black coffee and his system managed to right itself. Of course, Josh wanted to drive home himself, but I grabbed the keys out of his hand, beat him to the wheel, and locked the door behind me. He cursed me a bit, but eventually got in on the truck's passenger side.

As we were pulling out of town, I spotted Frank, our mystery biker. He was heading out of town down Route 214 on his Harley. I breathed a sigh of relief. He had all his road gear strapped to his bike. My unknown element was conveniently moving on just as I had hoped; a mystery unsolved but one I wouldn't have to worry about. At least that's what I thought, watching him roar up the road that Sunday morning. Now, I realize, he was just leaving to meet up with his gang. Frank had his triumphant return to Shandaken all mapped out. If only I had checked on him a little more carefully, I might have found out what he was up to. Then a lot of trouble could have been avoided, and some good people wouldn't have had to die. *If.* What a nagging little word, full of recriminations and regrets. But then again, maybe I've laid more guilt on my head than I deserve. Lapsed Catholics have a tendency to do that.

When we reached Josh's house, Smitty and Kermit were still sawing wood. Josh and I flipped them very unceremoniously out of the hammock. That did no more than change the pitch of their snoring. So I was forced to fire a couple of .45 rounds into the air to rouse them from their slumber. I was feeling rather giddy all of a sudden and acting nearly as childish as Josh. I think I was experiencing what you'd call a contact high.

The twin sleeping beauties slowly came to, wished us a good morning, and asked if they had had a good time. We assured them that they had and sent them promptly on their way. I walked them to Silver Hollow Road and pointed them in the right direction. When the blacktop ran out, they'd be at their respective homes, so it wasn't as if I was abandoning blind drunks in the woods. Besides, I was sure Smitty's wife was keeping an angry eye out for the prodigal's return.

By the time I returned to Josh's, he had taken up residence in the hammock and was snoring louder than both Smitty and Kermit put together. I couldn't figure out how he managed to stay asleep while producing such a ruckus. Josh is a mystery in a number of ways.

I looked around his untidy little homestead. Its condition left no doubt that Josh was living all alone here, without any women about. Next to the garage lay a V-8 engine that Josh had removed from his truck and replaced sometime last year. An assortment of other discarded auto parts surrounded it.

The house needed painting. Behind it were two split garbage bags and three boxes of junk that looked like they were never going to make it to the dump.

At the far end of the field, Josh's backyard, I could see the two stills he uses to cook his moonshine. Mass production. Every businessman's dream. Behind the house, three work shirts and a curing wild turkey hung from a clothesline. A fourth shirt lay on the grass below, a victim of poor clothes-pinning and harsh winds. The two graves, starkly alone, sat off to the right of all this, in a corner all their own. I walked over and looked down at the crudely hand-carved inscriptions. The names were just as I remembered. Jennifer and Marvin Woodward. The dates on the tombstones told me that Marvin had died at the age of thirteen, his mother at thirty-two. The dates also told me that they had died three years ago on July 17. Yesterday was July 17.

I turned and looked at Josh in his hammock. "Sorry, old friend. I didn't remember."

He had tried to tell me what it was like in words. It hadn't worked. They had come out as empty clichés. But Josh had finally answered my question. Looking at him lying there, passed out in his cluttered backyard, told me the whole story that he couldn't.

I felt an acid burning in my eyes. The wind must have changed direction and I was suddenly downwind from the still. That smell is enough to make anyone's eyes water. I rubbed at them with the back of my hand and headed over toward my place up the road. Maria would be awake by now. Today was supposed to be my day off. I was going to spend it with my lady and enjoy it.

The storm clouds hung over the horizon, but it didn't matter. My world was still bathed in the sunlight that was Maria. I was going to revel in it as long as I could. For I was beginning to accept the fact that she wasn't going to be with me much longer, and that she was going to be a memory for an awfully long time.

15

It had been a terrific day. Because if the truth were told, I'd have to confess that I've always enjoyed lying around doing absolutely nothing. Beneath this hardworking and responsible exterior, there lurks a hedonist who would be perfectly happy to never again undertake another useful task in this lifetime. He would be quite content to guzzle wine, get fat, and listen to Maria Burgos play the piano. And that's exactly what I'd been doing all day. A part of me was mildly surprised by how easily I'd pushed Rachel, Mayor Hayden, and all the rest of the bullshit out of my head. But the rest of me thumped me heartily on the back, saying, "Tom Laker, you devil-may-care sybarite, I always knew you had it in you."

That Sunday was something truly special. Maria hadn't even touched the ivories for nearly two months. She'd claim that she didn't feel inspired. I didn't buy that. Music had always been Maria's passion, as much an integral part of her being as breathing is to the rest of us. I didn't want, however, to poke into any dark corners, so I just let it go at that. But when I came home from Josh's that morning, there she sat at the Steinway upright. Maria played with happy abandon right on through the entire morning.

At noon, when she took a break for lunch, we joined forces to do some serious damage to a watermelon I had carted home the day before. I retrieved a bottle of Pinot Grigio I had stored in the basement. I'd been saving it for an "occasion," and Maria's return to the ivories seemed like a special enough event to me. So she and I polished off what was quite possibly the last bottle of imported wine in the Catskill Mountains. To be perfectly honest, it was I who worked with diligence to do justice to this fine wine. The small splash that Maria poured to cover the bottom of her glass went nearly untouched. She didn't need the wine. All she wanted was her music. She raced back to the piano even before I finished lunch.

Maria couldn't wait to cast her magic spell. The first number she dived into was Liszt's "Rakóczy March" with a power that made it feel like the whole house was vibrating. The manic look that glittered in her eyes as she played this number scared me a little. But then she drifted into "Valse Oubliée No. 1" and a new person suddenly emerged at the piano bench. This woman was as sweetly dreamy as the music she played. So I relaxed, sipped my rare nectar, and enjoyed the impromptu concert. The afternoon was spent with giants: Mozart, Chopin, Schubert, Handel, and others that don't come as readily to mind.

Maria took only two breaks during that entire session. She'd get up, stretch, come over and tease me about getting drunk in broad daylight, have a small sip of her own wine, then return to the keyboard. It was as if she were packing several months' worth of playing into a single afternoon. The music was beautiful, and yet there was a slightly disturbing quality to her performance. I drank some more wine to put that out of mind. This was going to be a sunny and enjoyable Sunday afternoon. I wasn't going to let my grim thoughts of the future or my paranoia ruin a lovely day.

But as it turned out, that afternoon was obviously not meant to remain idyllic. I "watched" with closed eyes a mild spring shower, as Maria made her way through Chopin's "Raindrop Prelude." When the music and downpour ended together, I remained as I was, waiting for the next number to begin. But the silence continued unabated. I waited . . . it continued. Finally I opened my eyes and turned to Maria. She was staring at me, rather intently.

"Something wrong, babe?" I asked uneasily.

"You weren't in bed this morning when I awoke."

"Couldn't sleep. I didn't want to bother you, so I took a walk."

"That never used to happen. I was always the light sleeper, remember? Now I seem to be constantly waking up to find you've gotten up before me. I find that kind of disturbing."

"I wouldn't worry about it. So you're not sleeping as lightly as you used to. It's no big deal. Probably means your body needs a little extra rest, that's all. . . ." My voice trailed off, it seemed to me, for lack of conviction.

"Yes, well . . . maybe you're right."

Maria started in on "The Minute Waltz." Her eyes closed as her supple fingers danced across the keys performing Chopin's sixty-second masterpiece. When it ended, her eyes remained closed as she quietly asked, "What happened to the pillow?"

"Pillow?" I said glibly, always able to think on my feet.

"Your pillow, Tom. It's gone. What happened to it?"

"I tossed it. Split seam. It was getting feathers all over the place. I'll pick up a new one tomorrow."

Maria opened her eyes and smiled at me as she started quietly playing "Für Elise." "I saw it in the trash bin outside. Looked like someone had gutted it."

"I caught it on my belt buckle."

Okay, I exaggerated slightly when I said I could think on my feet.

The look on Maria's face said she didn't quite believe me. She finished the piece without another word and glided smoothly into the first movement of Beethoven's "Moonlight Sonata." I've always found that particular bit of music slightly creepy, and Maria's low-volume, high-intensity rendition only managed to heighten that impression.

"Life hasn't really played fair with us, love. Has it?" Maria asked without looking over to me.

"I don't know. I've seen it treat other folks a lot worse. At least we have each other."

"You're right about that. But it seems to me that life used to come with something like an understood guarantee. It said that if I ate my vegetables and played by the rules, I'd get to lead the good life someday. So I studied hard and practiced my music endlessly. I tried hard never to hurt anyone and helped out whenever I could. I say my prayers at night to the God I still believe in, and love my husband. That's the way I always heard it should be.

"But something happened, and now there's no payoff left. Where are all the just desserts that used to make up the good life? I can remember the concerts and plays. Where are they now? What happened to the museums and art galleries? I remember how we used to hang around at little restaurants in the city. We'd meet friends and have lively conversations that would last until closing time. What happened to that world, Tom? Our world—"

"It died, Maria. The berserkers killed it. I'm sorry."

"That's only part of it. There's more. It's not just that half the world has gone crazy. I know how nutty it sounds, but . . . I can live with that. As long as you're by my side, I can. There's something else here. But I can't put my finger on what it could be.

"I think I first noticed it the day they told me that they wouldn't be needing my services as music teacher at the grade school anymore. I mean, I not only thought it was strange that they had decided to stop teaching music . . . but it was the way they said it. I knew they were lying to me. They seemed afraid of me. I know everyone's afraid of everyone else these days, but they stared at me as if they were absolutely sure I was dangerous. That was the beginning of it.

"Then people stopped coming over. All the friends we had made over the last three years. They all suddenly stopped calling. You told me it was because they were afraid of this berserker situation. That wasn't it, though, was it? I could tell there was more to it than that, by the way they acted when I came into town.

"So I stopped going into the village. I don't need those people, you know. All I need is you, Tom. Sometimes I think I'd be happy to spend the rest of my days in this house, dealing with no one but the man I love. But now there's even something unspoken hanging in the air between us. I'm not blind, Tom. There have been things going on here. I don't know what they are. But I can see them in your eyes . . . and there are too many questions left unanswered.

"What really happened to the pillow, Tom? And what about those cars and motorcycles across the road? Where do they come from? Why aren't they in the town's car pool?"

I remained silent, because I didn't know what to say. In fact, I was holding my breath. Maria was beginning to glimpse something in the whirling mist. I couldn't even imagine what would happen when she saw clearly and finally understood. There was no doubt left, however, that the moment of reckoning was almost at hand. What would the truth do to her mind? Would it cure her? I didn't dare to hope.

Or would she fall all that much farther into the madness that had been claiming her? There was so much I didn't know. So much nobody knew.

Could a berserker experience remission? I'd never heard of such a thing. That didn't mean it couldn't happen. Could it be that until now most, if not all, berserkers had met their deaths before the disease, which caused their homicidal behavior, had been conquered by their body's own defenses? Who would know if such a thing was possible? To my knowledge Maria and Charlie Benson were the only two berserkers ever to be kept under any extended period of observation. It had never occurred to me that some people might be capable of producing their own immunity to the disease.

It was heart-achingly apparent that Maria's condition was altering. Whether she was getting better or worse I couldn't say. Over the past few months she had become progressively more violent, but she was also beginning to sense her own condition. The changes in her seemed to indicate that the disease was taking two contradictory turns. What was I to do? Which way was I to go? Should I help her face the problem head-on? Or should I continue to go along with the subterfuge she'd been playing on herself for the last year?

Maria snapped me back to the real world with the single question needed to cut through all my uncertainties. She stopped playing.

"Is there something wrong with me?"

She wanted to know the turth. She'd always wanted to avoid it before. This had to mean a significant breakthrough. She had a right to know the true state of her mental health. I was going to give it to her, because I felt sure it would help. But we had to take it slowly. So I simply said, "Yes."

Maria let it sink in. I could see enormous tension drain from her face. The cat was out of the bag at last. Everything wasn't exactly roses and daffodils yet, but the simple fact that she hadn't merely imagined all this was, obviously, a relief.

"What's wrong with me? Is it mental?"

"Yes, but it's not easy to explain."

Maria suddenly rubbed the heels of both hands against her temples. This frightened me. It was apparent that Maria was getting a Class A headache. It was too much for one day. I shouldn't push her. Maria's headache made the words "brain tumor" flash across my mind's eye.

"I knew it! I just knew it! The way you'd been acting lately . . . you've been creeping around me as if I were a cancer patient."

"I wasn't sure what to do. Your head bothering you?"

"Yes, a headache. A real killer. It's been sneaking up on me for the last half hour. It just sandbagged me."

"Aspirin?"

"Please."

I got Maria a glass of water and a couple of tablets from our first-aid kit. She got up from the piano and stretched out on the sofa. The aspirins went down with no trouble. Maria eased herself back down again with her eyes squeezed shut and her forehead furrowed.

"What is wrong with me exactly, Tom? Do I vege out occasionally and not remember it?"

How far to go with the truth? How fast to take it? I took a look at the pinched expression on her face and made my decision.

"Yes, something like that. But it's not all the time . . . and I think you may be coming out of it."

"I've never heard of anyone being a part-time vege."

"It's a fact. Your condition's unique."

"Well, I'm glad it's finally out in the open. I've been going out of my head wondering what was wrong. Did I really just say that? Oooh! Bloody head. Damn . . . but those dreams were the worst. Lord, this head hurts."

"Maybe you ought to take a nap. You've been pushing it awfully hard today. You played for hours."

"Yes . . . that's a good idea. We can talk more later. At least now I know what's wrong. I imagined all sorts of terrible things. You wouldn't believe some of the things that crossed my mind."

I pulled a light blanket out of the nearby wardrobe and

covered Maria with it. Then I knelt beside her and massaged the back of her neck.

"That feels good," she whispered. Maria was fading fast.

"I'm glad. I want you to get better. I love you, Maria. I love you more than anything else on the face of this earth."

"That's sweet. And I love you. I'll get better. I promise."

She rolled over onto her side and I tucked the blanket in around her. She turned her head, so she could see me through eyes that were already mere slits. "Maybe now the nightmares will go away."

"Let's hope so."

Then she softly drifted off to sleep. After a while, I quietly got up off the floor and walked over to the easy chair on the other side of the room. I must have sat there for nearly an hour, watching my darling wife sleep. It was beautiful. My mind, ablaze with the possibilities of what tomorrow might bring, the doubts and hopes that were dancing across my consciousness, made me dizzy and, yes, a little giddy.

Was I losing my marbles too? Perhaps fantasizing that Maria might be getting better? I carefully tested my grip on reality. My inspection revealed that I was still on relatively solid mental ground. Nothing that had happened that day had any of the qualities that I figured a hallucination should. Maria had really said and done everything that I remembered. I would swear to that on a stack of Bibles.

The other possibility I had to consider was that I was reading this situation all wrong. Could I be seeing only what I wanted to see? Was I ignoring any facts that would contradict my new hopeful outlook? Once again I decided that I had it right. Maria was definitely trying to face and solve the problem. She wasn't denying its existence anymore. Over the past year or so I'd delved deeply, reading extensively about mental health problems. One of the constants I'd come across in all my research was the unanimous opinion of experts that you can't cure a problem until it is acknowledged as such by the patient. This is true of everything from alcoholism to paranoia. Denial is the first hurdle to overcome. It is the prerequisite first step to a cure.

But I also knew, from my reading, that confrontation with the patient isn't the way to get this admission. Maria would have to come to this realization herself, or it would do absolutely no good. So I had to continue to let my lovely, kill-crazy wife run free in her world of denial and fantasy. But deep down, I prayed that someday she'd come around. Today was quite possibly the turning point. I felt sure my Maria had taken the first step in returning to me and sanity.

I suddenly flushed with embarrassment at the recollection that only a few hours ago I had decided I'd finally have to accept Maria's inevitable destruction by this relentless disease. I'd given up on her. I felt ashamed. I had written off the woman I loved and readied myself for her death. So little faith.

Yes, that was it. Faith. I had broken faith with my lady. I had stopped believing and given up hope. There were many things I'd stopped believing in over the past years. Perhaps it was time for me to reflect on them again. Examine those beliefs that I'd disposed of along the way, simply because I'd had no proof of their existence. Beliefs that may have had more value than my young mind could grasp. These thoughts roused the sleepwalker, and when I awoke it was to find myself teetering on the brink of epiphany.

That's when the town alarm sounded. It wasn't the steady siren wail that summons the town volunteer fire department. No, it was the alternating blasts of three longs and three shorts which signal that a police emergency is taking place. Damn! It was the worst possible time for something like this to happen.

I stormed into the dining room and flipped on the CB. Ricky Skeats's voice instantly came blaring out of the Channel 9 emergency band. "Home Base calling Big Chief! Home Base calling Constable Laker! Please come in, Tom! It's bad, Tom! Call in!"

"I will, as soon as you get off the channel." I know Ricky couldn't have heard me, but he cleared the air as if on cue. Maybe it was telepathy. "Big Chief here. What's the problem, Home Base? Over."

"Officer Burton's dead! You've got to get down here, Tom!"

"Pull yourself together, Rick. What's happening down there? Give it to me slowly. Over."

"Berserker trouble. Burton went to check on it and got . . . oh, it's horrible, Tom. You've got to get down here. Over."

"Can't do that, Rick. Maria's sick and needs me here. See if you can get hold of Benny. Over."

Ricky's end of the line went dead. Then I heard movement behind me. It was Maria. She was standing in the archway between the living room and the dining room with the blanket still wrapped around her.

"Go. It sounds like they really need you. I'll be okay."

"Are you sure?"

"Positive. It's just a headache. Go."

I turned back to the radio. "Ricky, you still there? Over."

"Yes."

"Disregard what I said before. I'm on my way in. Where's the action at? Over."

"110 Post Road. Over."

"See you there. Over and out."

I raced to the gun rack, pulled out a pump-action shotgun, checked to make sure it was loaded, and stuffed some extra shells into my shirt pocket. Maria brought over my boots and a cap. I struggled into the boots, hurriedly plopped the cap on my head at a rakish tilt, and gave Maria a long, warm kiss. I headed for the door.

"See you as soon as I can. I'll try to make it quick."

"You can be as late as you want. Just be careful. I love you."

Rex jumped into the patrol car when I tossed the shotgun into the backseat. I noticed how spry he was looking and made a mental note to see how he'd manage without his splint tomorrow.

I caught sight of Josh Woodward coming down the road as I pulled out. He flashed his lights twice to let me know he'd heard the call and was coming along to back me up. This made me feel a lot better. I wanted someone with me that I could trust. Life, I realized suddenly, was very precious to me again. Maria was coming back from the abyss.

16

Officer Randolph Burton really was the stupidest constable I ever had. I know I shouldn't speak ill of the dead. But the unvarnished truth is that it was pure luck that Randy had survived as long as he did. Burton's death was absurd and could easily have been avoided. It was almost as though he had been asking for it. It was an incredibly foolish way to die.

Although Josh and I had arrived only moments earlier, it was excruciatingly apparent to me how Constable Randy Burton had met his end. Ricky Skeats and John D. were keeping the neighbors away from the crime scene. I left ol' Rex in the car. The place was enough of a mess without letting him loose. I was sure that my car's upholstery was going to suffer the consequences, but what could I do?

My head was still a little fuzzy from the wine I'd consumed earlier. As I looked up, I saw the sun creeping behind Mount Sheridan. That meant we only had about an hour of daylight left. I'd have to move quickly. But before I examined the crime scene I wandered over to John D. and asked, "All the scouts get off okay?"

"Yeah, they took off about noon. Don't figure we'll hear anything from them until tomorrow sometime. Nothing to do but wait and worry. I guess it comes with the job."

"Yeah. Well, I'd better get to this mess while there's still time."

John D. walked over to the house with me, but kept his distance from the porch. Can't say I blamed him. He looked away as he said, "I'm sure glad you're here to handle this one, Tom. You know whose place this is, don't you?"

I glanced over at Josh leaning against the front fender of his truck and nodded.

Randy Burton lay sprawled on his back across the front steps. His head had come to rest on the sidewalk. As I glanced over him, I consciously avoided looking too closely. Time enough for that gruesome task later. I looked up at the shattered glass in the front door, then over my shoulder at the slowly setting sun, thinking. Ricky had told me that Burton had arrived here to answer a possible berserker call forty-five minutes ago. The neighbors had complained of horrible screams coming from the house. "It sounds like someone's being butchered in there!"

Of course, the screaming had stopped by the time Randy arrived. That's why the stupid son of a bitch didn't wait for backup or even bother to pull the gun out of his holster. Only Burton found he couldn't see into the house to find out if anyone was home. The sun was directly behind him and the glare turned the panes of glass into opaque reflectors. So Randy leaned his face close to the window and cupped his hands around his eyes to peer in. He probably caught just a glimpse of the ax coming at him before it crashed through the glass.

The blade had come down with enough force to completely sever Burton's left hand then cut a huge gouge through his clavicle and deep into his chest cavity, as it caught the left carotid artery on the way. I could see by his face that Randy probably had a few seconds to think about how asinine he'd been before he passed out and from this world. His eyes were still half open in stunned silence. I reached down and thumbed them shut. Poor, stupid Randy.

Then I turned to Josh and said, "I'm going in. You want to come?"

"No thanks. I've been here before. I'd rather remember it as it was."

"Sure. I'll make it quick."

What was left of the door was open, so I stepped into the house. The kitchen was to my left. Its floor was spotless. He hadn't gone that way. I looked over to the room on the right. It was your typical rural living room. The only thing that made it special was the damp bloodstains on the rug.

This bloody trail led to the staircase, where it diverged in two different directions, one upstairs, the other one straight back. I decided to follow the one that stayed on this floor. At the end of it I found the lady of the house, in a half bathroom which had been added at the back of the building. He had really done a number on her. She was hacked to bits. He'd obviously been so frenzied that one of his blows had missed its mark and shattered the toilet bowl. A fine spray was shooting out of the porcelain, covering the entire room with a sweaty sheen. The bathroom was a step lower than the rest of the first floor. It was filling up with crimson water. Smaller pieces of the dead woman bobbed about in the three-inch-deep scarlet pool. There's something voyeuristic about seeing the fresh site of a violent death. I felt a twinge of something closely akin to guilt as I turned away.

Then I remembered. There was a little girl. Her name was Kathy or Karen. She was about six. I retraced my steps and walked up the stairs. At the end of the second-floor hallway, there was a splintered door. I peered through the opening. I could easily have walked in, but decided against it. Even from the hallway I could see the blood-splattered walls and the overturned bedframe and springs. The bedcovers and mattress had slid forward and now lay flat on the floor. Bloody footprints decorated the off-white bedspread. The girl had probably tried to hide underneath her small single bed. Of course, Daddy had no trouble flipping it over and getting to her.

A small sneakered and bloodstained foot stuck out from behind this havoc. A doll, off in a corner with its head splintered, stared with one remaining eye at the terrible carnage I couldn't see from my angle. I could tell from its expression that I could easily live without seeing anything more. The crime scene had burned off whatever alcohol I'd still had in my system. I was suddenly sober.

When I came back outside I spotted Josh following the blood trail across the street and into a neighbor's backyard. I ran to catch up with him. A bloody handprint showed us where the berserker had gone over the back fence. We did the same. The next street over was Cedar. We came out on it with our shotguns at the ready. But there were no more crimson signposts to tell us which way the killer had gone.

So we split the difference. Josh headed one way up the street, I went the other. I kept to the middle of the road, checking out the windows and driveway of every house I passed. I'd gone only a half a block when I heard the crying. I whistled over my shoulder to Josh and heard him running toward me.

I followed the sorrowful sound down the driveway of Ernie and Allie Jacobson's home. It was coming from the backyard. I waited for Josh to catch up, then we both raced around the corner of the house. He covered my blind spots. I did the same for him. We'd done this before. We always worked well together.

Our target was nowhere in sight, but he'd been there. Allie Jacobson sat in the middle of her backyard, by the lawn mower. Sprawled next to the mower was Ernie's still and slightly overweight frame. Allie had Ernie's head cradled in her lap. Ernie's skull had been cleft nearly in half. Allie looked as if she were trying to press the ugly seam back together and make everything all right again.

"Which way?" I quietly asked her.

She looked up, tears glistening on her cheeks. She gave a sort of small helpless shrug, then looked at Ernie and said, "Look what he did to him. Why? Ernie never hurt him or anyone else."

"Which way, Allie?"

I was surprised when she gently set Ernie's head down on the lawn, got up, and pointed over the back fence and toward the path leading to Main Street. I hadn't been sure my words were even reaching her.

Josh and I heard gunfire as we made our way carefully down that overgrown walkway.

"Sounds like it's coming from Tent Town, Josh."

"He's really covering some territory, then. Let's move it!"

We raced along the trail, no longer worried about ax-wielding assassins behind every tree. On Main Street we came across two men putting a tourniquet around a woman's leg. The ax blade had laid open the entire length of her thigh. She was in shock, but alive. Thank God. Some onlookers pointed toward Tent Town. We didn't bother to stop.

It seemed like everyone in that transient community was crowding around the center of the camp. I fired my shotgun into the air and yelled, "Make way! Let the law through!"

The crowd obeyed. The sea of faces parted. Josh and I found ourselves standing over a dead old man and a much younger fellow who was kneeling next to the corpse. He was desperately trying to stanch the blood flowing out of a nasty-looking wound in his right shoulder. A pistol lay beside him. The dead man had been badly chopped up.

"Which way?"

"Follow the creek. I put a bullet into him before he caught me. That ought to slow him down for you. Blow the bastard's brains out. That's Gramps he did in here."

"Will do! Somebody help this man with his arm!" I called over my shoulder to the crowd as Josh and I sprinted off.

He had crossed the creek but not followed it for too long. His diseased brain realized that he was too exposed there. Probably it was beginning to wonder why he had run off with just an ax. Why hadn't he grabbed a rifle instead? A firearm would be a lot more useful in the woods he was heading for. But it just wouldn't have been the same, killing his wife and child with a gun. Berserkers are sometimes very fussy about their mania. A lot of them get quite obsessive about the way they murder people. If they can't kill them in their favorite fashion, they'll occasionally not even bother. I was betting that was how it was with our prey.

He was leaving his own blood now for us to follow. It led us down to the old railroad track. At this point the track bed followed the creek around a sharp bend. On the other side of it we spotted our man. He was about a quarter mile out in front. I was surprised by the distance he had managed to travel since the shooting in Tent Town. He was losing quite a bit of blood but it didn't seem to matter.

Josh and I took a couple of quick shots at him even though the chances of a hit at this range were slim. What we really wanted to do was scare him off the rails. It would slow him up a bit and make our job easier. We stayed with the tracks as long as we felt safe, then slowed and melted into the forest that bordered the right side of the rails.

We could hear him scrambling through the woods ahead of us. He wasn't wasting any time trying to be cunning. It was speed he was going for, not stealth. There was an abandoned hotel and restaurant up ahead. That was where he was heading. A good move if he made it. We turned up the juice, hoping to catch him in the clearing that surrounded the old buildings.

By the time we cleared the trees he was already out of sight. There were two different buildings to choose from. I was betting he had made his way to the second and larger building. Blood on the floor of the hotel's foyer proved me right. We scanned the cobweb-covered room through the open and inviting doors. I recalled there was a reception counter off to the right and an information desk and bar to the left as you entered. He could be hiding behind one of those counters or just inside the doorway.

Josh and I came through the doors fast and low. We spun around, ready to blast anyone hiding by the doorjambs. No one was there, so we turned our attention to the bar. Josh took one end, I took the other. He did low, I did high. We came up blank. The reception counter and information booth also yielded nothing but dust.

The far end of the lobby had an upstairs gallery running its full length. Josh went over to the stairs to see if our boy had gone that way. He found only undisturbed dust—no blood. It had to be one of the two hallways that led from the lobby. I spotted blood a few feet down the first hall I checked.

We found a couple more drops every few feet. The shiny spots of crimson stood out brightly against the dry, gray, time-worn floor. The bloody trail ended at Room 108. There were a few droplets right by the door and a smear on the knob. The rest of the hallway was unmarked. Our quarry had set up residence.

Josh pressed his back to the wall across from the room. I fired a round through 108's door and immediately kicked it in. The place was a mess. An overturned bed leaned up against the wall. Over in one corner lay a broken chest of drawers and a chair. The blood led across the room to the bathroom door, which sat a bit ajar. I fired through it and was surprised when no one screamed from the other side. So I went over and kicked in the splintered door. The bathroom was empty.

I spun around. Josh had entered the room to cover the closet while I hit the bathroom. The gore-flecked berserker was coming behind Josh, through the hall doorway, with his ax held high over his head. I had no shot at the crazy. Josh was in the way.

"Drop!" I screamed. Josh threw himself down and I fired a round into the madman. It slammed him backward and out into the hallway. He thudded against the hall's far wall and bounced back toward the room. Somehow he was still alive and intent on burying his ax in my friend. Josh had rolled over onto his side. He saw the lunatic coming toward him and let loose a round that blew away most of the berserker's chest. I pumped another load into him, just to make sure.

The gore-spattered corpse stumbled back out of the room and took a few feeble steps down the hall, as though trying to outrace its own mortality, then collapsed. He still had a good grip on that ax. Even in death he wouldn't let go of his dark fixation.

Josh got to his feet and asked, "How?"

Now that I was turned around, I could see the clever trap our quarry had laid for us. He had obviously been much more familiar with this hotel than either Josh or I. We'd nearly come to as stupid an end as Randy Burton. As soon as the crazy had entered this room, he had flipped the battered old brass bed and its springs up on the headboard, resting them against the wall at an angle. This hid the door leading to the adjoining room from us as we entered.

He deliberately left enough blood outside the door to make sure we entered Room 108. He pulled the same trick with the bathroom. But he was already in the next room when we smashed our way through the hall door. He knew our attention would be riveted to the inside of 108. So he popped out of room 106 and followed us inside. I guess he had hoped to whack us both before we knew what was happening. Fortunately, we had moved faster than he expected. I had already turned around before he got his shot at Josh.

"Let's head back to town. I'll have someone come out for the body," I suggested.

"You go on ahead. I'll stick here until they come for him."

"You sure you want to do that, Josh?"

Josh sadly looked down at the dead body of his old friend and chess rival, good-natured Sid Douglas. "Yeah, I'd like to say a prayer or two over him, before they come to haul him away.

17

The sun set over Shandaken and a nearly full moon took its place. It took me several hours to get everything squared away. The death of several citizens is not something you can walk away from immediately, even if you have bagged the bad guy. The bereaved have to be comforted. The injured have to be tended. Statements have to be taken. Bodies have to be gathered up.

This had been a bad one. Most berserkers are brought down before they can add even one person to their body count. Sid had taken out five.

I decided to stick around long enough to see if Josh was going to be all right. It had been a rough couple of days for him. Having to shoot a friend the day after the anniversary of his family's death had to be tearing him up inside. I tried to get him to talk about it, but he wasn't in the mood yet. Maybe in a few days. All he wanted to do was head over to the Sportsman's Bar and tilt back a few. I assigned Ricky Skeats to keep an eye on him.

Maria knew I was okay. She had kept the CB on to monitor what was happening. When the last of the bodies had been taken over to the mortuary, I gave her a call. She was relieved and told me to take my time getting home. Maria knew what it was like after a shooting in town. She was going to stretch out on the couch and finally grab that nap, the one Rick's call had cheated her of earlier.

The last duty I had to perform, before I could head home, was to report to Mayor Hayden. She was a good enough administrator to know that she should stay out of my way while I was getting the job done. But she expected all the details as soon as I was finished, I found her up in her small, dusty and cluttered office. She was sipping a glass of Jack Daniel's. A portable cassette player softly filled the small room with Esther Phillips singing "Such a Night." Ruth reached over and lowered the volume. She listened to my report, only occasionally interrupting to ask a question.

Finally she turned back to me and said, "When's it all going to end, Tom? How much more of this does the good Lord expect us to take?"

"I've no idea, Ruth. Maybe it'll never end. Maybe it's something we're going to have to learn to live with, for the rest of our lives."

"Warren Green thinks things are getting better."

"How does he figure that?"

"Well, he's been going through the town records. You know how he likes to sift through facts and figures. He claims the frequency of violent incidents in town peaked about a year ago."

"Is he counting the trouble we've had with raiders?"

"No, he claims his calculations only include those events that can be classified as berserker incidents. He figured seventy-five percent of the unsolved homicides into his tabulations. Warren concluded that in the past year the number of berserker incidents has dropped by six percent."

"There could be a number of reasons for that. First off, we're better organized than we were a year ago. Word gets around. Maybe the crazies are avoiding our town for easier pickings. I mean, they're loonies, not mental deficients. Secondly, I don't know this for a fact, but I suspect we've got less people in this town than we had a year ago."

"Two percent less. I checked. Even with that factor figured in, though, it still leaves a definite drop in the number of berserker incidents we've had of late. Maybe it's just luck. Maybe it's a trend. Who knows?"

"Well, as chief constable of this burg, I'm going to hope it's a trend but expect it to be nothing but random chance that has given us a break this past twelve months."

"Yes, that's the prudent thing to do. Pray for the best, but keep that gun handy."

We drifted into an uncomfortable silence, staring at each other over her honor's large oak desk. I'd been waiting for her to bring up the subject, knowing she was hoping I would. Didn't see any reason to make it easy on her.

Finally, she cleared her throat and said, "I suppose you've already heard about the meeting of the town council I called for tomorrow."

"Yep."

"I can't let it go on any longer. I like you, Tom. Used to like Maria too. But she's gone now, as far as I'm concerned, and I can't stand idly by while you harbor the dangerous animal she's become. I'm the goddam mayor, Tom! I've got responsibilities!"

I silently glared at her for a few moments, letting her wait for my response. She was expecting a debate, but I wasn't going to give her that satisfaction.

All I said was, "I've got responsibilities too, Ruth."

Then I got up and walked out of her office. I had to. If I had stayed, I doubt I would have been able to fight off the urge that was beginning to overtake me. Despite our differences, part of me still believed Ruth Hayden to be a good person and a good mayor. So I left while I could still remember that fact.

As I drove home, Warren's hypothesis kept racing through my mind. Could it be true? Could the horror be slowly winding down? Please let it be true, I prayed.

Could it be possible that this marvelous machine we call the human body was finally developing an immunity to the madness that would otherwise eventually destroy us all? I remembered reading somewhere that human beings were the most adaptable creatures ever put on earth. Was something mutating within us, something to fight off the effects of Berserker's Syndrome and Schizophrenia X? Could that be why Maria appeared to be getting better?

It had been a long time since anything in life had gone from bad to better. Maybe the tide was beginning to turn.

When I arrived home I let Rex out of the car to do whatever it was he did all night long. There was only one light burning inside the house. My guess was Maria was still sleeping. So I decided to enter quietly and awaken her with many kisses around the neck and ears. That didn't happen.

The living room was a shambles. Its floor was covered with broken china, statuary, and scattered sheet music. Books had been tossed in every direction. Some of them, with pages ripped out, littered the room. Furniture was overturned. One of the dining-room chairs had been reduced to kindling by bashing it against a wall. A number of Maria's canvases had been slashed. It looked as if someone had had a fit.

I loosened the gun in my holster and softly called, "Maria?"

Something in the darkened kitchen stirred. I heard a chair scrape against the floor. Soft footsteps approached me out of the blackness of the kitchen. Maria stepped from the darkness and into the dining room. Her hair was disheveled and there were tear-stained mascara streaks running down both cheeks. But she wasn't crying . . . anymore. The Coleman lantern on the dining-room table cast chaotic shadows across her angry features. A glint of light reflected off the large and dangerous-looking butcher's knife she held in her hand.

I shifted my stance, to prepare for the attack I was certain I'd have to fend off within seconds. I'd taken that knife away from her before. I could do it again. But there was something different about her this time. She looked more alert. There was nothing dreamy about her stare as there had always been before. I suddenly wondered if I was going to survive this encounter. I felt my hand drifting uncontrollably toward my gun.

When she spoke I nearly jumped out of my skin.

"Damn you, Tom Laker!"

"Maria?"

"Damn you! You knew all the time and you didn't tell me!"

"You didn't want to know."

We stood there glaring at each other like a pair of angry medieval gargoyles. I had no idea what was going to happen next. Had I said the right words or was she going to explode and lunge at me?

Then the tension drained out of Maria and she dropped the knife on the floor. She walked over to the table, collapsed in a chair, and buried her face in her hands. I picked up the knife and joined her at the table. I could feel the heat of her passion on the knife handle. The thought of how it would feel having this modern-day dagger enter my body hit me. There'd only be a quick sensation of pressure resisted and surrendered to at first. It would take a few microseconds for nerves to send the message to the brain that the body had been violated. Then the pain would become overwhelming and total. My sensation of this was real, almost like reading a psychic imprint on the knife. I shivered and tossed the blade onto the table. Maria was still hidden behind her hands.

"When did you remember?" I asked.

"Just after you called. I went back to the couch to sleep. But I was so relieved to know you were all right that I couldn't drop off. I lay there thinking. I heard over the radio that Sid had been running around killing people with an ax. The very thought of dying like that made me feel sick, but I couldn't stop thinking about it. I kept seeing the ax blade cutting through flesh.

"All of a sudden, it wasn't an ax doing the damage any more . . . it was a knife. Then everything started to pour out. I couldn't push it back. I thought it was a dream or fantasy at first. But the details kept getting clearer. Finally I had no choice. I had to face the fact that these were all memories."

Maria looked over at the knife on the table and grimaced. "How could you have kept that thing in the house after what I did with it?"

"I buried it along with the first . . . victim. But its disappearance seemed to disturb you. You kept searching for it. So I dug it up and put it back in the drawer. You quieted down then."

"Yes, I remember now."

We fell into an uncomfortable silence. I could feel Maria struggling to figure out what to say or ask next. I waited. I knew we had arrived at a breakthrough, yet I had absolutely no idea what to do with it. A psychologist I'm not. I was afraid of saying the wrong thing and causing her to regress. I was sure that the best doctor for Maria was her own mind. So I decided that Maria herself should set the pace of her recovery. Her mind would show us the way, if it truly wanted to be cured. I thought it had been doing a fine job so far.

"You stayed with me despite everything. But why? I was

trying to kill you! For the love of God, Tom, I killed eleven different men! How could you stand it?"

"I love you, Maria. It wasn't you who did those things. It was the disease. You don't desert or stop loving someone because she's sick."

"But you're a lawman! You've sworn to protect this town from people like me."

"That's just it. You never hurt anyone from the town. The drifters you killed didn't mean anything to me . . . and you do."

"What if I had murdered someone from around here?"

"You never did, so I never gave it much thought. I probably would have tried to cover it up." I reached over and touched her hand. "You mean more to me than even the law, Maria. I would have done anything to help you and keep you safe."

The tears started running down her face again. She turned away, and we fell into another of those bottomless silences. I must have sat there for five long minutes, listening to her cry. I wanted to reach around and comfort her. I didn't. This was something she'd have to work through on her own. I knew I couldn't take the pain away with a hug.

Finally she turned to me sadly and said, "What are we going to do, Thomas?"

"We're going to go on . . . together. We're going to talk a lot and tough this thing out. I think you may be beating the odds, love. You've remembered what you've done. That's a gigantic step in the right direction."

"How can you be so sure of that? Maybe I'm getting worse. Maybe I'm learning to live with what I've become."

"You haven't become anything! Get that straight. The disease did those killings. It used you the same way I used my gun today. You were a weapon, not a killer."

"Do you think I might be cured?"

"Possibly. There's only one way to find out."

It took a moment for that to register. "No! I couldn't do that. Not now. I don't know if I'll ever want to have sex again."

"I wasn't suggesting that we jump in the sack right now, doll. I think we should give it a few days. I want to talk to Doc Rogers and maybe Warren Green about what's happened. The doc will probably want to run some tests on you. If you've beaten this disease, there may be something in your blood that will show us how to cure other people. Maybe some kind of a vaccine can be made up."

"Do you really think so?"

"All scientific discoveries have to begin somewhere."

"But what about us, Tom? How are you going to go on living with me after what I've done?"

"I've lived with you through the worst of this mess, Maria. I'm not about to leave you when it looks like you may be getting better."

"I guess the real question is how I'm going to live with myself."

Yes, that was the very heart of the matter. Maria had been raised in a strict Roman Catholic family. From the first day of her parochial schooling to the day she graduated Mary Immaculate High School in Brooklyn, the Ten Commandments had been branded on her conscience as the laws of Almighty God. And the gravest of these edicts, the one with consequences too terrible to contemplate if it was broken, was the Fifth Commandment, "Thou shalt not kill."

How Maria would live with her guilt worried me. Her adherence to Catholic doctrine had lapsed as she grew older, just as mine had. But deep within her was the same catechism-fed conscience that haunted me for the people I'd killed during the war and since then. Being absolved of those killings, because they had been in the line of duty, didn't help me during my sleepless nights. I doubted that Maria would find being a victim of Berserker's Syndrome much of an excuse, either.

The only hope I found in this situation was that the fifth commandment also forbade suicide.

"I've been there myself, Maria. Let me help you through this."

Maria looked up at me then, with so much love in her eyes that my heart skipped a beat. "Then how about starting by taking me over to that sofa and just holding me. I sure could use a little warmth and comfort. No sex. I just want to be close."

"I understand."

We never went to sleep. We spent the night in each other's arms, curled up together on the couch. We talked about a lot of different things, touching on everything from the soul to our first kiss. That night reaffirmed our love for each other. I'd never felt closer to her. A new day was dawning for us, I knew it. It wouldn't be easy, but together we'd manage. Maria was going to be okay, of that I was certain, and that was all that mattered.

A little before dawn the words finally ran out and we contented ourselves with savoring the warmth of our union. We sat and listened to the summer breeze rustling the leaves outside.

When the early-morning sun started creeping in on us, Maria got up to make us an omelette on our old kerosene stove. On the way to the kitchen, she stopped in front of the dining-room table. I watched her as she stared down at the butcher knife. She began to reach for it, then pulled her hand back. Her eyes sought me out, then returned her gaze to the knife. Finally her hand slowly drifted forward and closed around the blade's handle. She brought it up to eye level and examined it closely.

"It's just a knife, isn't it?"

"That's right, Maria, nothing more. Would it be better if I got rid of it?"

"No. I need it to chop onions for the omelette. It'll be all right."

She lowered the blade to her side, still dreadfully aware of its presence, and headed for the kitchen. When she reached the doorway, she turned and looked back at me.

"It's the only way we'll know if I'm getting better. I can't run away anymore."

The omelettes were delicious. Rex heard us moving around and started yelping for his breakfast. It was only quarter of six. He didn't usually get fed until I got up at seven. So I decided he could wait.

By the time I finished my meal, Rex's whining protest had escalated to howls of outrage. I began to worry about what he might do if he didn't get his breakfast soon. So I went in the back room and broke open a new case of Kal Kan dog food. When I first got Rex, I commandeered the town's entire supply of dog food. Rex was the only woofer around, and no one figured we'd ever get so bad off for food that the town would need it to survive.

So I ended up with a more than adequate supply of canine delicacies to last Rex through at least two lifetimes. I thought it was a wise move. Rex was just nasty enough to live forever.

Maria was out sunning herself on a lawn chair when I brought Rex's bowl out. He dug into it as if the last meal he'd had was sometime before the spring thaw. Rex made disgusting noises when he ate, a series of wet-sounding slurps and snorts, so I left him to enjoy his meal and walked over to join Maria.

"How you feeling?" I asked as I sat down beside her in the heavy oak love seat.

She answered in an exhausted monotone. "Tired, but good. I feel as if a great weight has been lifted off me. I guess it has. I'm not sure what tomorrow's going to bring, but it's got to be better than what I've been through already."

I pulled my socks and boots off as we talked. The dewy grass felt good between my toes.

"You're going to be okay, Ms. Burgos."

"Yes, I do believe I am, Mr. Laker."

I liked the way she grinned as she said that. I hadn't realized until then how long it had been since I'd seen her crack a real smile.

"Are you going in today?"

I rubbed my unshaven chin and considered the situation. "I should, but I don't think I will. I'll probably stick around here with you. There's some trouble in town, but I don't think it's anything to get excited about. They can get along without me today." I didn't think Maria had to know just yet that if Mayor Hayden got her way, the constable's office was going to have to get used to doing without me permanently.

"You don't have to play hooky on my account, Tom. I'm not suicidal or anything. Besides, I'm going to need to be by myself a little to come to terms with what's happened."

"Think you'll be able to do that?"

"If I'm really getting better, I will."

"Okay, I'll get out of your hair for a while, in an hour or so. I could use a little nap first. In case you hadn't noticed, we didn't get any sleep last night."

"Why don't you make that a two-hour nap. I'll write a note to your teacher explaining why you're late."

"Don't bother, I'll forge one. All these years in law enforcement occasionally stand me in good stead."

"Are you going to talk to Doc Rogers about me today?"

"I will if I can find him. He's hard to pin down sometimes."

Rex came over and started to worry at his splint. That reminded me that I had decided July 19 was the day for Rex's leg to be unveiled and tested.

"Speaking of medical treatment, how would you like to help me take Rex's splint off?"

"No way, José. I don't look good with bite marks. He's your monster and your problem."

"So much for helping each other with all our troubles, hey?" I kidded.

"Everything has its limits."

As it turned out, Rex was relatively cooperative about the entire operation. I guessed he sensed that he was gaining back his mobility. I untied the bandages, unwrapped the splint, and removed the second layer of bandages underneath it. Unbound, the leg was wrinkly, its fur matted. But it looked straight, solid, and healed.

At first Rex wasn't quite sure of what to do without his wooden leg support, but he soon felt confident enough to rest some weight on it. It held. The next step was just that. A step. He managed it without falling over. That step was followed by another and still yet another until Rex was racing around in circles on our front lawn. Happiness was written all over his pugnacious mug.

He finally walked over and looked up at me. He gave out one little gleeful bark, which I interpreted as "Thanks."

"Don't mention it. It was my pleasure," I answered.

Rex then trotted over to my boots and urinated in the neck of one of them.

"You bastard!" I screamed as I raced toward him with violence in my heart. But he ducked my kick, ran several circles around me to show how slow and clumsy I was, and then disappeared out the front gate.

"Where the hell do you think you're going?" I raced out of the yard after him. He didn't stop to answer, though. He just kept running down the road.

"Rex!"

That lousy dog continued at the same breakneck pace. About a quarter mile down the dirt road, he slowed and looked back at me. He let loose with a final yelp that either meant "Good bye" or "So long, sucker." Then he cut off onto one of the many deer paths that cross our road and disappeared. I never saw him again.

"Rex!"

I heard Maria walking up behind me and turned to face her. She had my boot in her hand. She smiled and said, "Let no good deed go unpunished."

Then she upended the boot and let a trickle of yellowish fluid pour out onto the ground.

All I could say was, "What am I going to do with all that dog food?"

Maria put an arm around my stooped shoulders and walked me back to the house. "There, there. It'll be okay. You've still got me. I promise that when I get better, I won't pee in your footwear and run away from home."

20

The old pair of Fryes I pulled out from the back of my closet didn't feel quite right. In fact, it was hard to believe I'd ever worn them. No doubt someone had slipped into the house, stolen the old comfortable boots that I remembered, and left behind these stiff and lumpy look-alikes. Such a heinous act, I decided, would not go unpunished. I was still mentally rounding up the usual suspects when I pulled up in front of the station house and found John D. sitting on the front steps, cleaning his sidearm. I got out of the patrol car and sat down on the step below him.

"How's everything going, John?"

"Quiet. Just like you figured. The scouts are all out in the field. I had them dirt-bike five miles into the hills, stash their wheels, and continue on foot from there. They each called in a radio check at that point."

"Any contact since then?"

"Willie Platen and Dutch Sutton, they're up in the park.

Claim they hear the sounds of engines way back in the hills, getting closer."

"That makes sense. The raiders are probably coming in on three-wheelers and four-by-fours, as far as they safely can. They'll ditch them before they get too much closer to town."

Without looking up from reassembling his gun, John D. nodded thoughtfully. "That's what I thought too. Told the boys to keep going deeper into the hills but to stay off the main trail. They know all the little deerpaths up that way and should be able to get a good look at what's coming our way without getting spotted themselves."

I got up, turned, and headed for the station's front door, but didn't quite make it.

"Tom, Dirk came up with something new while playing with his crystal sets."

"Yeah? What?"

"I don't know. He popped out of his hole about half an hour ago, all excited. I tried to find out what was up, but the self-important little prick went all mysterious on me, clammed up. He said he didn't want to talk about it with no one but you. Knew you'd be in soon, so I let it ride."

"Thanks, John," I said. "I'll let you know what's going on as soon as I find out." Then I finally stepped through the door.

I admit it. I enjoy making a dramatic entrance as much as the next guy. But I sorta like to know in advance that it's going to happen. When you don't know that, it becomes a surprise. And I hate surprises. Four of my deputy constables were inside the station house. As I came into the squad room, they all froze in their tracks. Four sets of eyes fastened onto me as if they expected me to burst into flames. You could hear them breathing in the heavy silence. It didn't exactly take a mind reader to know that they'd all heard about Mayor Hayden's plans to oust me from office.

Clearing my throat as I walked to my desk, I said to no one in particular, "We've got raiders heading toward this town. I'm sure everybody has something that needs doing."

The room became a vortex of activity. I wandered over to the day log and read last night's entries. Nothing out of the ordinary, so I looked around the room to see what everyone was up to. Officers Gibson and Moore were taking scatterguns out of the station's firearm locker, getting ready to clean them. Rick Skeats was pushing colored pins into a large map of the county. It had been tacked to the wall since the last time I'd set foot in the office. Yes, everyone, it seemed, was suddenly busy except one officer, at his desk at the back of the bullpen. Benny Hollaster sat, still as a statue, a shit-eating grin creasing his ugly features. His eyes, with their slightly feverish gleam, followed me with noticeable pleasure across the room.

I was sure Benny was really getting off on my trouble with the mayor. Somewhere in that little peanut-size brain of his, he was probably accepting the job as my replacement from Mayor Hayden. Though she'd threatened exactly that in order to get John D. to back her play, I knew it'd never happen. I think Ruth knew I'd put a bullet into Benny before I'd ever let him take over this town. As I stood there, my eyes locked with Benny's malevolent stare, the idea took on an increasing appeal. But finally, good sense prevailed. The raider trouble meant Benny's expert services would be extremely valuable over the next few days. After that, well, it was anybody's guess.

The door to the com center opened about eight inches and Dirk Parker's unshaven mug poked out through the opening. His eyes looked for and found me. A pudgy hand snaked out from under the haggard face, its forefinger beckoning, accompanied by a furtive "Pssst!" Both head and hand disappeared, leaving the door slightly ajar in their wake. I took this to be a invitation.

I entered Parker's sanctum, closing the door behind me. It looked like he had every radio in his tiny cubicle turned on. I'd never seen it like this before. The drapes on the room's lone window had been pulled shut. Glittering lights and illuminated dials bathed the room in an eerie light. Static cracklings filled the air. Dirk sat in the middle of the room, a wild-eyed expression on his face. Obviously I was not the only one going without sleep around here. An eager childish grin creased his face as he said, "You're never going to guess what I've stumbled on."

"You're right. I'm never going to guess. So you're going to just tell me without us playing twenty questions. Okay, Dirk?"

Dirk's expression of disappointment was almost laughable for a moment, then he recovered, shrugged his shoulders, and turned to a nearby tape recorder. "I was monitoring the raiders' transmissions earlier when a fourth party came on the band. It was a very clear signal. I'd say he was probably transmitting from just outside the town. Wait till you hear this . . ."

Dirk flipped the recorder to play. We sat in silence, straining to catch every word of the conversation between party number four and his confederates. The talk was a mix of military jargon and the group's own little code-speak, but their code just didn't quite cut the mustard. It would have been painfully apparent to just about any fool that party number four was filling his friends in on what was currently going on in town. There was a trace of a Brooklyn accent in number four's voice. Though I'd never heard him speak, I had a fair idea of who that voice belonged to.

"We've got a spy in town. A viper in our bosom, Tom!" Dirk whispered in alarm. "What are we going to do?"

"Arrest him as soon as he sets foot back in town."

"You know who it is?"

"Yep, I think so."

I stepped over to the door and called out to John D. A moment or so later he was silently filling the com center's doorframe, a questioning look on his face. "What's up?"

"That biker, Frank—you talked to him, didn't you? Did he have any kind of accent?"

"Yeah, a touch of Brooklyn."

"Put an APB out on him. He's with the raiders. Have the boys try to bring him in alive. I'd like to question him."

"Will do." And John D. was gone. I was about to follow him out when Dirk rolled his office chair to one of the radios and turned up the volume, announcing, "Tom, it's Dutch and Willie calling in from the park. You want to take the call?"

"Yeah, sure." I reached for the mike, marveling at how Dirk could pick up the station's call signal out of all the din that filled the room. A very strange little man, this Mr. Parker.

"Home Base to Cat Two, come in," the radio pleaded.

"Home Base here. What's up, Cat? Over."

"That you, Tom?"

"This is Home Base. A little radio integrity, all right, guys? Over."

"Sure, sorry. We got trouble out here, Home Base. Over."

"You been spotted? Over."

"No, it's nothing like that. We're up well away from the main trail, and it's a good thing we are. We finally came up on the main body of . . . uh, uninvited guests. Looks to be about thirty of them, and they're really well armed. Over."

Thirty! Three groups . . . that'd make roughly ninety raiders heading our way, twice as many as Shandaken had ever had to deal with before. "How well armed? Over."

"Machine pistols, Ingrams! I'd say they've got about ten of them. Everyone else is toting shotguns and hunting rifles, some scoped, some not. Plenty of sidearms too. Over."

"Shit! You sure they're Ingrams? Over."

"Yeah, seen pictures of them in some old rifle magazines. They're supposed to be terrific little guns, can fire something like ten rounds a second. Where you figure they got them? Over."

"Probably from some big-city arsenal. They used to outfit SWAT teams with those babies. What are our uninvited guests up to now? Over."

"Looks like they're setting up camp for the night. Makes sense. From here they're less than a day's walk into town. Over."

"Yeah, they'll want to rest up before coming in to party. They still got their ATVs with them? Over."

"Uh-huh. But they're hiding them in the bushes. Looks like they're planning to hoof it from here. Over."

"Then get yourself situated ahead of them. Let us know when they're on the move again, Cat. Over."

"You got it, Home Base. Talk to you later. Over and out."

Parker and I exchanged glances without saying a word. When you're up to your neck in cow manure there's no need to point out the obvious. I got up and headed back to the bullpen.

En route, I had to pass Benny's desk. He probably hadn't expected me to come popping out of the com center the way I had. Benny started visibly in his chair as I walked by and clutched something small to his belly; something which he had been fingering under his desk, where no one else could see. I slowed my pace, staring back at him. He had the nervous yet defiant look of a man caught with his hand down his pants. Whatever it was that he'd been fooling with got shoved into his desk drawer and slammed out of sight.

I decided this mystery wasn't worth delving into right then and continued my way over to the map on the wall. I called my men over and briefed them on the latest developments. All thoughts of my trouble with Mayor Hayden were forgotten. Temporarily.

Following some give and take, it was decided that Moore and Gibson would round up the posse we'd need to go out and meet the raiders on their way into town. That way we'd hit them in the woods, long before they'd be expecting any trouble.

I impressed it upon Gibson and Moore that all this recruiting would have to be done in complete secrecy. They were to go quietly from one house to the next informing only locals of what was going on. The recruits would be told tomorrow morning when and where to meet. No outsider was to know about this operation. Frank was probably our spy, all right, but he might not be the only one in town.

John D. was in charge of keeping the map up to date, tracking the raiders and scouts. He was also to compile the list of posse members as Gibson and Moore reported them in. "Split them up into three groups, John. You and I will each lead a band. I think Josh can handle the third."

I was expecting Benny to take loud exception to this idea. When he didn't, I turned away from the map for the first time in several minutes. It was only then I realized that Benny was no longer with us. "Any of you boys see where Benny went?"

They all looked around and shrugged. No one looked terribly surprised. As good as he was in a fight, everyone knew of Benny's lack of enthusiasm for the more mundane aspects of police work, like planning and preparation. This wasn't the first time he'd pulled this vanishing act.

I assigned Rick the job of making sure the station's arsenal was ready, with the understanding that if Benny returned, he was to help Rick out. Rick grimaced and said he wasn't going to hold his breath waiting.

In the meantime, I'd check each of the town's outer fortifications and personally inform the guards of our current situation, with the stern reminder that they keep their yaps shut about it once they got off shift. They were to tell only the relief personnel about it. No one else, and that included girlfriends, wives, and drinking buddies. At least that's what I intended to do, but there's a saying about the best-laid plans of mice and men. As I was walking toward the door, Tad Wilson, one of the town board members, stepped into the station house.

A tall, reed-thin man, Tad had a hard time looking imposing. Nonetheless he gave it his best shot, standing there attempting to fill the doorway. He cleared his throat in what he must have considered his most official manner and announced, "Mayor Hayden has called an emergency town meeting. Your presence is requested at the town hall immediately, Constable Laker."

"Tell her honor that I'll be along in a moment."

Tad squared his shoulders and tried to puff up his rather sunken chest. "I'll wait. I'm to escort you to the meeting."

I did manage to not break out laughing, but I just couldn't suppress a rather nasty smirk. Tad's face became a scowl. Mr. Diplomacy strikes again. Here was one of the folks who were about to vote on whether I kept my job or not. So what do I do? Antagonize him . . . what else.

I was trying to think of some way to smooth over the damage I'd done to Mr. Wilson's pride when a meaty hand came to rest on my shoulder. I turned to look up at John D.

"These damn pins can wait for a while. I'm coming with you."

"How come?"

"I've been thinking all last night about this nonsense. Decided I don't want your job. Aside from all the trouble we've got with these raiders, the chief constable has to deal with Benny. I'm too old for that kind of grief."

"Raiders!" Tad Wilson looked as if someone had poured acid down his pants.

John D. and I smiled at each other as I said, "I'll explain at the meeting, Tad. Be right with you. There's something I want to check on before we go."

I strolled over to Benny's desk. The top drawer opened without any trouble. I knew he'd lost the key to it a long time ago. The drawer contained all the usual things you'd expect in a cop's desk: paper clips, pencils, a box of

bullets, rubber bands, even a couple of girlie magazines.
One thing did puzzle me though. I picked it up and stared
at it.

Now what the hell was Benny Hollaster doing with a
rosary?

21

Mayor Hayden's carefully orchestrated public display of righteous indignation was already in progress by the time Tad, John D., and I arrived at the Hotel Phoenicia, the new town hall. They were seated at a group of tables pushed together in the middle of the hotel's dark wood-paneled bar. Ruth, sitting in the seat of prominence, had them spellbound. Even the deer heads on the walls seemed to be hanging on her every word.

As we walked in she was methodically listing all of Maria's dastardly crimes. Ruth knew the precise date each new cross appeared across the street from our home. There were stern warnings that it would only be a matter of time before Maria took the life of one of the local citizenry, possibly a young teenage boy who wouldn't know any better.

I let Ruth go on uninterrupted while I went behind the bar and helped myself to a cold beer, well aware of the icy glares this simple act was generating. I offered one to John D. He refused with a shake of his head and a look that warned of doing foolish things, like digging my own grave.

I bellied up to the bar and listened to Mayor Hayden drone on. The rapt attention everyone gave her was astonishing. Each board member looked like this was the first that he or she had heard of "Maria's violent acts." You'd never guess that Maria's thinning of the transient population had been the main topic of gossip around town for months. Each of them had an expression of outrage and shock on his or her face. And they were all prepared to do their civic duty and vote me out of office.

Ceremony. That's what it was all about. Tribunal. The eight good citizens sitting within the circle of power, doing what tradition demanded: interpreting justice to fit their own personal biases and wishes. Theirs was an outmoded vision of reality, completely out of step with this new age. I must have gaped at the spectacle they presented. Didn't they realize the world had turned itself upside down? That the games they were playing had gone out of style a long time ago? Yet none of them seemed to recognize that fact, including John D., obviously. If he had grasped the truth, he wouldn't have been worrying about me the way he was.

But none of them had come to grips yet with the reality of the post-berserker world. Not one single person there realized that the only reason they were able to go about having their special meetings and setting forth their endless picayune little rules and regulations was that they had someone like me to keep them safe from the outside world. Their learning the facts of life was long overdue.

So I sat back, sipped my beer, and let the pageantry run its course, knowing I would eventually get my say and that it would be the last word.

I finished my drink and was setting the glass in the bar's sink when I finally noticed Benny Hollaster. He was standing at the back of the room, next to the rear exit, his arms folded over his chest, as still as an old cigar-store Indian. I was sure he had not been there when I came in. I finally decided I'd been so intent on listening to Ruth that I hadn't heard Benny's entrance. But even then I knew that conclusion had a hollow ring to it.

My attention was drawn back to Ruth's diatribe when I heard her address me. Mayor Hayden was on her feet, and all eyes were turned to me with the funereal air of eight hanging judges. An interminable silence hovered in the air. I let it stretch on, enjoying this test of wills. Apparently Ruth didn't share my appreciation of it. She blinked first.

"Well, Tom, this is your chance to defend yourself. What have you got to say before this committee votes on whether you and your wife should be posted from town?"

"Nothing."

"Does this mean you've come to recognize that your position on Maria is indefensible?"

"I always knew it was, Ruth. That's why I'm not wasting any breath here. But I think the time has come for you to realize that your standing is just as precarious."

Silence descended again. But this time it didn't last long. One by one the "judges" began whispering to their neighbors until the rhubarb's pitch hit an all-time high. Only Ruth remained silent, still standing, staring at me. She let things go on like this for nearly a full minute before she slammed her shiny little gavel down on the table and coolly asked, "Tom, are you threatening the members of this committee?"

"No, ma'am. But you committee members are threatened all the same. I suggest you ask John D. what's been happening over at the police station today before you have your little vote."

John D. glared at me, not at all pleased to be put in the position he found himself in. But he pulled himself together and told the gathering all about it—how we'd discovered the raiders' plot and what we'd done thus far to counter it. He ended his little speech by reminding them to keep their mouths shut about what they'd just learned. It was apparent, by the way he phrased this admonition, that in relating the truth about our grave situation, the implications of that truth had finally sunk in on John D. The veil was lifted. He realized now that the council and the police force were equal partners in this little outpost of civilization. And that the only way this arrangement was going to work was if we stayed out of their hair in the everyday affairs of running the town and they, in turn, let us be. The way my predecessor and I had run things had kept this fact a virtual secret. Now the time had come to let the scales drop from their eyes, so that everyone on the committee could blink, squint, and finally see the light.

The awful truth was that we all lived in a police state. True, in Shandaken it was a sort of benevolent dictatorship, but that didn't change the spots on the cat. The only reason these eight solid self-important citizens were able to carry on the way they always had was that men with guns, like me, were willing to keep the wolves off their backs. But that kind of protection doesn't come cheap. They were about to learn that putting up with my crazy wife was the price they'd have to pay.

Of course, Ruth wasn't about to take this lying down. "John, you don't really expect us to buy this wild story about raiders, do you? The timing on this seems mighty convenient for Mr. Laker."

John D. narrowed his eyes and leaned back against the bar. "Ruth, you and I grew up in this town, went to school together. Everyone at this table has known me for years. Does anyone here think I'd go along with such a story if it weren't true?"

The silence said it all. Still Ruth refused to give it up. "Then we'll just have to handle this emergency without Tom. You're going to be in charge here, John. You've handled raiders before."

"Ruth, you haven't been listening to what John D.'s been telling you," I said as I came out from behind the bar. "You've got nearly one hundred trained fighting men heading for this town with automatic weapons."

"So what? Are you claiming that your gun is going to make that much difference?"

"No, but my head will."

"What are you talking about?"

John D. stepped forward, shook his head sadly. "Ruth, the best we can hope to raise, in the time we've got, is about sixty men, tops. The only way we're going to stop these characters is to head up into the hills and outfox them. To do that we've got to split our forces into three groups, each commanded by someone with a bit of tactical fighting experience. There ain't that many folks around with that kind of background, Ruth."

"That's nonsense. We've plenty of combat veterans in town."

I stared down at Ruth, suppressing a smile, and said quietly, "That's true, but most of them were grunts—followers with no tactical training. John D. was a shavetail in Korea. I was a sergeant in Nam."

"Who's going to be the third commander?" she wanted to know.

"Josh. His training came from running with street gangs in New York. Granted, it's not West Point, but it'll do."

Ruth waddled her angry little self over to me and glared up into my face. "Then we don't need you, Mr. Laker.

We've got Benny Hollaster! He was a real hotshot with the Green Berets or something, as I recall."

Every eye in the room slowly turned toward Benny, still lounging at the back of the room. The wooden Indian was smiling now. I waited until Ruth turned back to me before answering her challenge.

"I'll be glad to step aside and let Benny take my place. All you have to do is find twenty men who'd be willing to follow him into battle."

That got their attention. Everyone in the room stared at Benny, remembering. Old brutalities were recalled, as were men who'd gone out on patrol with Benny and never returned. It was common knowledge that Benny was hard on partners. They didn't last long. That was why I hadn't paired him with anyone in over a year.

The statue scowled across the room at me. It had never occurred to him that his presence at this meeting might prove to be my ace in the hole. I hadn't needed his ominous presence to drive the point home, but his being there had stated my case more eloquently than mere words ever could have. If he had a list, then this undoubtedly put me at the top of it.

I could see that Ruth was casting about for some way to salvage this situation. But she never got the chance. Ricky Skeats came bursting into the bar all out of breath, having run from the station house. "Tom, you'd better get back to headquarters. Dirk's made contact with the other scouts. One of the other bands of raiders has got a flamethrower!"

Seeing no reason to wait for Ruth to officially end the meeting, I headed for the door, disturbed by Rick's latest news flash. But I stopped in my tracks when I heard Mayor Hayden suggest that they adjourn this meeting and follow me directly over to the station house to learn, firsthand, how bad the situation really was. I couldn't help cracking a smile. Ol' Ruth just didn't know when to quit. So I mentally shrugged and headed off. I figured the town board wouldn't get in the way . . . too badly. If they did, I'd just have Benny chuck them out. He'd be in the proper frame of mind for that kind of work about now. I glanced over to where he'd been standing. Of course he was gone.

Ruth and her gang behaved themselves okay, once we had all settled down at the station house. Chairs were provided for them, and they had the good sense to stay out of our way. I got on the horn with the scouts. The ones up in Woodland Valley confirmed my worst fears. It was true. The raiders really did have a flamethrower. I kept wondering where the hell they could have gotten it.

Josh was at the map when I came out of the com center. I wandered over to him. "Welcome to Constable Laker's three-ring circus."

He turned to me with a sardonic smile. "You ain't going to keep this operation a secret very long with those clowns sitting around," he said, indicating the town council.

"Yeah, I know. But if I kick them out right away I'll have a revolution on my hands. You can't win a two-front war. Just ask Napoleon."

"Guess they'll get bored and wander off on their own after a while. How's things hanging here?"

"They keep going from bad to worse, Mr. Woodward. Turns out the creeps have a fucking flamethrower."

"I heard. So now what do we do?"

I leaned over close to Josh and whispered, "I've been thinking. Do you still have that nightscope you got off that soldier in Arkville?"

Josh stepped back, his face a perfect mask, all innocence. "What nightscope?"

"Come off it, Josh. One night while we were tying one on, you told me how you won it in a poker game."

"I did?"

"You did. Do you still have it?"

"Yeah. I don't like to use it often, though. Don't know where to get replacement batteries."

"Forget the batteries. You're going to use it tomorrow night. You're leading a posse after the raiders coming in from Woodland Valley. Use the nightscope to take out the guy with the flamethrower and the rest of it will be a piece of cake."

"Some piece 'a cake. Those suckers got Ingrams."

"Just keep your head down." I walked over to where Rick and John D. were standing, adding names to a list on a chalkboard. "How's the recruiting going?"

Rick beamed broadly as he reported, "Got twenty-four so far. At this rate, there's a good chance we'll get as many as eighty men by the time Gibbons and Moore get done canvasing the town."

John D. made a face at Rick. "Keep dreaming, son. Most folks in this burg still think protecting hearth and home is the job they pay us to do."

"Any word on Frank the Biker?" I asked.

"No sign of him. He must have decided he'd done his job and headed off to join his boys."

I glanced over at Mayor Hayden, standing by the map, as I said, "Too bad. Frank could have proved a very useful source of information." The back of my neck suddenly prickled. I sensed a last-ditch effort to get rid of me coming my way from Ruth's direction. I didn't have long to wait.

A few minutes later she turned to me and asked in a voice loud enough for everyone in the room to hear, "Why do we have to go out into the woods to face these raiders? Why can't we set up fortifications on the outskirts of town to hold them off?"

I didn't even bother turning around to answer her. This game was beginning to wear thin. "Because they'd just skirt around any fortifications we'd set up. Then we'd have ninety men running around town with automatic weapons and a flamethrower. Is that what you want, Ruth? Having half the town go up in flames is going to raise hell with the real estate values around here."

Everyone waited for the retort I knew would never come. You can only drive stupidity so far before it runs out of gas on you. Tad Wilson was suddenly at my side. "Constable, the rest of the board members and I are leaving now. We ought to get out of your way. But let us know if there's anything we can do to help."

That neatly removed my neck from the chopping block. Now came the tough part, mending fences. So I reached into my bag of tricks and pulled out the Tom Laker who was part diplomat, part big brother, part priest.

"I'll do that, Tad. Thanks. Remember, though, don't breathe a word of this to anyone." I didn't have much hope that no one would. But maybe our luck would hold and Frank would turn out to be our only spy.

I watched the board members slowly file out through the front door, certain that it'd be some time before they thought about voting that nice Constable Laker out of office again. Ruth was the last to leave. I could tell by the look in her eyes that nothing had been settled between us yet. What a tough old broad. At that moment, I really felt kind of bad about the fact that we disliked each other so much. She'd probably be a hoot to have a few drinks with.

For the next half hour I kept busy trying to map out the best place for us to set up our three ambushes. It'd been a while since I'd been up in the woods, and my recollection of the terrain was a bit hazy. So I finally gave up and called in Josh and John D. We put our heads together and figured it out.

Only then did I remember that the town's outer fortifications hadn't been warned about the trouble in the wind. It wasn't a top priority, since our uninvited guests weren't going to be putting in an appearance along the main highway, but I decided it couldn't hurt to put them on alert anyway. I looked around the room for someone I could delegate this job to, but everyone looked like he had more than enough on his plate.

Of course, there was one likely candidate who immediately came to mind, someone I was relatively sure would not be doing much of anything. When a quick glance around the room failed to turn up the "statue," I yelled. "Where the hell is he? Where's Benny?"

I really didn't expect an answer.

22

The rest of the day seemed to stretch on forever. I wanted to get off early and catch up on the sleep I'd been missing. I'd need all my wits about me for the following night. But every time it looked like I could possibly split, something else came up. There were still people to contact and brief, plans to solidify and questions to answer. I might have made good my escape if Hollaster had ever returned, but he didn't. There was just too much to do for me to jump ship as well.

As the day wore on, my nerves began to fray. I had to squelch the urge to bite off the head of anyone who came near me. A short time after lunch I was forced to raid the cache of toothpicks I have hidden in the bottom drawer of my desk. I transferred half my stock to the shirt pocket and stuck one between my teeth. I'd quit smoking over a year ago, but stressful situations still brought out the oral obsessive in me.

Toothpicks were the best noncarcinogenic pacifier I'd been able to find. A friend of mine swore the best substitute for a cigarette was sucking a plastic bar straw—without the drink, of course. But as chief constable, I had my reputation to think about, and I didn't want to look like a perfect fool with it hanging out of my mouth. So for me it was definitely toothpicks.

The sun finally set over Shandaken, and the things that absolutely had to be done immediately ran out. I left the night shift in charge, said my good evenings, jumped into my patrol car, and headed home. I was so exhausted by then that I knew I wouldn't have any trouble sleeping tonight. Worrying about the upcoming battle could wait until tomorrow when I could think straight again.

As I drove through the deepening darkness, I could still see bits of the fading day peeking over the edges of Mount Sheridan's silhouette. Part of my numb mind marveled at how beautiful it was. Once again I found it hard to believe I was actually living in the mountains, the Catskill Mountains no less. When I was a kid, I always thought of the Catskills as this mystical vacation wonderland that the folks took us off to once a year. It seemed to be this sanctuary Dad would rush us off to when things on the job got just too much to bear. Of course I'd learned, since then, that that was nothing but a childhood fantasy. The Catskill Mountains were never a place where you could let down your guard completely.

Back in the twenties, the Catskills had been Legs Diamond's territory. He and his gang had buried more than one rival bootlegger in these hills and valleys.

Even a small chunk of the revolutionary war was fought in these mountains. And before that the French, British, and their Indian allies had done a pretty good job of killing each other for possession of these lands. I've always found this especially strange, because the Indians seemed to be the only ones who ever found any real use for the mountains. The English and the French only wanted the Catskills for their never-to-be-realized potential.

You see, back then everyone imagined that the Catskills would prove to be a treasure house of mineral riches. How were they to know that the greatest treasure these mountains would ever bear in abundance would consist of slate for pool tables and fresh water for New York City? Even the oil pumped from the hills was paltry, valuable only because of its extreme rarity.

No, the Catskill Mountains always looked too big and tempting to newcomers, so they always wound up trying to grab a piece of the mountains' riches . . . without ever realizing that the mountains themselves were the treasure.

From their very earliest recorded history, these mountains were a hotbed of double dealers and shady characters. Probably the worst rascal of all was Johannis Hardenbergh. It was back in 1708 that old Johannis petitioned the crown to grant him ownership of the Catskill Mountains. This petition or patent, as it was called, was signed by Governor Lord Edward Hyde Cornbury, who used to enjoy parading around the battlements of Fort New York while dressed like his cousin Queen Anne. Of course, Lord Cornbury had no idea how much land he was actually signing over to Hardenbergh. Johannis had taken the government's surveyor general in as a secret partner. For some inexplicable reason the official inspection of the patent showed the Catskills to be only about one-tenth the size they actually were. Fancy that.

But in the end, all of Johannis Hardenbergh's scheming gained him very little. By the time he actually gained possession of the mountains, he had so many secret partners and under-the-table commitments that nothing could be done with the land because of the legal mess he had created by his machinations. It took over a century to unravel this real estate scam.

It all seems kind of funny now. No one really owns the mountains. The Catskills let us play hide-and-seek within their protective folds with the madness that plagues this world. But we have no claim any longer on these proud hills and valleys. We're here only at the whim of Ma Nature. The wilderness has quietly reclaimed its own.

*   *   *

I was abruptly roused from my historical reverie as I pulled up to my house. There was a car parked out in front of the place. I immediately recognized it as Mayor Hayden's huge white Cadillac, a monstrous fuel burner. Only Ruth's position as mayor allowed her this extravagant luxury. That Detroit monster should have been scrapped for parts ages ago.

I parked behind it, wondering what Ruth was doing there at that time of night, instead of holding court at Ricardella's. Was she looking for a rematch? That didn't seem likely. More likely she'd stopped by to bury the hatchet. At least, that was what I hoped. I didn't have the strength for another fifteen rounds.

But then everything became crystal-clear to me as I stepped into the driveway. The door to the garage stood wide open. My personal car, a 1984 Camaro SS, was no longer parked inside. I felt the adrenaline surge into my bloodstream, and everything in me went cold. The walk to the front porch took forever. Then I opened the door and stepped in. There was Ruth, sitting on the sofa, illuminated by two Coleman lanterns burning on the mantelpiece.

"Evening, Tom," was all she said.

"Maria?"

Ruth stood up and took a few steps toward me. "I stopped over here this afternoon and had a long talk with her, Tom. I told Maria how things were in town, made her see what trouble she was causing for everyone. She was very understanding about it. I helped her pack up. She's gone, Tom. Maria doesn't want you coming after her. It will be best for everyone if—"

There was no conscious thought involved in the act. In fact I felt as if I were completely out of my body, watching the incident like a disinterested third party. But some part of me must have been exerting a little bit of control, because I pulled the punch. If I had let all the anger boiling within me lash out unchecked, it would have reduced Ruth's jawbone to shards and sprayed her teeth all over the room.

As it was, the blow spun her around and dropped her face first onto the couch. For an eternal moment, everything in the room froze like some grotesque tableau. I stood there staring down at her, reveling in the insane rage berserkers must feel. There was no question in my mind but that I was quite capable of killing that meddlesome old fool.

But then Ruth groaned and rolled over. She looked up at me. Blood trickled from her mouth, and I could see in her eyes the shocked realization that she had woefully miscalculated my reaction to her most recent tactic. Ruth was still counting on civilized responses in a world teetering on the edge of the abyss. The recognition that this was quite possibly a fatal error also showed in her frightened gaze.

Fortunately for her, that terrorized look was enough to diffuse my anger. I turned away from her, grabbed one of the lanterns, and walked back to the bedroom.

All of her drawers were empty. So was her closet for the most part. I walked over to the night table, on her side of the bed, and was relieved to find Maria had taken her little pearl-handled Beretta along. At least this showed her departure wasn't a subconscious means to suicide.

When I checked the gun rack in the backroom, I discovered one of my shotguns missing. I grabbed up one of the others and a rifle and got a backpack from a nearby shelf. As I slung the pack over my shoulder, I could feel the weight of the boxes of ammo I always kept stored in it. All I needed was some food.

Ruth was in the kitchen when I walked in, a moist towel filled with ice cubes pressed against her rapidly swelling jaw. She stared open-mouthed at the rifles I was carrying. "You going to shoot me or just knock me around some more?"

"Don't tempt me, Ruth."

I went to the pantry and began to stuff cans of food into the backpack. Ruth stepped over and surveyed my progress. "Just what the hell do you think you're doing?"

I saw no reason to answer her, so I didn't. Instead, I walked over to the front room's closet and started rummaging for a set of binoculars I thought I remembered storing there.

"You're going after Maria, aren't you, Tom?"

"What did you expect?"

"You can't do this, Tom. You've got to stay here and help against the raiders."

"Should have thought of that before you guilted my wife into hitting the road, Ruth."

Mayor Hayden plopped onto the couch, defeated, crushed by her own stupidity. She muttered, "But Shandaken needs you . . ."

"Screw Shandaken!"

She just sat there, an empty husk, watching me hustle around the house looking for those damn binoculars. Ruth must have fried several million brain cells trying to salvage something from this mess she'd gotten herself into. I could almost hear the wheels grinding as she came up with one perfect strategy after another, only to discard them when it became apparent they wouldn't work. If she couldn't talk me into staying, how would she ever explain my departure to the town board? How?

Then she hit on it. But it obviously took a bit of doing for her to come up with it. It was pretty straightforward and honest, qualities politicans hate to have to rely on.

I finally found the binoculars in the back room, stored them away, and was heading for the door when Ruth said, "You know it wasn't the town that drove Maria out. It was me."

That stopped me in my tracks. The simple uncluttered truth that my anger hadn't allowed me to see. Ruth saw she'd hit her mark and pressed the advantage. "Sure, you'll be getting back at me, in spades, taking off like this and leaving the town to fend for itself. There's probably a good chance we won't be able to fight off this attack without your help. I guess that'll show me, won't it?

"But when those raiders hit town, I won't be the only one to die, Tom. A lot of other good people, folks you haven't got any argument with, folks you swore an oath to protect, are going to go down the tubes with me. Some of them you might even say are friends."

Yes, she knew she had me, damn her. Ruth had dug deep to unearth this truth, this thing that a person like me hardly ever speaks of. I should have seen it coming. The lady had always been a shrewd judge of human nature. She knew I was bound by those intangibles called responsibility, integrity, and honor. Maybe I didn't wear them on my chest like battle ribbons, but to a trained observer they were stamped on me just the same. And Ruth knew exactly how to use that fact to suit her needs. She'd snared me with the one thing I'd always considered to be my major strength.

I had been so peacock-proud of the way I'd handled her earlier in the day. Big Tom Laker had rubbed her nose in the fact that little Mayor Hayden couldn't get along without his guns and brains. Well, Ruth had just executed a pretty neat little end run around Big Tom. The tables had been turned, and now the score was not 1-0 Tom Laker's favor, but 2-1 Mayor Hayden's. She'd gotten rid of my wife and still had me under her thumb.

I dropped heavily into an easy chair. "Ruth, I've got an overpowering urge to pump a few rounds of buckshot into you. Don't know how much longer I can suppress it. I think you'd better leave."

I've got to hand it to her, Ruth did manage to keep a straight face as she made her way to the front door. That must have taken a tremendous amount of self-control. But she just didn't have the good sense to quit while she was ahead. When she was halfway out the door, she stopped and turned around. "Tom, you've got to realize that I had no choice in this matter. As mayor, it's my responsibility to ensure the public safety. If there had been—"

I cut her short by jacking a cartridge into the shotgun I was still holding and leveling it at her. You wouldn't believe how quickly she disappeared.

After a while I heard her car start up and drive off. I didn't move for a long while, just sat there amid the terrible stillness of the house. Maria was gone. The only sound was the persistent ticking of the mantel clock. From somewhere I found the energy to get out of the chair, drop the backpack and rifles onto the couch, and bump my way numbly into the kitchen.

The bottle of Smirnoff's vodka was exactly where I remembered. I brought it and a glass back into the front room and set them on the side table next to the easy chair. Then I dropped into the chair, feeling every muscle in my body turning off, worn out from overuse.

As I was reaching for the vodka, my eye was caught by a photo of Maria. I couldn't see it very well, because it was on the far end of the mantelpiece from where the Coleman lantern sat. But there was enough light for me to see her dark eyes peering joyfully at me . . . those beautiful eyes and soft lips surrounded by a pitch-black mane of hair.

I never cracked open that bottle of Smirnoff's. Guess I fell asleep staring at that picture.

I woke up with someone's hand shaking my shoulder and a voice cutting through eight miles of fog. It took me a while to get my eyes to focus, and when they did, I thought I was still dreaming. Josh Woodward and Rick Skeats were standing in front of me, staring around the room, loaded shotguns in hand.

Always able to grasp a situation at one glance, I said, "Whatthefuckisgoingonhere?"

Josh stepped over to the kitchen, staring past it down the hall leading to the bedroom, tense and alert. "Got worried when you didn't show up for work on time."

I glanced up at the mantel clock and was surprised to see that it was nearly ten-thirty. It looked like I'd finally caught up on my sleep in a big way; fourteen hours straight. But that still didn't explain Josh, Rick, and the guns. "Don't you think this is overreacting a bit to someone getting a little extra shut-eye? What's with the popguns?"

Josh turned somewhat reluctantly back to the room and sat down on the couch, apparently assured that whatever danger he was worried about wasn't present. "You weren't the only one who didn't show up for work today. Benny missed morning muster. No one worried about you, 'cause judging by the way you looked yesterday, you were home catching up on some much needed Zs.

"But John D. figured Benny's absence was just more malingering and drove up to the Hollaster place to find out what was going on. When he got there he found evidence that Benny has berserked out on us."

"What do you mean? How?" My brain refused to process this news.

"Not sure myself. Haven't been up there yet. John D. radioed in the report. He said we'd better get over here and see if you were still alive. It's common knowledge that you ain't exactly Benny's favorite person. John figured if Benny berserked out, he might have given you a late-night visit before splittin' town."

"No, the only visitor I had last night was Mayor Hayden." As Josh talked, everything about the previous evening slowly came back into focus. I could feel all my will draining away. Apparently this process had a visual aspect to it. For as I turned to look back at Josh, I found him giving me a long, hard once-cover. He then glanced around the room, spotted the rifles and backpack sitting on the sofa next to him, and asked, "Where's Maria?"

"Gone."

"Mayor Hayden's doing?"

"Yeah."

Josh got up, grabbed me by the arm, and pulled me to my feet. "Come on, let's get out of here. Rick, grab that backpack and the guns and drive Tom's car down to the station house. We're heading over to Benny's to see what's going on."

Before hustling me out the door, Josh scooped up the bottle of Smirnoff's and brought it along. Rick followed us out, jumped into my cruiser, and took off without saying a word. Smart kid; he recognized a potentially sticky situation and decided to put some distance between it and himself. He was only an employee. Josh was a friend. Let the friend deal with me.

The two of us sat silently in Josh's truck, watching Rick disappear down the road. Finally I turned to him and said, "Don't I, at least, get to brush my teeth before we go?"

Josh returned my stare, grimaced, twisted the cap off the bottle of Smirnoff's, and handed it to me. "One rinse and one hit. That's all. I need you in working order. You can go to pieces later if you want, but not today."

I took the bottle, spit the first slug out the window after giving the gums a good sudsing, and then donated the second hit to my empty belly. It didn't appreciate the donation and immediately began to rumble. I returned the bottle to Josh's outstretched hand. He recapped it and tossed it behind his seat. As he started up the truck, he said, "There's a turkey sandwich in the glove box, if you're interested."

I was. When I had half of it down, I felt human enough to talk again. "Don't worry about me, Josh. I'll pull my own weight today. What happened last night ain't the end of the world, though it sort of seemed that way then."

"I suppose you're going after her?"

"As soon as we get done with these raiders. If Maria won't come back, neither will I."

"And if she does come back, how you going to deal with Hayden?"

"I'll worry about that when the time comes. I've got to take this one step at a time."

Josh took his eyes off the road long enough to examine me. He apparently decided I'd live and he could stop mothering me, at least for the moment. "Guess you got more sense than I gave you credit for."

"That's only because you've been such a swell role model. *Really . . .*"

"Screw you, Laker."

We gave each other the meanest scowls we could muster, to show we meant business. On cue we broke up, roaring with laughter. The tension dissipated, I turned my attention back to the turkey sandwich with renewed vigor. So the quiet intensity of Josh's voice caught me by surprise when he said, "If you need any help, after this mess with the raiders gets straightened out, you let me know. Okay?"

"I'll do that. Thanks, pal. Now what say we find out what's happening up at Benny's."

It was too bad I didn't really feel anywhere near as chipper as I sounded.

Benny's place was a good fifteen minutes away, up a steep dirt road on the other side of town. As we pulled up, I could read relief in the faces of the men standing around Hollaster's dilapidated little mobile home. How he had ever managed to get it up here was beyond me.

John D. and Officer Gibbons ran up to us as Josh and I stepped from the truck. John D. grabbed my arm and looked me square in the face. "Boy, am I glad to see you're still among the living."

"So am I, John. What have you got here?"

"Looks like Benny berserked out last night and killed his wife."

"You sure he's gone berserker? I mean, Benny's not the most stable person, you know. Maybe he just lost his temper last night and did his wife in before he got it back under control."

"Come see for yourself," John said as he turned and headed toward the mobile home. Josh and I followed him around behind the place, neither of us having any idea of the horror we were about to see. My years on the job had hardened me to a point where I figured I could handle just about any sight without being affected. But I was wrong.

As we rounded the trailer, I saw Officer Moore and some civilians standing about. A few with terrible, stricken expressions glanced our way. One of them was sitting on a tree stump, looking shaken, wiping his mouth with a dirty handkerchief. But now that their curiosity had been settled as to who the newcomers were, most of the bystanders turned back to the thing they'd been steadily staring at before our arrival. My eyes automatically looked there, too.

About fifty feet to the right of this group, I saw a short ladder leaning against a tree. On it was Pete Canfield, a local lumberjack. He was busy doing something that his huge bulk concealed. At the foot of the ladder stood Doc Rogers, giving Pete instructions that I couldn't hear. Doc finally spotted me coming and called up to Canfield, "Tom's here, Pete. Get on down. He's going to want to get a look at this before you take her down."

Pete obeyed Doc Rogers's orders and slowly climbed down the rickety old ladder. As he did so, I could see that something was hanging from the tree behind the ladder, but I couldn't quite make out what it was. Even after Canfield picked up the ladder and moved it out of the way, my mind still refused to recognize the mysterious hanging object. It's amazing when you think about it, really. But the mind often, like a good friend, tries to let us down easy. As I moved closer, though, I felt my heart drop with a loud thud.

The heap hanging from the tree had obviously once been Maggie Doyle Hollaster, Benny's wife. Even my medically untrained eye could tell that she'd probably been killed early yesterday evening. The blood that covered her, nearly from head to toe, was clotted and a deep sienna. Even though she was nearly unrecognizable, I knew it had to be her. The body was the right size, and you could see her bleached-blond hair sticking out from under all the dried blood. She was hanging about three feet off the ground. When I stepped closer, I noticed the three large nails, driven through her right wrist, holding her pinned to the tree, like a grotesque broken butterfly. I found myself staring at the hand at the end of that wrist, the last recognizable vestige of her humanity. It seemed to be the only part of her body that hadn't been beaten out of shape.

Lying on the ground, about ten feet from the tree, was a crowbar, caked with dry blood and bits of unidentifiable matter. I walked over and picked it up by the end, being careful not to smear any fingerprints that might be on it. I didn't really think there'd be any need for forensic evidence in this case, but it's hard to break old police habits. I looked back at Mrs. Hollaster's dangling body and said, "I've seen enough. Take her down."

The ladder was put back in place and Pete Canfield returned to his precarious perch. It took him several minutes to work the nails out of the tree with a pair of visegrips. Josh and Officer Moore grabbed hold of the lower part of the body and waited for the last spike to be extracted. When that nail came loose, the body flopped bonelessly down across Josh's broad back like a piece of cloth. In Josh's arms, it was painfully apparent just how small and vulnerable Margaret Hollaster had been in life. I could never understand what such a frail and gentle flower had ever seen in the coarse and brutal Benny. Maggie had obviously taken that secret to her grave.

Josh set her body on the ground, as gently as he could manage. Doc Rogers bent down beside her, with me looking over his shoulder. He lifted her left arm at the elbow, and both upper arm and forearm drooped away from his grasp, accompanied by muffled grinding sounds. Doc let the arm drop and probed about the body's ribs and jaw with the

tips of his fingers. With a grunt of disgust, he got back to his feet and walked away from the body. I followed. Like him, I'd seen more than enough. "Josh, see if you can find something to wrap her up in, so we can take her body into town."

Doc Rogers was lighting up a cigar by the time I caught up with him. His complexion looked as ashen as the smoke that drifted from the tip of his stogie. "Got anything to tell me, Doc?" I asked, not really wanting to know. She was dead. Wasn't that enough?

"Looks like Benny broke every bone in her body, and I don't mean that figuratively either. I bet when I get her back into town, I don't find a single bone that hasn't been shattered, except maybe in that one hand. Guess it was out of Benny's reach. He had to have continued beating on her long after she was dead."

"How do you suppose he got her up in the tree like that?"

"Probably knocked her out and hauled her up there. As you well know, Benny was strong enough to pull off such a stunt. God, I pray she was still unconscious when he started in on her with that crowbar."

Knowing Benny, I didn't think there was much chance of that being the case. He would have wanted to hear her scream. It made an unspeakably ugly mental image. And I thought I'd seen it all.

"Tom! Come here and look at this!"

It was Josh calling from the trailer. I glanced at Doc to see if there was anything else he had to say. He shook his head and said, "I'll have a full autopsy report on your desk by the end of the day. If there's anything else you ought to know, I'll fill you in then."

"Thanks," I said as I walked off.

The inside of the Hollaster residence proved as disturbingly fascinating as the horrors on the outside were gruesome. I had no idea what I expected Benny's home to look like, but this certainly wasn't it.

There was no mistaking it, though, as I walked through the door. I'd seen this particular equation before. Insanity + obsession = one berserked-out killing spree. Familiarity had made it far too easy to decipher the handwriting on the wall. And that's exactly where the message was written this time. On the walls. The little trailer was wall-to-wall cruci-

fixes, holy pictures, religious pamphlets, and rosaries. There
wasn't a square inch of space that wasn't covered. But what
was even more disturbing was the guns. There appeared to
be hundreds of them scattered all over the mobile home:
shotguns, standards and sawed-offs; hunting rifles; pistols, all
makes and models. Mixed in among the piles of firearms
were various other instruments of death: knives, nunchakas,
throwing stars, a couple sets of hunting bows, and a few
items I didn't even recognize.

Josh and I wandered through the trailer in stunned silence. Who would have suspected that Benny had squirreled
away such an arsenal? No one, I guess. We all had known
he was crazy, but no one had had any inkling that he'd been
this far gone. It was hard to accept these facts, even with the
overwhelming evidence we had staring us in the face.

I watched Josh tear a missal card down off the wall and
stare sadly at it. "Guess the guns were Benny's and all this
religious stuff was hers. Quite a couple."

"No, I think the God paraphernalia was Benny's also," I
said and then related the incident with the rosary, back at
the station house, to Josh. "Looks like this has been going
on for quite a while, too. Seems incredible that no one
picked up on it."

"Well, if nothing else, Mr. Hollaster has contributed
nicely to the town's defense system. Once we get this stuff
hauled to town, it'll be a sizeable addition to our firepower.
Where do you suppose he got all this shit?"

"I've got a fair idea where some of it came from," I said,
picking up a shotgun I'd been staring at in disbelief all the
while Josh had been talking. I handed it over to him and
pointed at the name carefully engraved into the stock: Noel
Bearsly.

Josh stared at it for a few seconds, a confused look on his
face. Then I saw the circuits light up. "Holy shit! This is
Noel Bearsly's gun! Wait! He was supposed to have had it
with him when he disappeared on his way back from
Woodstock!"

"That's right. I think we just uncovered the identity of the
212 Spook."

"Benny?"

"Makes perfect sense. The victims would have stopped
for him along the road, despite the fact that none of them
probably liked him. They all knew him as a lawman and

they probably thought he was having trouble with his wheels or something. Not a one of them would have suspected a thing until it was way too late."

"But why would Benny do it?"

"I think that answer's painfully obvious. So obvious, in fact, that you know it, whether you care to admit it or not. I think Benny berserked out a long time ago. It's just that the rest of us never noticed. How long have we been having people disappear along 212? Almost a year now, isn't it?"

"You really believe that, Tom?"

"You bet. We both know that there's a rather wide swing in the way berserkers behave. They don't all act alike. Take Maria, for instance."

"Yeah, I guess so. Benny didn't have that far to go to become a homicidal maniac, either. He could easily have taken that last step without any of us noticing it. Damn."

"That's it, all right. Benny was used to operating on that level, always playing it close to the vest, always trying to conceal the monster within. That's why he was able to keep it so well hidden when the berserkerism finally claimed him. The mania hit him, but he didn't let it show."

"Jee-zus Christ, man. You think we got any others running around like that?"

"Let's hope not."

It took us another hour or so to finish up at Benny's. A work detail was dispatched to collect his arsenal, a job that took up most of the day. In his own way, Benny had contributed most generously to our little community before departing its ranks. The furor over discovering that a berserker had been living in our midst for months, undetected, kept a lot of folks' minds off the coming evening's activities. It also helped keep people from thinking about the fact that some of the locals would probably not be returning from our little excursion into the hills.

As for Benny himself, it was concluded that he'd undoubtedly split for parts unknown. Even in his state, he must have realized that he'd never be able to cover up what he'd done to his wife and so decided it was time to move on. Or perhaps it was just possible that the murder of Maggie Hollaster had tipped him over the edge completely, and he could no longer hold it together enough to pass for normal. I myself didn't think this was the case. Upon further examination of his home, Josh and I found that Benny had been clear-headed enough to take the time to load up a couple of backpacks and that his Ford Bronco and favorite shotgun were missing. There was no telling what else he might have taken along. I felt sorry for any poor soul that had the misfortune to happen upon him on the road now.

Later in the day I made the rounds of the town's road fortifications, to find that no one remembered Benny's passing by. That didn't surprise me, though. The guards on watch never logged official police comings and goings in their journals. Constables were constantly zipping in and out of town. As a result, we became invisible. Why take note of something or someone you see all the time?

What I did learn was that Maria had gone through the Route 214 checkpoint about seven-thirty the previous night. This meant she was heading toward Hunter, and that would make my job easier. The fact that the population was a lot thinner in that direction than in any of the others she could have chosen, together with her striking good looks and my jet-black Camaro, would make her stand out in anyone's memory. She'd be easy to track.

I kept myself busy the rest of the day, with preparations for tonight's outing that I could easily have left for someone else to do. But it was imperative that I keep moving, keep my mind occupied with minutia. If I'd hung around the office all day, I would have gone out of my mind worrying about Maria, out on that road by herself. And I was determined not to let myself think about that until I had the time to go after her. That's why I let John D. hold down the fort while I attended to any trivial detail that needed attention.

But four o'clock finally came, and I headed back to the station house. It was time to gather my gear and rendezvous with my posse over at Park Road. The members of my contingent had been quietly drifting out of town since noon. I'd be the last to join them, since it was generally agreed that I'd be the one any remaining spy would be keeping an eye on.

That's why I was surprised to find John D., Josh, and Dirk Parker in a huddle in the bullpen when I arrived. The prearranged schedule called for them to have left, to meet their own groups, fifteen minutes ago. It was apparent from the look on their faces that something had gone wrong. "What now?" I asked, expecting to find a truly alarming

new development on the horizon, something on the order of
the Russian army having joined forces with the raiders. It
wasn't quite that bad. But it was close.

"We've lost contact with our scouts up in Woodland Valley," John D. said in a dismal tone.

"When'd you hear from them last?"

"About three o'clock this morning," Dirk answered.

"Why didn't you tell me before this?"

Josh shifted uncomfortably in his seat. "I told them not
to. Figured you had enough on your mind. Besides, we
don't know for sure anything's happened to them. Their
radio may be on the fritz."

"Or they may be dead. Or captured. For all we know,
those raiders may be setting up an ambush, right now, for us
to walk into."

Once again Dirk jumped in. "No way. I've been monitoring their radio traffic all day. I haven't heard a beep about
them capturing or even spotting anyone. The three groups
are too far apart to communicate in any way other than the
radio. If they'd captured Updike and Smitty, I would have
heard of it."

"Unless they had a prearranged code signal they could
work into a conversation unnoticed, something that would
let them know to switch over to another wave band?"

Dirk conceded, "That's a possibility, but I doubt that
happened. I've been monitoring all the nearby bands with a
scanner and haven't picked up a thing. I mean, even if they
were sending in Morse on another frequency, I would probably have come across it. I don't think they're on to us."

"Then what do you think we should do?" I asked, already
knowing the answer.

"Go on as planned," Josh answered with some hesitation.
John D. and Dirk nodded their agreement. There was nothing else to be done.

I thought out loud about switching posses with Josh,
wanting to be where trouble was most likely to pop up. But
Josh vetoed the idea, arguing that he was familar with the
nightscope that would be needed to take out the guy with
the flamethrower. It was a tricky gadget that I could easily
screw up in the woods at night. In the end we decided to go
as planned.

John D. and Josh took off at the same time, each going
his separate way. I gave them three minutes, then hauled

my duffel bag full of gear out to the car. Anyone spying on me would have seen me toss the bag casually through the car window, stretch lazily, check the air in my left front tire, and head off in the direction of home just as I usually did. Nothing suspicious. Nothing out of the ordinary.

Except, of course, that the duffel bag sitting on the seat next to me belied that notion. In it rested my old service .45, a set of camouflaged fatigues, a flashlight, hiking boots, a tin of bootblack, a pump-action shotgun, a clip-fed .30-06 bolt-action, and enough ammo to blow apart a Mack truck.

The waiting game was over. We were committed. There was no turning back now. People were destined to die that night and I was going to be a part of this action. The years began to slip away, gradually at first, until I could once again clearly feel the emotions that stirred a certain nineteen-year-old draftee from New York on his first patrol into the bush. As I drove along, the leafy foliage out the window began to take on a junglelike aspect. Welcome home, soldier.

24

   We were all ready for them and set to go, waiting. Everyone was in position and psyched for a fight. All we needed was someone to shoot at. But our prey seemed to be taking its time about arriving for the slaughter. I'm sure it was getting on everyone's nerves. It was on mine. According to my calculations, the raiders should have been along about a half hour ago.

I stayed crouched behind a fallen tree at the top of a steep slope, about twenty feet high. From where I sat, I had a good view of the trail below. It was the perfect place for an ambush. The ground rose at a sharp angle on either side of the path, a natural washout. My men, positioned along a sixty-yard stretch of the trail, were spaced far enough apart so they would be able to cover the entire length of the raiders' procession once the shooting began. I was situated on the bottommost rung of the ladder, the lowest point on the trail. Everyone was to wait until I opened fire before joining in on the turkey shoot. Marty Kuntsler shared my cover. The two of us had the job of making sure nobody rabbited out of the ambush and escaped. There was a similar setup at the other end of our trap. The full moon over head illuminated the scene with surprising clarity. Unfortunately it didn't look like this advantage was going to last.

Ever since we'd started our trek up the mountain, thick clouds had been appearing and disappearing across the night sky. Each time they covered the moon, the entire forest was momentarily enshrouded in an impenetrable blackness that reduced visibility to zilch. Fortunately we'd made it most of the way there before the sun had set completely. It was beginning to look like the clouds would be settling in for a good long stay.

When I rendezvoused with the posse, I had filled in Officer Moore about our loss of contact with the Woodland Valley scouts and what that might mean. Yet Moore took the point position as we hiked up the trail without so much as an idle gripe. Apparently Dirk's reading on the situation was correct. We made it to the ambush site without incident and linked up with Willie Platen and Dutch Sutton. That meant we were now twenty-one strong. Willie and Dutch claimed that the raiders were about an hour behind them at most and that this, logically, was the only way for them to come. But then they'd given me those assurances two and a half hours ago. So where the hell were those raiders?

I kept telling myself that they'd probably been slowed down, to an intermittent crawl, by the pitch-blackness of occasional cloud cover. They wouldn't dare use flashlights to light their way, not this close to town. Okay. They'd be along soon. All we had to do was sit and wait. Yes, that's what I told myself, all right. But I kept picturing them skirting around us and entering Shandaken unchallenged. I imagined us sitting up there in the darkness, like roosting pigeons, with the sounds of their attack on the town drifting up the valley to us. The longer we waited the blurrier the edge became between reality and that fantasy.

I suppressed my tension as best I could, keeping an ear

cocked for any sound of the approaching enemy. All I
heard, though, was the noises of my men fidgeting up on the
trail. Everyone had been warned to keep quiet, no talking.
Unfortunately, two and a half hours is a hell of a long time
to sit silently in a damp, dark forest.

I killed a little time applying a bit more bootblack to my
face. This was the third time I'd done it. If the raiders didn't
show up, I'd have a quarter-inch coat of shoe polish over my
features, which would take a hammer and chisel to remove.

Suddenly my worst fear was realized. The moon disappeared behind a thick cloud and didn't return. A few minutes later it started to rain. It was only a light shower, but
enough to muffle any sound made by the raiders while they
were still some distance away. We wouldn't know they were
there until they were right on top of us. Worse yet, it'd
make the waiting that much more miserable. I could already
feel my clothes getting drenched and sticking to my body.
None of us had come prepared for rain. That's another one
of those niggling inconveniences of a post-berserker society.
No more boob-tube weather forecasts. Never thought I'd
miss them. But I'd actually reached the point where I felt a
certain nostalgia for that annoying weatherman from New
Jersey who always used to bleat, "Haloooooo . . ." at the
beginning of his reports.

Then I heard it. It cut through the soft patter of the rain.
The sound was definitely not that of someone shifting his
weight behind cover. It was the noise of a foot kicking a
loose stone. I crouched lower behind the dead tree, chanc-
ing a glance over toward Marty Kuntsler. Though he was
less than five feet away, I couldn't see him.

I soon realized that what I was listening to was the sound
of two men doggedly, and as silently as they could, making
their way along the trail toward me. They weren't exactly
succeeding at this stealth business. It wasn't their fault. The
exposed creek stones that covered the trail together with the
darkness made a quiet approach damn near impossible. I
began to feel my pulse throbbing rhythmically in the tensed
muscles of my jaw. The fireworks were about to begin. For
a brief second I wondered whether I'd survive the encounter. Then I pushed that dangerous thought from my head
and focused on the job at hand.

The point men stumbled their way past my position. I let
them go unharmed. There was a man stationed down the

path to take care of them once we engaged the main body of the raiders. Simply scaring the raiders off wouldn't solve our problem. Like bad pennies, they'd turn up again in no time. We had to wipe them out while we still knew where to find them. I hated this realization almost as much as I hated the kind of world that demanded it.

As soon as the point men got past, I reached down and unsnapped the holster cover on my .45. I flipped off its safety, then I did the same to my rifle and settled back.

The main group was following hot on the heels of their point men, no more than a hundred paces behind. Shoddy discipline, I decided. Then again, what could be expected from scum who lived off the hard work of others? It didn't matter how military and official they sounded on the radio; the truth of the matter was that what we were dealing with was a band of vultures, scavengers.

In the dark, they were like a herd of elephants crashing toward me, tripping and stumbling their way down the washout. I waited until the sound of the lead footsteps was directly below me. Then I swung my rifle over the top of my fallen tree and aimed into an ebony void. I saw nothing. All I heard was the clomping of raiders' boots below me. I squeezed back the trigger and the forest filled with the cracking report.

The flash gave me a quick look at the group below me. I think maybe I saw someone hit and falling. Before I could jack another round into the chamber, the night was filled with gunfire. The posse's barrage strobed light and dark across the scene below. I fired again, this time sure I hit my mark. As I pumped another round into the rifle, I realized I was in trouble.

The raiders were bunched together in a tight knot on the trail, probably because of the dark and the rain. I had expected them to be spread out more along the path. But they weren't. In fact, most of them were grouped up right underneath my position. That meant the men I'd stationed farther up the trail had no targets. My hope was that they'd be able to reposition themselves, without getting shot by one of their own men thinking they were being attacked from the rear.

But I didn't have the time to worry about that. I had to concentrate on my work. Killing. The raiders started to return our fire, not sure yet of our position. Their Ingrams

sprayed the woods above and below me, searching. Once again I took aim, fired, and was rewarded with a cry of pain from below. But that shot gave away my position. Bullets sang off my cover, sending splinters of tree bark into the air. I buried my face in the dirt, waiting for the onslaught to lighten. It did so after a few moments, as the raiders turned their attention to other gunfire that was decimating their ranks.

I popped up into a sitting position, took aim, and downed another raider, noting methodically as I did this that there seemed to be as many of the enemy on the ground as there were standing. Once again an Ingram sprayed my hideaway. I ducked, glancing over at Marty. I could see him there. He had chosen that moment to poke his head up to take another shot at the raiders. It was the last thing he ever did. In the glare from the gunfire below, I watched as the bullet struck Marty in the face, exploding his head into an unrecognizable bloody mass. The raiders were obviously using explosive bullets. Any wound our side received, it seemed, would be a bad one. Damn! Poor Marty.

This realization got me a little crazy. I went a bit John Wayne. Getting back into firing position, I started pounding the raiders with nonstop volleys. I made every shot count. Bolt back, bolt forward, fire. Bolt back, bolt forward, fire. Those sons of bitches. More than once bullets tore up the turf and deadfall around me in return, but I didn't have enough common sense to hit cover. I merely identified the source of the gunfire and coolly eliminated it with my next shot. To tell the truth, I felt pretty near omnipotent when the hammer of the rifle clicked down on an empty chamber.

Of course, that's when three of the survivors from below decided to rush my position, leaving me no time to put in a new clip. I guess they figured that charging up into my gunfire was preferable to remaining where they were, waiting for their turn to be mowed down by unseen shooters. At least they had half a chance this way, or so they thought. I quickly unholstered my .45 and took aim. Unfortunately their dash up the slope had taken them out of the illuminating glare of the firefight. It was hard to get a bead on them in the poor light. But somehow I got two of them before I ran out of bullets.

Again I ducked behind the dead tree, as an Ingram chopped at it like some monstrous ax. The barrage stopped for a moment and I slapped another clip into my rifle, assuming that the raider was also reloading. I wanted to save the shotgun's five shells of buckshot as a last resort; if I was about to be overrun they would cut a broad swath. Then I heard footfalls as he struggled his way up the slope. I poked my head up, hoping to get off a shot at him, and nearly pulled a Marty with an Ingram blast. Oddly enough, that gave me an idea.

Realizing he had zeroed in on my position, I started to crawl up to where Marty had been fighting. I found myself climbing over his warm corpse and edging my way around the roots of the fallen tree. Every few seconds bullets raked along the top of the deadfall, showering me with bits of debris.

I flattened myself as best I could next to the roots and waited, listening to the raider scramble his way closer, blasting at the tree every few steps to keep me pinned. I wondered why someone from my group hadn't knocked him off already. But then the gunfire in the background told me that my boys were rather busy with other matters. This was my own private little war. The only person who was going to get me out of it was me.

In a final burst of automatic fire, the raider came hurtling over the top of the dead tree. He spotted Marty's body and began emptying his Ingram into it, just as I knew he would. In the glare of the machine pistol's blast, I could see Frank the Biker's face. It was twisted into an incongruous mask, a parody of determination.

The Ingram's clip hit empty and I took careful aim at Frank's dimly outlined form. He was nothing more than a lighter patch of darkness amid the black sky, but it was enough. I pumped three slugs into him and heard him hit the ground with a very final sounding thud.

In the darkness, I heard someone pleading for mercy, begging that we stop firing. His screams were punctuated by an occasional shotgun or rifle blast. I called out for our men to hold their fire, and after a while they did. Creeping back to where I had originally been fighting, I found my flashlight where I'd left it, stuffed under some leaves. Keeping low, I shined it down onto the trail. My beam was soon joined by two others, dimly illuminating the carnage below.

A fifty-foot length of the trail was littered with dead, bloodied bodies. I began to wonder which of these corpses had been pleading for mercy a moment ago. I called out for any survivor to get to his feet and put his hands behind his neck, wondering if I'd get any takers. Much to my surprise, I did. One of the dead stumbled to his feet, which wasn't easy to do holding his hands high. He linked his fingers together and looped them behind his noggin. He'd been there before and knew the routine. The lone raider stood stock still amid his dead comrades, probably wondering if he was about to join them. A few seconds later, several of my men stepped into the light and covered the survivor with their flashlights and guns.

I turned my beam to where I guesstimated Frank should be lying and found him on the first sweep. He was lying face up, staring at the starless sky, three bloody holes in his leather jacket. I relieved him of his Ingram, backpack, and all the ammo he had on his person. After making a perfunctory stop at Marty's body, to make sure he was as dead as I expected, I joined everyone down on the trail. I felt terribly old and awfully tired.

25

Officer Moore already had our prisoner in handcuffs by the time I joined him. The survivor was a burly thug with long, wet, matted dark hair and a full beard. He was wearing camouflage fatigues, as were most of his dead comrades. The man was clearly scared. Good. His eyes looked like they were about to pop out of his head. I walked past him and strolled over to Moore, who rather matter-of-factly had the prisoner covered with another of the captured Ingrams. In a low voice I asked, "Do you know how to use that?"

In an equally hushed tone, Moore answered, "No, but he doesn't know that."

"Marty Kunstler's dead, up by that fallen tree. He's the only one of our guys that I know of. I'll keep an eye on the prisoner. You check around and get me some numbers on our casualties. Then have someone bring Marty's body down."

Moore nodded and wandered off to take care of business. A couple of my men were going over the dead bodies of the raiders, stripping them of their weapons and anything else that might come in handy. The prisoner and I were in the way, so I led him over to a nearby boulder and sat him down. He thanked me. Obviously shock was beginning to set in and the bozo was about to collapse. I asked him his name.

"Jerry Franklin."

"Where you from, Jerry?"

"New York City."

"Where in New York?"

Jerry decided he'd said enough and just stared nervously at me. It was at that moment that one of my posse members, a lumberjack named Bruce Bocson, came over. His timing was perfect. "Got another live one over here, Tom."

"What shape's he in?"

"Gun-shot."

I looked into Bruce's eyes and said, "You know what to do."

Bruce shrugged his thick shoulders and turned back toward the mass of bodies lying on the trail. I turned back to face my prisoner and watched his eyes follow Bruce. After a moment or so, I saw them widen in disbelief and then I heard the shot. Jerry winced and lowered his head.

"I asked you what part of New York you're from."

His stammering reply was barely a whisper. I had to strain to hear him. "Manhattan, Fourteenth Street. We've got a commune in the old Ma Bell Long Lines Building. About four hundred of us living there. Mostly ex-cops."

"Cops, eh? Frank, the spy that was in town, was he a cop?"

"Yeah, used to be part of some kind of SWAT team. That's all I know about him."

"Then that's where you got the Ingrams. Nice guns."

We sat there in silence for a while, Jerry waiting for the next question, me digesting the fact that I'd just participated in the butchering of some of New York's finest, my former brothers in blue.

"What was the plan, Jerry?"

"We were going to clear out your food stores, get a couple tanker loads of fuel, and hightail it down to the thruway. We were only trying to get by, like everyone else, mister."

"Sure, by wiping out half my town and leaving us to face starvation in the coming winter. You're breaking my heart, Jerry."

"You going to kill me too?"

I let him thoroughly chew that thought before shaking my head. "No, Jerry, we're going to release you . . . after a while. We want you to go home and tell all your friends what an impossible nut Shandaken is to crack. You're going to spread the word not to fuck with us, Jerry. That's the only reason we're going to let you live."

"But . . . but . . ." Jerry stuttered, looking over at the pile of bodies scattered along the trail.

"Your buddy had a stomach wound. He wouldn't have made it. It would have been a slow and painful death. We did him a favor, Jerry. We put him to sleep."

I delivered my lines in the coldest manner I could muster. It was important that Jerry leave us believing everyone in Shandaken was a psychokiller. He was to be the town's PR man to the outside world, so I wanted him thinking that we all ate babies for breakfast. The stories he'd tell when he returned home would be our front-line defense against a gasoline-hungry population, normal and berserker alike. You see, I was very serious about this business of myth-making.

Litters were slapped together for the dead and the wounded. Fortunately there were only two injuries, Ron Marz, who'd taken a load of buckshot in the left shoulder, and Pete Canfield, who'd caught a sliver of wood in the eye. It had happened when one of the Ingrams tore into the tree he was hiding behind. The consensus, among the amateur physicians present, was that he'd lose the eye, but live to tell about it. That was more than could be said for Marty Kuntsler and Max Duratte, a mechanic, who had caught one of those explosive rounds in the chest. There'd be two new widows weeping in the town of Shandaken tonight.

Before heading back to town, I got on the radio to find out what was happening with the other two posses. No word had come in yet from the Woodland Valley group, but Dirk Parker glumly informed me that the Mount Tremper contingent had closed with their band of raiders and wiped them out to the last man. That posse had suffered only one fatality, but had four wounded, John D. among them. Dirk had no idea what shape John was in and wouldn't know until that group returned to town. I over-and-outed, feeling angry and helpless. This evening was costing us good folks.

I placed the prisoner in Geoffrey Austin's charge. Sometime between our starting up the mountain and now, Geoffrey had donned his mime makeup. It was just the right touch to keep Jerry Franklin in a perpetual state of high anxiety, a-fearin' for his life. I honestly couldn't think of anything more frightening than being led down a mountainside in the middle of the night by a gun-toting, capering

lunatic in black-and-white pancake makeup who never spoke
a word.

Everyone loaded up with weapons and gear stripped from
the dead raiders and we began the long march back to town.
I kept my load light. I had this sinking feeling that it would
be a long time before this evening was over for me. Why
hadn't we heard from the Woodland Valley posse yet? What
was going on up there?

The dead raiders? We left them where they fell. Their
bones would discourage anyone who happened along this
trail from thinking this might be a short cut to some easy
pickings. It was a tough and ugly world out there. You
couldn't get by without a little of it rubbing off on you.

26

It was nearly two o'clock in the morning when we got back to town. The rain had stopped about twenty minutes earlier. I locked the prisoner up in our holding pen and had the weapons transferred to the town arsenal, with the exception of a half-dozen of the Ingrams. Turned out we might still have some use for them. Josh's posse had finally called in; they'd yet to have any contact with the raiders.

I got on the horn and told Josh to hold his position. He was relieved to hear that I'd be joining him with some backup firepower. Josh had no idea why the bad guys hadn't shown yet. No, they hadn't heard any of the gunfire from the other two firefights. The mountains had obligingly muffled the sounds of the distant shots.

By the time I came out of the com center, most of my posse had disappeared to join the survivors of John D.'s group over at the Sportsman's Bar—in order to celebrate their continued status of being among the living. As a result, I was only able to recruit Officers Gibbons and Moore, Geoffrey, and Dominic Varrez as backup. Lucky for me that Dominic had stuck around to help stash the new weapons. He was an ex-marine, familiar with the Ingram machine pistol. I left him in charge of showing the rest of the group how to operate them while I went to check on the wounded.

The doc and his three draftee nurses had their hands full with six patients, so I didn't bother trying to get in a word with any of them. From where I stood, it looked like John D. was the worst of the lot. He lay over on a cot in the far corner, his right thigh wrapped in bloody bandages. When I went over for a closer look, I was surprised to find him conscious. His eyes fluttered open as I approached, and he greeted me with a slurred voice but an obviously clear head. The first thing he wanted to know was how things were going against the raiders. I squatted on the floor next to his cot and filled him in, using twenty-five words or less, then asked how he was doing.

"They caught me on the run, while I was trying to change positions. Damn explosive bullet clipped me in the back of the leg and went off like a grenade. The doc's got me doped to the gills and says he has to go in again to probe for more fragments. Guess I was lucky it didn't hit a major artery. Would never have made it down the mountain if it had."

"Well, you just rest now. You'll be back on your feet in no time."

"Not quite the way I used to be, I'm afraid. Got a bit of cartilage and ligament damage. Going to be on crutches for quite a while, from what I hear. I'm probably going to need a cane for the rest of my days. Looks like Mayor Hayden's going to have to find someone else to replace you with."

"You shouldn't have gone to this trouble, John. I think Ruth and I could have worked out our differences without you hobbling yourself."

"Very funny. You still heading off after Maria?"

"Soon as I find out what's happening in Woodland Valley."

"Then put Josh in charge while you're gone. Rick, Moore, and Gibbons are all too young to handle the job."

"I'll do that, even though Josh ain't going to like it. I don't think growing up to be a policeman was ever one of his fantasies."

Geoffrey abruptly materialized at the door and signaled me. This meant the group had loaded up the cars and was ready to go. I said goodbye to John D. and headed off. As I reached the door, I turned back for one last look. He'd closed his eyes and was resting again. Big John looked so small and broken, lying over on that cot. I'd never realized how much I'd come to depend on him over the years. It wouldn't be easy getting along without him. But neither of us had been fooled by his "prognosis." John D. was permanently off the active-duty roster, and we both knew it. You need two good legs for the type of work we did. From now on John D. was relegated to the paper-pusher brigade. He'd still be more than useful, of course, but it would never be like the old days again. I knew John wasn't going to make peace with that fact easily.

As my group drove out of town, I wondered why I hadn't seen Mayor Hayden since my return. My guess was she'd decided to keep a low profile until everything quieted down. Smart woman. I doubted I'd feel kindly toward her again until I got Maria back to town.

Maria. It was the first time since that morning I'd let myself think of her. There'd been no time before, and I had put all my gentler emotions on hold, including my concern for Maria, in order to survive the battle. All the worry came back in a mad emotional rush. Where were those slow-ass raiders? Didn't they know I had a wife out on the road who needed rescuing? The longer they took showing up to be slaughtered, the farther away my wife was getting.

A long, poorly tended dirt road snaked up through Woodland Valley. It ended about halfway up that winding gorge. From there the hills, valleys, and lots of woods stretched on for I don't know how many miles. All the small towns in that direction were deserted a long time ago, too out of the way and tiny to defend properly. That was our wilderness frontier. The raiders had probably made their way down along the outer edge of it from either Margaretville or Arkville. This was tough country we were heading for. That could be why the raiders were late. It'd be easy to underestimate the time it would take. But for some reason, a little voice in the back of my head kept warning that that wasn't the case.

Another hour on foot brought us to Josh's stakeout. Everyone except Josh was out of sight and quiet. Josh positioned the new arrivals where he needed them, and then he and I walked back down the trail to talk. We sat on a couple of large rocks under a huge pine tree, the only dry spot we could find.

"What do you make of this, Josh? What's happened to them?"

"No idea, really. Maybe they tried reaching their pals on the radio, couldn't get them, and decided to go home."

"That occurred to me too. But Dirk tells me he hasn't picked up any radio activity on their wavelength, none at all. Nothing. Zip. Bubkes."

"Then that means they should still be on their way. You think they got lost in the dark?"

I thought about this possibility for a while and finally rejected it. "No, these guys had planned this out too carefully to have that kind of a screwup. In their own way, they're pros at what they do. Pros don't get lost in the woods. Something's happened that we can't even guess at."

"Then that means the only way we find out what's happened is to wait for first light and go up and investigate, eh? Makes sense, don't it?"

I didn't want to hear that. Not even from Josh. No matter how much sense it made. To me, all it meant was more time wasted on these damn raiders. But Josh was right; it was the only solution to the problem. After some talking and then some arguing, it was decided that I'd take two men up with me, come dawn, and find out what was going on. Chances were we were walking into a trap. That's why the main body of the posse would remain behind. Josh thought he should be the one to take the scouting party up, but I finally convinced him that he should stay and command our main force. After all, he knew how they were deployed, and he still remained the only one familiar with the nightscope. There was no telling how this was all going to shake out. That flamethrower might still have to be taken out from a safe distance at night.

I know, my reasoning was pretty flimsy. But Josh was a good enough friend that I didn't press the matter. Mr. Woodward must surely have realized that my nerves were in no shape for sitting around with the posse, waiting for him to return from the patrol. I'd probably have blown my stack. The way I see it, when time's grating against your nerve endings, keeping busy is the best tonic, even if that means putting your life on the line.

I figured Dominic and Geoffrey were the best choices to join me on this recon, so I had Josh send them back to join me for some rest before the sun rose. I knew this decision wouldn't sit well with Ricky Skeats, who was also part of Josh's pack, but the kid just didn't have the experience for this kind of job. Besides, I'd lost enough of my constables over the last few days as it was.

The most useful thing the service taught me to do, during my two-year stint, was to catch up on my sleep whenever the opportunity arose. So I was already out when Josh returned with Geoffrey and Dominic. I didn't stir until Josh shook me awake two hours later.

Geoffrey, still in mime makeup, was stretching and doing deep knee bends, trying to work out the stiffness his nap had bequeathed him. It was pretty apparent that Dominic hadn't bothered with sleep. Why should he? He was only twenty-two years old. Sleep, like youth, is wasted on the young. Me? I felt like someone had broken my mainspring, my joints popping and creaking as I got to my feet. I was still working out the kinks when Josh said, "I've got something to show you. You're not going to like it."

He headed up the trail, with me following morosely, silently cursing the fact that I hadn't had the sense to bring along a thermos of hot coffee, something to kick-start my engine.

Josh stopped about fifty feet up the trail and pointed to the soft earth at his feet. I walked up beside him and looked down at the rain-filled tire tracks. The clear markings of the treads were readily apparent. An enormous hemlock sheltered the spot I was standing on. That was why the rain hadn't washed these tracks away. They looked awfully fresh.

"Just didn't see them in the dark last night. I guess these tracks go a long way toward explaining why the raiders didn't show," Josh said as he bent down beside me for a closer look at the impressions.

I scratched at the stubble on my chin, trying to put it all together. "You thinking the raiders had another spy in town . . . and he drove up here in some kind of four-wheel vehicle yesterday, after finding out we were onto them?"

"Looks that way to me."

"Then why didn't they warn off their pals in the park and Mount Tremper?"

"Maybe the news flash didn't reach them in time."

"Yeah, that might be what happened." But I just couldn't

buy it, for some reason. It didn't feel right, even though all signs pointed to it.

I got to my feet and stared up the trail. "We don't know if they hightailed it out of here or are waiting up the path to make a run at us after dark."

"Yeah, tonight would be the time to hit us," Josh agreed. "Everyone will be laid back, fat and sassy from our victory the night before. A surprise attack with those machine guns and a flamethrower would tear us up bad. They'd have a good chance of pulling it off."

"Then we go on as planned. If we run into any resistance, we'll fall back and regroup with you. If it turns out the raiders are still up there, we get more backup from town and go in after them. Can't have them hanging over our heads like some damn Sword of Damocles."

Josh followed us up the trail until we reached the area where he had his men deployed. Then he melted into the bush without another word. There was nothing more to say, so no breath was wasted. Josh and I knew the score. Geoffrey, Dominic, and I trudged on silently, spotting only a few of the twenty-odd men we knew were hidden about us.

With every step possibly leading us closer to an explosive bullet, all systems were on full alert. The woods were coming alive for the day, and that made it tough going. More than once we almost sprayed an innocent squirrel with Ingram fire. At one point, a grazing deer nearly gave all three of us heart failure. I'm not sure who it was rougher on, us or the wildlife.

Every so often I'd spot another set of those tire tracks, dug into the soft earth of the trail where the loose creek stones didn't cover. Something about them kept setting off an alarm in my head, but I couldn't put my finger on why. From the width between the tracks, I concluded that it had been some kind of camper that had been through here, probably a Blazer, Bronco, or Samurai. Try as I might, though, I couldn't remember any such vehicle in town, recently, that would have fit the bill as a possible candidate. I think that fact, more than anything else, bothered me the most.

Then I saw something that froze me in my tracks. Ahead and off to the left was something gleaming in the woods. A little beam of light had broken through the overhead foliage and was playing off something shiny. Nature doesn't produce reflective surfaces in the forest. Whatever was producing that gleam was definitely man-made.

I stepped off the trail into a clump of bushes. Behind me, Geoffrey and Dom followed my lead. Dom was at my side within a few heartbeats. I motioned for him to head off to the right. Geoffrey and I slowly made our way through the undergrowth toward the place the gleam had come from, using the uneven terrain as best we could for cover.

It took about five more minutes of this slow going before I finally spotted the answer to our little mystery. But even then I approached it carefully, ready to unleash the deadly power of the Ingram at a moment's notice.

The Ford Bronco was deserted, a thin shaft of light playing on the driver's door handle. There was nothing to indicate which direction its owner had taken. He'd simply driven it off the trail and abandoned it, disappearing into the vast woods that lay beyond. He could be anywhere by this time, and that really worried me.

Because I knew this Bronco, had seen it almost daily for the past two years. It belonged to one Benny Hollaster.

27

The list of possibilities that ran quickly through my mind at the sight of Benny's wheels made it reel, as if drunk, out of control—for about the first fifteen seconds. Then something clicked and I suddenly found myself thinking logically once more. Okay, say Benny had to split town. He knew he'd never be able to cover up the death of his wife now, not without my checking into it. And her "condition" would give lie to any story of her berserking out and his having to put her down. So his guise as a normal, if not very likable, human was blown all to hell and back again. Add to this equation the fact that he not only knew about the raiders, but also knew which way they were coming from. So what did he do?

He drove up here and abandoned his vehicle—long before he had to, if he was planning to make his escape through the wilds. Why? It would have been a lot easier and smarter staying to the main roads and putting a few hundred miles or so between himself and Shandaken before anyone discovered his wife's body.

But maybe his twisted mind felt safer in the forest. Benny always did spend a lot of both his on-duty and off-duty time in the woods. He was sort of the town's unofficial perimeter patrol for those areas not easily reached by car. Benny was the only one crazy enough to take that assignment and as a result knew these woods better than anyone else in town. Perhaps that was why he'd chosen this unlikely escape route.

Then why had he chosen that particular direction to run in? He knew the raiders were coming that way. He could have come up with a dozen other alternatives easily. That left only one conclusion. Benny was going out to meet the raiders. But why? What was his secret agenda?

To join up with them, maybe? Perhaps show them a route to sidestep the intended ambush, so they could hit town from an unprotected direction? But if that was the case, why hadn't they done it already? Were they waiting for nightfall? No, none of this made any sense.

There'd be no reason for the raiders to trust Benny. Trust wasn't something the man normally engendered in people. They'd think he was trying to lead them into a trap. Berserked out or not, Benny would realize this. And somehow I couldn't see Hollaster meekly wandering into their camp asking for sanctuary, knowing he'd be killed. The man was too wily for that.

Maybe his idea was to skirt around the raiders and put them between himself and an imagined danger, like someone coming after him. No sale. This theory, too, was easily shot full of holes. Why would he think anyone was after him yet? He knew we had enough trouble on our hands without adding tracking him to our list.

I reluctantly had to admit to myself that there was no way to anticipate what Benny was up to. I was dealing with a man whose mind had flown the coop. And here I was determinedly straining my logical little brain trying to anticipate his moves and motives based on **rational** patterns. Deciding this intellectual exercise was a complete waste of time left me free, though, to get on with the necessary next move. Sad to say, but in hopeless situations like this, more thought rather than less usually equals paralysis. So without another speculation, I headed back to the trail with Geoffrey and Dominic. We had to find out what was going on up in the woods, and as much as I hated the idea, the only way to do that was to move on.

As we slowly edged our way along the path, Benny's army record kept drifting into mind. I tried to remember everything I'd heard over the years about his tour in the Nam. He'd been in Special Services, a hard-core, behind-the-lines outfit. I seemed to remember some mention of two tours of duty before he got into that trouble with the prostitute. Then there were all those on-the-job killings for the constable's office. There had never been a more enthusiastically brutal and savage blue knight. But these times called for a few monsters in uniform. I'd needed Benny and had used him shamelessly. Just how shamelessly was beginning to dawn on me with every step. The realization that Benny was first and foremost a human killing machine was sinking in, at this moment, with a relentless clarity. Of course, I'd known it all along, but had overlooked it because he'd been *my* killing machine. That was all changed now.

It was insanity, I realized, to be going after him with anything less than half the town along. The only sensible thing to do would be to turn around and head home. But we didn't. We might have done just that in another quarter mile or so, but something happened to keep us from ever reaching that decision.

The Ingram was lying in the middle of the path, all by itself; no one was anywhere in sight.

We approached it slowly with silent anxiety, totally alert, with our weapons trained on the nearby undergrowth. Anyone foolish enough to jump out of that foliage would have been cut to ribbons in an instant. I positioned myself next to the fallen weapon, covering my partners as they checked out the brush. When they signaled the all clear, I stooped down and picked up the machine pistol.

It was fully loaded and on safety. The weapon was already beginning to pit from its night's exposure to the elements. But it yielded no clue to how it got there. Geoffrey and Dom rejoined me, keeping an eye on the woods, occasionally glancing at the second Ingram in my hand, as if it were a poisonous snake they didn't want to turn their backs on too long.

Dom finally broke the silence. "I give up. What's it doing here?"

"Beats me," I answered as I jammed our discovery into my backpack. "But it sure looks like the raiders made it at least this far. Where they've gone from here, though, is anyone's guess. That Ingram might have been dropped while they were retreating up the path. Maybe they ran into big bad Benny and he scared them off."

"You don't really think that, do you, man?"

"It doesn't seem likely, does it? If Benny had stumbled upon the raiders, his body would be lying here together with a number of theirs, instead of just this one gun."

"So, we go on?"

"Yeah, at least a little bit farther. I've got to get some idea of what's going on here before we head back."

I took the lead as we continued, not really crazy about this, but knowing I'd react faster than either of my companions should any danger pop up. I tried to make my steps completely silent, even though I knew all the stealth in the world would mean precious little if Benny was somewhere up ahead waiting for us. We rounded a bend in the trail and came across . . . another discarded weapon. A shotgun this time.

A quick glance at the gun was enough to convince me it wasn't worth taking my eyes off the woods long enough to carefully examine it. We moved on without comment.

It was Dominic who spotted the glistening blood on the creek stones. I had walked past it without noticing, keeping my eyes on the woods ahead. It wasn't my last chance to spot some. Every two hundred feet or so we found more. At one point, the crimson droplets veered away from the path and up an embankment. We chose not to follow them, however. It felt safer on the trail.

Then all at once we came around another bend and stumbled upon our first body. He was lying on his back, staring blindly up into the trees, his throat slashed open. There was a surprised expression on his face. Dominic turned to me and asked in a whisper, "Benny?"

"Probably."

There was another body two hundred feet farther up the trail. This one lay facedown. I could clearly see where the blade had been slipped past the corpse's upper vertebrae and driven through the opening at the base of the skull, into the brain. Death had been instantaneous. The Army had also taught me this neat little trick. But Benny's handiwork had the clean, crisp look of someone who had kept his hand-eye coordination honed with long hours of practical application. From where we stood, the three of us could see a third body.

We continued until we'd passed eight corpses, each with its brains scrambled by Benny's knife. I couldn't believe he'd gotten away with it. He must have concealed himself along the trail and allowed the entire band to walk past him in the dark. I could see Benny silently counting off the passing raiders until the last man came by. Then he would have stepped in behind him, murdered him, and taken his place in line.

Each raider would have thought it was just the guy behind him, getting a bit too close, as Benny stepped up and dispatched him into oblivion. He'd have had to make it quick and then gently lower the body to the ground so as not to alert anyone to trouble. Then he'd be up and after the next man. There had been thirty men in this group. I didn't have to continue counting bodies to assure myself that they were all dead.

So I figured it was time for us to head back. The threat of the raiders was over as far as I was concerned. Benny was the only trouble we had to contend with, and I didn't want to take on that problem with just two men at my side. I motioned Dom and Geoffrey to turn around. I'm sure the expressions of relief on their faces were mirrored on my own features. We needed backup, lots of backup.

This grisly display of Benny's prowess had put him in another class altogether. I mean, a man who's killed thirty men at a clip with only a knife deserves some extra respect. And fear. This was an impossible feat; no human could have accomplished it. We'd been ready to risk our lives against run-of-the-mill raiders, but this was a different matter. I sensed I shared an unspoken realization of this with Dom and Geoffrey. Merely getting killed we could handle. But death at Benny Hollaster's hands . . . now that was something to be avoided at all costs.

We hurried back down the trail, choosing speed over stealth. It was only after we failed to pass the first body we'd come across that I screeched to a halt. I backtracked to where I remembered it being and found telltale scarlet smears marking its recent resting place. Dom and Geoffrey nervously came up behind me. I turned to look into their puzzled faces.

"Why the fuck we stopping, man?" Dominic demanded.

"Look. The guy with the slit throat. He's gone."

"So what? Let's get the hell out of here!"

"Use your head, Dom. Benny's come back for the bodies. I don't know why yet, but he has. This guy didn't just get up and walk off on his own."

"Like I said, so what? Why don't we follow his example and burn rubber outa here?"

"Because it also means Benny probably knows we're here. He couldn't have missed that mad dash we just made down the trail."

"So what are we going to do, Tom?" It was the first thing Geoffrey had said all day. I didn't like the sound of his voice.

"Getting off this trail is probably a good idea. If Benny's planning to bushwhack us, standing out in the open like this is an engraved invitation."

The three of us scrambled up the embankment and into the safety of the undergrowth without standing on ceremony. We squatted there, listening to the sounds of the woods, all sensory indicators registering in the red zone. It sounded like Geoffrey was hyperventilating. I let us sit there until he got control of himself.

Then I took the lead, snaking us through the brambles and bushes. The trees were sparse along this stretch, so the undergrowth was pretty thick. It would serve us well for cover. Unfortunately, it would do the same for Benny.

We continued like this for about a quarter mile, until I came across a deerpath. It was a narrow little strip, worn away by the passing hooves of hundreds of does and bucks in their daily trek through these woods. I decided this was just what the doctor ordered. It would simultaneously quiet and speed up our departure from the area. I let Dom take the lead here, figuring any trouble from Benny would more likely now come from behind. Of course, I was wrong. Taking the rear guard saved my life and cost Dom his. I'm really sorry about that.

We hadn't gotten a hundred yards down the path before I heard Dominic scream out in pain and horror. I raced forward, hoping to get my chance to cut Benny in half with the Ingram. What I found instead was Geoffrey staring fixedly into a large hole in the ground at his feet. Dead leaves were scattered all along the edge of the eight-foot-wide pit.

I approached slowly, keeping most of my attention on the deathly still forest around me. When I got close enough to Geoffrey, I nudged him in the ribs with an elbow and hissed, "Snap out of it, Geoff! Keep an eye on the woods!"

Geoffrey seemed to hear me as if from a long way off and began to inch his way around the pit. I took this opportunity to make sure, although I was already certain, there was nothing I could do for Dominic. There wasn't. It looked like he had dropped into the pit at a near run. Two of the pungi sticks had gone clean through his torso. Another was sticking out the back of his neck. A fourth and fifth pungi impaled his left arm and right leg. Dom was still twitching, bits of dirt and dried leaves falling off him. But he was no longer among the living.

Benny had learned his lessons well in Vietnam. It was a classic death trap, right out of the jungle warfare textbooks. But when, I wondered, had he had the time to set it up?

28

Once again I took the lead position. Dom's death had mercilessly driven home the pointlessness of trying to second-guess Benny. I found another concealed pit two hundred feet down the trail. Fifty feet past that, I spotted a nearly invisible length of fishing line stretched across the path. We stepped over it, preferring not to find out what lethal surprise it would trigger.

The mind forgets nothing about surviving in the jungle. I was back in the Nam. The decades melted away as if they had never happened. Survival mode was the only thing that was going to get Geoffrey and me out of here alive. Concentrate on nothing but the terrain. Don't let anything distract you. Be prepared for any eventuality. Be ready to dive to the left or right at a moment's notice. Don't, repeat don't, take anything for granted. Or assume anything is as it seems. If something above you attracts your attention . . . quick look down. That's where the danger probably is.

Some part of my brain refused to stop mulling over Benny. It noted that this wasn't just some remote area that Benny had blindly run to. This was his hideaway, his stronghold. It had taken him a long time to set up these traps. They probably dotted our surroundings. There was a reason for his coming here. Something more powerful and precious to Benny than the safety of the open road. Now what could that be?

I'd never been this far back into these woods before. I wasn't familiar with the area. But by now I had a powerful desire to know what lay hidden away in this remote stretch of forest. What drove Benny to go to such lengths to protect it from prying eyes? I thought I remembered there being a ranger station or something back here somewhere. No, that couldn't be it.

A sound to my left stopped these stray thoughts dead in their tracks. I fell into a crouch and stared out over the undergrowth, hoping to catch a glimpse of the author of that noise. No go.

Then I heard something hit a tree, sharply, and clump to the ground. The old thrown-stone trick. Sorry, Benny, not buying it. I wasn't about to fall for that old chestnut. But evidently Geoffrey was.

Before I could stop him, he was spraying the woods with his Ingram, mowing down saplings and shredding bark. I hit the dirt, sure that return fire would be coming in at any moment. Wrong again.

Geoffrey emptied his clip and, before I knew it, was hurtling over me and racing blindly down the deer trail. I made a grab for him and missed. "Geoffrey, no!" I yelled.

But Geoffrey wasn't in the mood for listening. To me or anyone else. Blind panic had seized him. All he had ears for was the siren call of flight. Geoffrey disappeared around a bend, and then all I could hear was his feet thudding along the hard-packed dirt. Then there was a loud wet noise that sounded a lot like someone hitting a side of beef with a baseball bat. And, like magic, his footsteps were gone. Empty silence echoed loudly in their place within my head.

I sat there a long, seemingly eternal time, enshrouded by that deadly silence. That Geoffrey was dead I had no doubt. But I had no burning desire to join him, so I remained where I was, unmoving, desperately taking stock of the situation. Inexperience had killed Dominic. Panic had ended Geoffrey's days on this earth. What about me? Did I have a fatal flaw I wasn't even aware of? Like Freud, I didn't really believe in mistakes as such. I guessed I'd find out soon enough.

Benny was ahead of me, of that I was sure. That left me two choices. One: double back and hope to sneak around him. Two: take it slowly and carefully and blast the bastard off the face of this planet with the Ingram. Sure, he had taken out thirty trained fighters last night. But he had done it in the dark, with no advance announcement of his coming.

It was daylight now and I had an Ingram machine pistol in my hand with the safety off. That evened the odds some between Benny and me. So I quietly moved forward, making each step whisper.

A full five minutes later, Geoffrey's body came into view. As I spotted it, I dropped back into a deep crouch, listening for any sound that might betray Benny's presence. More of that same dreadful silence greeted me. I raised myself enough to peer above the nearby brambles, but spotted nothing.

Then I began to feel sort of vulnerable with nothing but the brush for cover and quietly inched my way over to a nice sturdy-looking oak tree. With the tree for both practical and moral support, I chanced standing erect for a better view, keeping the oak between me and the territory ahead. But another few minutes of peeking around this side of the tree and the other gained me nothing. I finally settled down onto my haunches, back to the tree, wondering what to do next.

That's when Benny decided to put in an appearance. His standing up smacked of an apparition rising from the grave. He'd been hiding in a thicket not more than two feet from me all along. At any point during the last few minutes he could have reached out and tapped me on the back or shoved a knife between my shoulder blades. I just squatted there, staring up at him, my jaw hanging slack, not believing my eyes.

He was completely naked, save for a small black bib or dickey. A tiny inch-and-a-half window of white clerical collar peeked out of the part that ringed his thick neck. The rest of him was covered from head to toe with camouflage paint. Most of his dark hair had been hurriedly hacked off, and even the exposed scalp underneath was painted. Benny towered over me like something straight out of my worst nightmare. And what's worse, he grinned down at me rather mischievously, like a mad Cheshire cat.

I snapped out of it and was bringing the Ingram around at him. But I was too late. Something flashed in Benny's right hand and reality splintered all about me. I felt myself dropping into the black void, that void no one ever returns from. Goodbye, cruel world.

The first thing I remember was hearing the Hail Mary. I thought at first it was an elusive childhood memory from my parochial grade school days. But the voice kept distinctly repeating the prayer over and over again. There was something familiar about that too, although I couldn't say exactly what it was.

"Hail Mary, full of grace, the Lord is with thee; blessed art thou amongst women, and blessed is the fruit of thy womb, Jesus. . . . Holy Mary, Mother of God, pray for us sinners now and at the hour of our death. Amen . . ."

It finally occurred to me that someone was reciting a rosary. I decided to open my eyes to see who it was. That was a mistake. The world was a fireworks display of popping yellow-and-white flashes. I tried to blink them away and eventually succeeded. It didn't help much. My surroundings remained a mystery, blurred and unrecognizable.

Right about then I started to notice the pain. Something was cutting into my arms, and my head felt as if a five-inch

nail had been driven into it. I tried to reach up, to pull the spike out, but found I couldn't move my arms. The unseen voice finished another Hail Mary and started in on an Our Father just as my vision started to clear.

"Our Father who art in heaven . . ."

My first semirational thought was that there was someone standing across from me. But I realized, almost immediately, that I was still cooking on only one burner when I noticed that that someone's jaw hung slack and he was missing an eye. It looked rather unpleasantly as though something had eaten it out. The corpse was lashed by the arms, to some type of crossbeam.

". . . hallowed be Thy name . . ."

The realization hit that I was similarly tied. I twisted around, trying to see what this structure was that I was bound to. The effort of movement was rewarded by several minutes of blinding pain. Then my head and eyes cleared again and I saw the rest of them.

"Give us this day our daily bread. And forgive us our trespasses . . ."

There must have been more than fifty bodies tied to the framework of the tower. Most were men, but I spotted two I thought might have once been women. A few of them were so badly decomposed it was hard to tell their gender. But half of them were fresh, no more than a day old, dressed in bloodied camouflage fatigues. Some distance down the scaffolding I spotted Updike, Smitty, and Dominic, dangling like dreadful Christmas ornaments. All that was missing was the tinsel.

Random animal carcasses were lashed here and there amid this ghastly collection of human cadavers. A fox to the right of me, a dead dog overhead. They hung at odd angles all about me, looking strangely disjointed.

My mind registered and recorded the horror, but some part of me refused to accept its reality. A timely case of shock has saved more than one mind from shattering into a million tiny slivers that all the king's men couldn't put back together again.

For a moment or so, it occurred to me that I might be dead myself. Why else would I be here in this charnel house? Then the pain in my head squelched that silly notion. I couldn't possibly feel this bad and be dead.

". . . as we forgive those who trespass against us."

I decided that this had to be an old Park's Department fire tower I was tied to and that I was hanging about halfway up its scaffolding. I twisted around to inspect the ropes that bound me and was pleasantly surprised to find I was loosely secured. So I painfully wiggled my way to freedom in mere seconds. My captor apparently hadn't realized he was hanging up a still-living trophy.

Yes, that's what this bizarre scene reminded me of. A hunting-lodge trophy room. Then the prayer being intoned above me drifted down and like the turn of a kaleidoscope, forever altered how I saw the scene before me. This was not simply Benny, the great white hunter gone berserk, that I was dealing with. This was something worse . . . much, much worse.

"And lead us not into temptation, but deliver us from evil . . ."

I examined the blood on my forehead and found it was dried and matted. I'd apparently been hanging about here for some time. My pistol and ammo belt were gone. I felt rather helpless and light-headed as I swung myself over to another crossbeam and sat down. When I looked up, I found myself sitting next to Geoffrey Austin. God, what a mess! Whatever Benny had used on my head had proven much more effective on the mime. His skull had been cracked wide open. Dried blood streaked his pancake makeup. The flies were making a picnic lunch of him. My stomach revolted. I turned away quickly to avoid losing the breakfast I'd never had.

". . . Amen."

Benny's familiar guttural voice was coming from the platform directly overhead. I figured there must be a small enclosure atop that platform, from which park rangers used to search for signs of forest fires. The tower had a much darker function and purpose now. I started to climb down from that open-air crypt as quietly as I could. It wasn't easy. My body kept trying to quit on me. Fear and pain kept whispering that unconscious oblivion was the way to go. I fought off the suggestion.

"Why? Why, my Lord?"

That sudden plaintive wail, full of agony and frustration, froze me momentarily in my descent. I held on to the simple thought of escape. I didn't want to have anything to do with the owner of that voice until my head was functioning again and I had a gun in my hand.

"Have I not set the pattern just as You bade? Why do You not speak to Your most loyal servant?"

I started down again, relieved that the outburst had been directed toward a Being more supreme than myself. I could hear Benny moving around above me and hoped his eyes were raised in the direction of his entreaty.

"I don't understand, my Lord! I've arranged the sacrificial objects according to Your will, which was revealed to me in the dreams! I've said the prayers as You ordered. What is amiss? What have I done wrong? How have I transgressed Your laws, that I am still denied the glory of Your voice?"

On my way down the scaffolding I spotted the cabin, wood planked with a sturdy cedar-shake roof. It was about a hundred yards from the base of the tower. That was where I'd find my guns, if I could reach it.

"Speak to me, my Lord!"

At last I reached the ground. I clung unsteadily to one of the tower's vertical beams. There was no cover between the fire tower and that shack. If my former deputy constable, turned God's servant, had a rifle up there with him, I was dead meat. I looked up to see if I could spot him. The tower's platform hid Benny from view. Good. With any luck, if I couldn't see him, he couldn't see me. At least I hoped it worked that way. It had really unnerved me the way Benny had stood up from out of nowhere back on the trail. The frayed ends of my nerves were still jangling.

"What is it you wish from me? How have I displeased you, my Lord?"

My best bet, I decided, was to walk calmly to the cabin as quietly as was humanly possible. With a little luck I could reach the shack, get my Ingram, and blow that maniac off the tower before he finished his little conversation with the Almighty.

I took a deep breath and stepped out into the clearing. Neither bullets nor lightning bolts struck me down. I set each footstep down as if I were treading on rice paper. But to my overly alert ears, the dry, rustling grass underfoot sounded like breaking two-by-fours. The dirt that shifted beneath my feet sounded like major construction taking place. I felt a rising panic. I pressed on. As long as I could hear Benny carrying on the way he was, I knew I was safe. But if it got quiet suddenly, then it would be time to run like hell for that cabin.

"What do you want, Lord? More bodies? Have I not brought you sacrifices in sufficient numbers? Tell me, Lord, I beseech you!"

I chanced a glance over my shoulder to see if Benny was in view yet. Big mistake.

His head turned toward me.

"THE ANSWER!" he bellowed and pointed an accusing finger at me.

Our eyes locked. I felt my bowels loosen and decided I'd better get moving before I befouled myself.

"Walking dead, return to your station!" he commanded, rather regally.

This walking dead broke into a run instead. The cabin looked to be a thousand light-years away. My legs became rubber. The ground tilted and without warning hit me in the face.

"Damn you, dead! You'll not cheat me of the glory!"

As I pushed myself up onto my hands and knees, I saw him bounding with astounding speed down the tower's ladder. Benny's arms looked incredibly long for his body. I'd forgotten how thickly muscled they were. He moved like a great ape. I could hear my heart pounding in my ears. Somehow I managed to regain my footing and resumed my footrace with the grim reaper.

Suddenly I was at the cabin. It looked impregnable up close. All the windows were shuttered. I rushed to the front door. It was locked. I looked back toward the tower. Mighty Joe Young had reached the ground and was picking something up out of the tall grass. I slammed myself against the door with every ounce of my strength. It didn't budge.

Benny was beginning to run toward the house now, yelling something I couldn't understand and swinging whatever it was he'd picked up. I rammed the door again. A sharp pain seared my shoulder, but the door held firm and I suddenly realized I was going to die.

"No!" I screamed and rushed around the house tearing at the window shutters. They held fast. *Please, God, save me!*

I couldn't help myself. It was complete, out-of-control hysteria. I'd seen their heads—Geoffrey, Updike, Smitty, Dominic. I'd seen those shattered skulls, dripping blood and gray matter. The scariest man I knew was coming after me with something that could do that, and I had to face him empty-handed.

Benny, crazed man of the cloth, what little there was of it, was halfway across the field now. He was death, and he was steadily gaining on me. I could finally make out what the weapon that he swung over his head with such abandon really was. It was a metal ball, about the size of a large orange, at the end of a thick wire. The wire was secured to a taped wooden grip. The crazy son of a bitch had a morning star!

Catholic bishops favored the morning star during the Crusades. Back then the ball was covered with dozens of rounded metal bumps. Supposedly the macelike weapon could kill a foe without splattering gore all over the place. That was important to the bishops. Their vows demanded that they not shed blood. Killing infidels was all right as long as you didn't shed blood. Causing massive internal hemorrhages was just fine . . . but you had to make sure you didn't shed blood. Benny had certainly collected enough evidence to disprove that ecclesiastical theory.

I couldn't understand how my head had escaped being reduced to mush the last time that macabre weapon had been used on me. An absolute truth dawned on me at that moment. I wouldn't be that lucky twice.

What I needed was a weapon of my own. Immediately. But there was nothing in sight. No forgotten ax or hammer, no sword in a stone. Nothing. I backed away from this angel of death charging at me and bumped into something.

It was a huge wooden crucifix, sticking out of the ground, with a porcelain figure of Christ secured to it. The cross stood about four feet high. I would have been much happier if it had been made of steel, but it would just have to do. I frantically ripped it out of the ground. If felt solid in my grip.

Suddenly, Saint Benny was only steps away. Take that, Nosferatu, I thought as I brought the cross up in front of me to ward off the shiny meteor that I sensed rather than saw whirling for my head. The porcelain Jesus shattered into a million shards, but the weathered wooden cross held. I swung my crossed staff at my assailant, but he easily avoided the clumsy attack.

I saw his arm snap forward quickly and barely got the

cross up in time. This go-round the heavy metal ball broke off one of the crucifix's arms. The naked madman quickly followed that up with a sweeping horizontal swipe at my midsection. I didn't manage to get completely clear of it. The fatty part of my hip took most of the impact, but that still sent me flying heels over ass.

As quickly as I could, I rolled to my knees. He was already springing at me. The metal ball whirled with ugly menace over his head, ready to split my skull and send its contents flying to the four winds. This seemed grossly unfair to me, so I wordlessly bellowed my outrage and threw myself in his direction. Better to spit in Death's eye, I thought. If I was going to die, it would be as a man and not as some whipped dog. In my heart I knew this was the adrenaline talking.

I don't even remember deciding to use what remained of the cross as a sword. My world was too full of the naked man's evil face. He knew he had me. There was no way to save myself. I was his . . . so he smiled his awful smile triumphantly as he closed on me. I stared with fascination at Benny's one gold-capped tooth. Had I really never noticed it before?

The metal ball zipped past my ear, then the full weight of its owner crashed into me. It knocked the wind out of me. I slammed onto my back gasping for air, but I still managed somehow to roll away from where I landed. As I lurched to my feet I realized I'd also managed to lose my cross along the way.

Benny had it. My old enemy stood no more than five feet from me. His trusty mace no longer cut the air. It hung limply at his side. He clutched the shattered cross to his chest. I stood weaponless and helpless before him. There was still fire in his eyes, but I realized there was also something radically different about him. I tried to force my addled wits to put a finger on the change in my foe.

Well, for starters, he wasn't attacking me anymore. That was a definite change for the better, although I doubted it was going to last long. But that wasn't all of it. There seemed to be a complete transformation in the monster's demeanor. He had a daft sort of smile on his face. I guess you could call it beatific, but my thoughts were running more to the bovine. He dropped his mace, pointed a finger toward the sky, and asked, "Can you hear Him? Can you?"

Then he coughed once and spit out a bloody glob. "Of course you can't hear. His words are only . . . for the Chosen."

When he turned back toward the tower, I saw what was left of the cross sticking out of him fore and aft. Benny hadn't been pressing his beloved cross to his bosom as I had first thought. Somehow I'd managed to run the bastard clean through. It was only then that I noticed what a sharp point the end, which had come out of the ground, had. The berserker's blood dripped freely from the spiky end.

He dropped his mace as he started back to the tower. He kept muttering, "Yes, my Lord, I hear. I understand. I . . . I . . ."

Then he fell over dead, and I heaved up my guts.

30

Releasing the horror and pentup tension left me feeling a bit better, but I was still pretty shaken by how badly I'd misjudged the situation. The only reason I was still breathing was my hair-trigger reflexes. If there's a number-one rule for survival, it's stay calm. Don't let the bad guys rattle you. I had really blown it. Any rookie, straight out of the academy, would have held it together better than I had. I'd lost my head, panicked. That grotesquely painted lunatic had gotten to me.

You can't let that sort of thing happen. That's the easiest way to end up dead. You've got to keep a situation under control at all times. Once it takes control of you, you might as well kiss it all goodbye. But he had popped up out of nowhere so casually and mystically that he had scared the bejesus out of me. There was something almost paranormal about that feat. I've always enjoyed the woods. In fact, I pride myself on the extensive knowledge I've gathered, over the years in and out of the service, about surviving out in the wilds. No human or animal had ever crept up on me like that. That incident made me take a good hard look at myself. The thought occurred to me that maybe I was getting too old for this kind of work.

I stared angrily over at Benny's body, but with no small sense of satisfaction. Well, he wasn't going to sneak up on anybody ever again. I'd fixed his wagon. I wondered if he had a key on him for the cabin. I doubted it. No pockets. So I grabbed his mace instead. I had some no-nonsense breaking and entering in mind.

Six good whacks with that fifteen-pound wrecking ball and the cabin's door yielded to me. It swung inward with a whoosh and a crash. I felt pleasantly illegal. A quick look back over my shoulder assured me that the cabin's owner wasn't going to object to my entry. Even in death Benny scared me . . . dammit.

It was pitch-black inside. The morning sun was slanting in from the wrong direction, so the open doorway didn't illuminate the depths of the shack's interior all that much. It was enough, though, for me to spot a kerosene lantern sitting by the door. I tossed the mace behind me and dug into my pants pockets for some matches. The lantern's cloth wick caught easily and cast a soft, eerie light into the darkness of the cabin.

From where I stood the cabin appeared to be one large room, about twenty feet wide by thirty feet long. The lamplight didn't reach to the far wall. Too bad. I know it seems crazy, and I was still all raw nerve endings, but there seemed to be something terribly wrong with that darkness. It was denser than it should have been. Then there was the smell. The place reeked of decay. I spotted another Coleman lantern sitting on a table and headed for it. I didn't realize I wasn't alone until I had the second lamp lit.

He was sitting in a chair over in the far corner and seemed to be smiling at me. Of course, he was quite dead. That didn't stop me from nearly jumping out of my skin. My guess was that he'd been there for about a year at least. The cabin's cool, dark, dry interior had mummified him. His clothes were terribly tattered, but I could still make out the clerical collar around his neck. I guess that explained why he wasn't strapped to the tower with the rest of the stiffs.

This discovery put a new light on Benny's mania, though. Somehow that lunatic had managed to conceal his changeover from merely disgusting human being to card-carrying berserker for much longer than I would have thought possible. He'd carried it off long enough to conceive and assemble that ghastly monument to his death-based religion. It was mindboggling.

My mind conjured up images of Benny having long theological discussions with his leathery counterpart. The concept of the tower of death probably grew out of those sessions. I wondered if my sanity wouldn't be better served if I just turned tail and ran as fast and as far away from this evil and rancid place as possible. But I couldn't do that yet. I needed my guns. Benny might not have gotten all the raiders, and it was a long lonely walk back to where I'd left Josh and his band.

I found them on a table over by the door. Seems I'd passed them on my way in. They were sitting atop a full-scale arsenal, the haphazardly stacked collection of the raiders' weapons and others. The firearms near the bottom of the pile didn't look well cared for at all. A thick layer of dust covered all the weapons that lay below today's arrivals.

As I buckled on my cartridge belt, I noticed on the wall behind the gun collection a reproduction of a painting of Christ ascending into heaven. Directly above the rising figure, a dove showered fiery tongues upon a group of amazed apostles. I remembered clearly looking at this picture in a missal when I was a kid.

. . . and on the third day He rose again from the dead . . .

A chill ran down my back. I raced to the doorway and looked out. I felt foolish. Benny lay on the grass outside the door, where I'd left him, with the cross still protruding front and back. I shook my head, told myself what a jerk I was, and turned back to the room.

On a bureau against one wall sat what I took to be the washroom amenities, a shallow pan, a towel, and a bucket of water. I wet the towel and began to dab at my head wound. The blood was thickly encrusted. I'd reopened the wound during my recent strenuous physical activity. Cleaning up was slow and painful work.

As I worked on my forehead, I dispassionately examined the room. It was a study in obsessions, merging and vying for supremacy. Everywhere I looked, religious artifacts abounded. Holy pictures, crucifixes, and rosary beads hung from the walls. The tops of tables and chests were littered with small plastic statues of the Madonna, Jesus, legions of saints, and stand-up crucifixes. I spotted a dozen Bibles.

But everywhere amid this sacred display were the weathered remains of the dead. Benny had lavishly decorated the place in human skulls. A number of crossed femurs hung from the walls. The total effect caused Jolly Rogers and poison bottles to dance through my head. Hundreds of other bits of bone lay helter-skelter throughout the cabin. He must have hit a local graveyard for his supply. I noticed one of the "chests" I had glanced at earlier was actually a coffin. I didn't open it to see whether it was empty. I didn't want to know.

Benny had obviously been maintaining this abandoned ranger's station for some time. On his days off, he must have used the place as a religious retreat. Benny Hollaster's secret life. I think what bothered me the most was that I had never suspected a thing.

My head wound was clean by now. It wasn't nearly as bad as I had feared. I examined it with the help of a hand mirror I found next to the water bucket. It would leave a mean-looking scar, but I'd survive. I'd been more than lucky.

Now what? I leaned against a table and pondered my next move. I was in no shape to do anything for Geoffrey, Dom, and the other poor wretches on that tower. Josh could bring a work detail up here tomorrow. Proper burials would wait until then, and the township would graciously accept yet another addition to its store of weapons.

A quick check of my Ingram assured me I was ready to hit the road. I had no idea how long it would take me to get back to town. My hope was that I could get back and hit the road after Maria by noon. The horror that had been Benny Hollaster was already beginning to fade from my mind. Back to business as usual. One crisis down, one to go.

As I stepped out of the cabin, I wondered which way was out. Even though I'd heard of the place, I'd never been up to the fire tower before. Nor had I paid much attention coming up here this time, probably slung over Benny's shoulder. I was greatly relieved when I spotted it. A well-worn path began at the tower and wended its way toward the woods. That had to be the way back to Shandaken.

I must have taken a dozen steps in that direction before it hit me. I came to a staggering halt, swallowed hard, and slowly turned around. The broken and bloody cross lay on the grass, all by itself.

31

The Lord is my shepherd; I shall not want.

Benny was gone! And the mace—it was gone too! But how?

He'd come back from the dead. That was the only possible answer. I'd seen him impaled on that cross. No one could have survived that kind of damage. Benny Hollaster's work for the Lord wasn't finished yet. I'd screwed up his holy pattern, so he'd come back, to put me up again in my proper place on the tower.

"Get a hold of yourself!"

I forced myself to visualize that cross sticking out of Benny. It was much easier to conjure up that frightening image than I had expected. The broken crucifix had passed through his midsection. It had gone straight through, just below his rib cage, probably through the stomach and the intestines. It had clearly missed the heart and lungs. That was it! The wound, then, wasn't immediately fatal. He'd probably only passed out from pain and shock. The only small and exceedingly cold comfort in all this was that it meant there was nothing supernatural about his surviving.

Yes, Benny had survived his injuries, but it was only a temporary reprieve. He was dying. He had to be. He couldn't live long with what I'd done to him.

But just how long could he survive like that? Minutes, hours, days? Long enough to strap me back onto the tower?

I tried to imagine him pulling that holy sword from his middle, the lurid wet sucking sound it must have made as he yanked it free. The pain must have been unbelievable. I couldn't understand how he could have done that without crying out and alerting me. And how did he walk right up to the cabin to retrieve his mace without my hearing him? I had convinced myself that he was mortal, but he certainly wasn't human anymore.

He'd apparently decided it was too risky trying to take me on in close quarters or on my way out of the cabin. I had my guns again.

I walked over to the path leading to the woods. Telltale droplets of blood marked his passing. Benny was in the forest waiting for me. The invisible demon of the green had returned to his natural element.

So what were my options? I could wait at the cabin for him to come for me. Some would call that a smart tactical move. Or I could try to sneak around him once it got dark. A chancier play but still well within the "wise move" range.

As far as I was concerned, though, neither option was any good. I could easily see both scenarios ending with Benny coming for me in the black of night. The idea of him suddenly and silently appearing out of the darkness with that whirling mace chilled me to the marrow. There was no way I was going to sit all day waiting for death's painted angel. Of course, he might die before sunset . . . but then again, he might not.

Besides, every moment I spent here put more miles between Maria and me. She was out on the road, alone. I just couldn't wait.

But I couldn't afford to rush things, either. That madman was out there in the woods. He was invisible and wanting to kill me. That made for a mighty slim margin of error.

He maketh me to lie down in green pastures: he leadeth me besides the still waters.

There had to be a way to get past him. Going after him to finish him off wasn't a consideration. I'd survived that folly once. What I had to do was think and think clearly. The path was out of the question. He was bound to be waiting along that route. After making my best guess at where he would be, I decided I'd try to circle around him. If he caught on to my game, he'd have to come out of his hiding place to chase me. That would greatly increase my chances for survival. He couldn't possibly be as quiet in pursuit as he would be lying in wait. All I needed was one clear shot with the Ingram. Now that he was injured, I'd surely hear him coming. Wouldn't I?

I cut through the tall grass to the edge of the woods and stopped. He was in there somewhere. Could he see me? I listened to the sounds of the forest, but I heard only a distant bluejay's screechy cry. I stepped into the trees with the machine gun's safety off.

At that moment the forest stretched on forever. There were at least a billion trees between me and safety. I had to remind myself that Benny's camouflage body paint wouldn't be quite as effective as it once was. It was streaked with a scarlet blaze now. Blood red would stand out nicely among these forest colors.

Then my inner voice warned, "Careful—he's probably smeared his wound with dirt by now to hide the bloody mark."

The lay of the land was working against me, too. Many of the trees were thick enough for a man to hide behind. And there were way too many boulders and fallen tree trunks for Benny to crouch beside. Spring run-off had cut dozens of concealing trenches and small ravines. Hollaster could be a mile from here or only steps away.

Something made a sound behind me and to the left. I spun around and fired. Ten rounds from the Ingram whizzed over a frightened chipmunk's head. He squeaked, leaped behind a log, and scurried away to safety. I stood there feeling very foolish and scared, remembering Geoffrey, fighting the mad urge to run. Well, so much for concealing my position. Benny surely knew where I was now and was busy leapfrogging ahead of me to set up an ambush. Damn! I could see his gold-capped smile in my mind's eye.

Fear, real fear, can make you stupid at least as often as it can make you cunning. I couldn't take back my grievous tactical error. There was nothing else to do but go on. I treaded as quietly as I could, but the deadfall that littered the forest's floor made stealth almost impossible. Every few steps I'd stop and listen, to hear if I could catch Benny approaching.

Nothing.

Maybe he was dead already and all my caution was foolish. At the moment, feeling foolish had no place in my universe. If I let down my guard in the least, I could find myself stone cold dead and tied securely to God's little tower of power. Now that would be foolish.

So, each tree and rock had to be approached cautiously.

My nerves drew tighter with every step. It took literally everything I had to stop myself calling out to Benny, demanding a showdown. I wanted it all to be over.

The only thing that stopped me was the memory of that gold-capped smile. It was something I never wanted to see again. There was still a chance that I could escape these woods without having another encounter with the nightmare holy man of Shandaken.

He restoreth my soul: he leadeth me in the paths of righteousness for his name's sake.

The forest floor fell away in a continuing slope. I had to slow down and feel my way along. My footing became less sure and noisier. I prayed for a deer trail I could follow. A path would quiet my descent, even if it did increase the chances of my meeting up with Benny or falling victim to one of his booby traps. It was a risk I was willing to take. As it was, my escape down the slope sounded like the approach of a thundering herd of moose. But my bad luck held. No trail.

A nerve-racking half hour later, the ground abruptly leveled off and became a ridge. I walked over to the ridge's edge. It dropped twenty feet to the ground below. I considered climbing down, but decided against it. Not having a sling for it, I'd have to toss the Ingram ahead of me, and that would leave me terribly vulnerable on the way down. I'd need both hands to navigate that steep cliff face.

So I walked along the rock ledge, hoping to find an easier way off it. I headed to my left, hoping that was away from the direction from which Benny would come looking for me. The more distance we had between us, the better I'd like it. I wanted to make it down off this ridge and set some new land speed records on my way out of here. I'd be back. I'd probably wait a week or two. Maybe three. Benny would certainly have died from his wound by then. Of course, I'd bring a small army along with me just in case. It never hurts to err on the side of caution.

I finally came upon a washout that cut through the ridge. Its gentle angle would allow me to walk down with both hands free. I didn't like the number of thick trees, though, that sat on the other side of it and thought about checking them out before proceeding. But I decided there was no way Benny could have determined I'd come this way. The odds were with me.

Yes, though I walk through the valley of the shadow of death, I will fear no evil: for thou art with me; thy rod and thy staff they comfort me.

I was halfway down the washout when it occurred to me that I might have had another grievous lapse in logic. This might be the only way past the ridge, aside from the trail. Benny would know this area very well. This was his domain. But even so, could he have beaten me here? The answer, uncomfortably, was yes if he had raced here directly. Had I walked into a trap? This was the perfect place to spring an ambush. He could either pelt me with rocks from above or be waiting for me around the corner of the washout's mouth.

There was a noise above me. I froze. What was it? Another chipmunk . . . a falling limb . . . Benny . . .

I stood there for close to five minutes, listening. No other sound came to me. It had to have been just a harmless forest noise. My fear kept endowing Benny with supernatural powers he didn't possess. I had to remind myself that nothing had happened to give credence to my fears of the supernatural. I only felt as off-balance as I did because he was even better in the woods than I was.

True, he was bigger, craftier, and crazier than any man I'd ever faced, but he was still only a man. In fact, the fool was probably squatting next to that trail leading away from the cabin and bleeding his guts out while waiting for me to show up. I smiled at the thought and started down the washout again.

My foot knocked a small stone loose. It sounded like a ten-ton boulder bouncing down the ravine. There was another sound above and to my left. I caught sight of a shadow flashing across the topmost edge of my peripheral vision. I raised the Ingram over my head and fired.

It was Benny! He had jumped down into the washout from above. But apparently the god who watches over drunks and fools was watching out for me. The machine-gun blast caught his right hand and the mace. The hand pretty well vaporized into a bloody mist. I caught a glimpse of the mace spinning wildly through the air, its grip shattered.

Benny bounced off the right wall of the ravine and onto me. He slammed me down onto the rocky ground. My Ingram was pinned between us, useless. The fact that Benny had just lost most of his right hand didn't seem to bother him at all. Without missing a beat, he latched onto my

throat with his left and began to squeeze. I clenched my teeth and tightened my neck muscles to keep that powerful grip from crushing my larynx. But I realized immediately that it was only a matter of seconds before this measure would prove useless. Benny was built like a professional wrestler. I'd never known anyone so massive and strong.

Without warning, he began to beat on my head with the ruin of his right hand. He was oblivious to the pain that must have caused him. I raised my left arm in a pathetic attempt to ward off the blows. One of my eyes was already blinded by the blood he was losing every time he struck me.

I fumbled for my pistol with my free hand. The gun was still there. Thank God! It hadn't bounced out during the attack. Benny hit me once more. The blow rocked my entire body. I felt the gun's butt slip in my hand. So I tightened my grip and pulled the .45 out of its holster. That's when I felt something pop in my neck. I jammed the gun into Benny's side and pulled the trigger twice.

The shots sounded muffled and distant. Benny shuddered. That vise crushing my throat relaxed and Benny's hand fell away. I looked up at his face. There was still some life and anger left in it. He was scowling at the two bullet holes in the left side of his midsection. A thin wisp of smoke curled lazily from each of them.

He raised both his stump and the good hand above his head. A fist clenched. Its purpose was apparent. One last blow which would certainly shatter my skull against the hard ground it was resting on. I raised the pistol and emptied it into his snarling face.

Thou preparest a table before me in the presence of mine enemies: thou anointest my head with oil; my cup runneth over.

Benny fell over backward. I hurriedly kicked his dead weight off my legs and scrambled to my knees. Then I frantically yanked my hunting knife out of its boot sheath and began to plunge it into the body, over and over again. About a minute and a half of this activity finally convinced me that Benny Hollaster was dead at last.

I wearily pushed myself to my feet and looked down at the corpse. It was pretty badly butchered. I didn't feel the least bit sorry about the carnage. I couldn't quite believe it. I was alive and it felt great.

Surely goodness and mercy shall follow me all the days of my life; and I will dwell in the house of the Lord for ever.

32

That terrible feeling of elation stayed with me most of the way down the mountain. I was numb to all of the bruises and abrasions I had acquired during my fight with Benny. Even my head had stopped throbbing. I was alive and invulnerable. I had gone through hell, faced the devil, and survived. I was Superman.

A small pond afforded me a chance to clean up a bit. I had to take my shirt off and soak it to get out Benny's blood. Then I used it as a washcloth to wipe away some of my own. Unfortunately, I then made the mistake of checking out how I looked in the pond's reflection. I was a wreck. My forehead was hideously knotted and gashed, one eye was nearly swollen shut, and my lower lip was split. The forgotten pain immediately began to creep back into my body. I quickly got to my feet and started off again before I convinced myself that I was in no shape to do so.

The summer heat had dried me off fairly well by the time I reached Josh and his group, a half hour later. They all had a million questions to ask, so I sat myself down on a boulder and slowly filled them in. I could see faces and hearts drop when I told them of the fate of Dom, Geoffrey, and the others. The deaths of the raiders and Benny did little to ease this loss. When I finished, I asked Josh to assign ten men for burial duty and to gather up the weapons cache at the ranger station. They could handle it without my supervision. There were more pressing matters awaiting me in Hunter and points north.

Josh left Ricky Skeats in charge of the men so he could accompany me back to town. I guess he thought I might not make it on my own. I let him do most of the talking on the way back to the cars, since I was beginning to feel about a thousand years old at that point. Josh said they had heard our machine-gun fire. Everyone wanted to rush out to help, frustrated by the fact that the only right thing to do was to wait and see what happened. I was glad I'd not let him take my place on the patrol. As bad as I felt right now, I preferred it to having gone through what Josh obviously had. There's nothing worse, nothing, than sitting helplessly and waiting.

As soon as we reached the vehicles, I crawled into the passenger side of Josh's truck and collapsed, staying awake only long enough to inform Josh that he was in charge of the constable's office while I was on the road, searching for Maria. I drifted off, without even half listening to my friend bitching and moaning about how he wasn't no capitalist tool pig and where I could stick this battlefield promotion.

When we reached town, Josh shook me awake and immediately hauled me over to Doc Rogers's office. I went along without resistance. The place was deserted, except for the doctor. All his earlier patients had apparently been transferred to their own homes for further treatment. As our grumpy neighborhood physician began the painful task of putting a couple stitches into my damaged forehead, I asked Josh to head over to Brio's for sandwiches. He left grumbling about first being drafted into a fascist police force and now being treated like some damn waiter.

Once Josh was gone, I filled Doc Rogers in on my plans to go after Maria. As I expected, he thought I was crazy, since I was in no shape to get behind the wheel of a car. I argued that I was, if he could supply me with something to keep me going. This launched the doc on a ten-minute harangue about medical ethics and the evil effects amphetamines have on the human body. I let him run his course, then calmly informed him that I was still going whether he helped me or not. It would be on his head if I napped out at the wheel and smashed into a tree. This led to another five minutes of argument, which finally came to an end with the doc sadly shaking his head, going off to the adjoining room, and coming back a few moments later with a small plastic jar containing ten little white pills. "Hold off on these until after you eat something," he warned as he handed them to me.

Josh returned with the grub, and I scarfed it down while Doc Rogers finished poking and prodding me. As he continued with his work, the doc filled me in on the condition of the patients he'd worked on earlier in the day. He confirmed my suspicion that John D.'s injuries would force him into the ranks of the armchair warriors. The leg would never again be what it was. What a waste. John D. had been one of the best.

Josh and I said our goodbyes and he drove me over to the station house to pick up a patrol car. I wanted one of the older cars, official emblems on the doors, gumball on the roof. I figured this sign of legitimacy would make it easier for me on the road, dealing with local sheriffs and constables.

It took me a while to convince Josh that I didn't want him along on this trip. What I really needed was someone to run the constable's office in my absence, and he'd been tagged for the duty. There just wasn't anyone else I could turn to for this job. Then he needed reassuring. If there was anything Josh had to know, he should ask John D. That old warhorse would have the answer, and being consulted would keep him from feeling he'd been put out to pasture.

In the end, I took off down the road, Josh in my rearview mirror, glumly watching my departure. Even at a distance, it was apparent how unhappy he was with this arrangement. Once again he'd been forced into the waiting position, holding down the fort, not sure if he'd ever see his friend alive again. Sorry, pal. I promised the receding image that I'd make it up to him somehow, one day.

I stopped off at home on the way out of town to load up on food and extra weapons. I'd brought along two of the Ingrams, but figured there was no such thing as leaving home with too much firepower. I couldn't predict what I was going to run into out there. On my way out the door, I washed down one of the doc's magic white energizers with a glass of water.

The pill kicked in twenty minutes later. I roared down Route 214 at a breakneck pace, cutting the usual two-hour drive to Hunter to an hour and a half. My watch said four-fifty when I pulled up to the first of the former resort town's outer checkpoints. As I expected, the sentries on duty remembered a woman fitting Maria's description coming through two days before in a black Camaro.

I cut through Hunter and learned that Maria had left town in this direction. From the time notation in the checkpoint's log, it looked like she'd passed through without stopping. I did the same.

Tearing up the road, I started to rehearse what I'd say to Maria when I finally caught up with her. It wasn't going to be easy convincing her to return home, of this I was sure. But I'd manage it somehow. I had to.

I'd gone through a dozen different scenarios and rejected them by the time I reached the next little town. Once again I discovered that Maria had shot through without stopping. The lady was obviously bound and determined to put more than a little distance between herself and her past. Undaunted, I pressed on.

Three small towns, another speed bean, and five hours of talking to myself later, I pulled into Blennum. This time when I reached the far side of town I found that Maria hadn't left town in that direction. I asked the sentries on duty for the locations of their town's other checkpoints. It took a bit of cajoling to get this info out of them. Mine wasn't a familiar face this far out of Shandaken. I think it was the patrol car that finally convinced them it'd be all right to give me the locations. Of course, the nearly full bottle of Smirnoff's I laid on them sweetened the deal. A half hour later, I was satisfied that Maria hadn't left Blennum yet. My lovebird had finally chosen a place to roost. So it was time to get acquainted with the local law enforcement officers.

I knew I wasn't going to like Sheriff Elmore Towner even before I met him. You can usually judge a law officer by the kind of town he runs. This dirty little village spoke volumes about the man. It seemed to me that Blennum had more bars than any other kind of business. Drunks littered the sidewalks wherever I looked. Main Street was filled with hookers and Johns hoping to make a deal. Bikers, in full colors, wandered about in packs, looking for excitement. It was obvious that this burg had gone down the tubes, lost any sense of morality and hope for tomorrow. I kept one of the Ingrams on the seat beside me, safety off.

Towner was a big, overweight man, mid-fifties, balding and half in the bag. But even lying back with his feet on his desk, eyes at half mast, I could sense the savage power in him. Here was a brute in uniform, only keeping his job because he was the meanest dude in town and because who else would want to rule over such a cesspool. The menacing Ingram that I'd had the good sense to bring along with me into the station house was probably the only reason I was able to get any civil answers out of him. There were two deputies with him, but one was asleep and the other drifted in heroin heaven, his works still on top of his desk.

I filled Towner in on why I was in his territory, leaving out that Maria was my wife, claiming that she was wanted for questioning in the homicide of a prominent citizen back in Shandaken. Towner didn't give a shit about my problems, but apparently bought the story. His attitude cooled some when I asked if he could help me with any leads on my prey and gave him a description. He fell silent, made a big production of rolling a cigarette and lighting it.

Finally, after what seemed like a million years to my racing, speed-strung nerves, he blew out a cloud of blue smoke and said, "Yeah, I've seen the little lady you're looking for. She was over at the Black Tie Bar earlier this evening."

"You think she's still there?"

"Might be, but I kind of doubt it."

"Why's that?"

"The Donovan brothers were hitting on her while I was there. Looked to me like she was going for their line, too.

Barney and Chet probably have her over at their place by now, having a private little party of their own, if you know what I mean."

I fought down the urge to knock Towner on his ass and asked where the Donovan brothers lived. The controlled calm in my voice surprised me.

"They got themselves a place on Kreel Street. It's a dead end. Go down to the end of the main drag, make your first left. You can't miss the place. It's a big piss-yellow house. There'll be a couple of choppers in front of the dump."

"What can you tell me about these boys, Sheriff?"

"Only that if you're thinking about going down and rousing those two, I'd advise against it."

"How come?"

"They're our local heroin suppliers. Got no idea where they get the shit, but they've got the market cornered in this town. Being in that line, you can figure out for youself what kind of disposition they've got."

"Don't like cops, eh?"

"Those suckers don't like no one, and they're mean enough and got more than enough firepower to get away with that attitude. They ain't going to be impressed with that little toy gun of yours. They've got themselves a Thompson machine gun, a nasty-looking black bastard."

"Guess it would be foolish to ask you for backup, as a professional courtesy?"

"Save your breath, Constable. You want to butt heads with the Donovans, you go right ahead. But don't expect me to get involved. You end up killing those boys, you'll be doing me a favor. But I ain't taking a hand in this business. You don't have to stay around here after the smoke clears. I do. Whoever kills the Donovans is going to have a lot of strung-out junkies pissed at them, my own deputy over there among them."

"So in other words, you don't mind if I do a little house-cleaning for you, just so long as I don't use your name, right?"

"You got it, boy."

I turned and headed for the door. Over my shoulder I said, "If you ever get down to Shandaken, Sheriff, stop by. I'll see if I can return the favor. Don't bother getting up. I'll see myself out."

* * *

Stopping by the Black Tie Bar proved to be a waste of time. The sheriff's guess at the Donovans' timetable appeared to be on the money. Maria was nowhere in sight, and when I asked a rather bleary-eyed hooker at a corner table about the Donovan brothers, she amicably informed me that they'd gone home for the night, but if I was looking for a fix I should talk to the bartender. Great, I thought, one-stop shopping.

The sheriff's directions to the Donovans' digs were flawless. I spotted my Camaro parked in front of the darkened house and drove by without stopping. About a quarter mile beyond, I found a place where I could pull the patrol car off the road, out of sight. Flipping off the lights and ignition, I sat back and wondered how I should proceed from there.

Showing up at their doorstep, in the dead of night, would only instigate a firefight. Maria could end up getting cut down in such an encounter, so that plan was out. It looked like I'd have to wait until dawn to see if I could get Maria out of there, before she completed her rites of lovemaking by trying to skewer the brothers with whatever sharp object might be handy. It wasn't that I was worried about them. Their deaths would be no great loss to society. But a double play might be more than Maria was capable of pulling off. The Other Mind had obviously raised the stakes again. I had no guarantee that Maria was up to the challenge.

So I snuck back to the house and quietly scouted the lay of the land. I soon discovered that the place was overgrown with wild bushes and that the Donovans' idea of waste disposal was to create huge mounds of garbage in their backyard. I'd have more than enough cover if it came to a fight. It seemed to me, though, that for dope dealers these boys had a very casual sense of self-preservation. Apparently their rep and a few years of being at the top of the heap had made them careless. In the old days, dealers turned their homes into fortresses. It looked like now that dealing dope had become just an accepted business like any other in the community, this new breed of pusher didn't feel the overpowering need for self-protection that their predecessors had had. Then again, the Donovans might just be their own best customers and were too spaced out to care. I figured I'd find out which way the wind blew on that subject in the morning. But then I might not have to wait that long. It sounded awfully quiet in there.

I silently made my way up to the house, carefully checking to see whether a door or window had been left unlocked or open, keeping my fingers crossed that the Donovans didn't have a dog. They didn't. But they also didn't leave any easy access into their home. After two trips around the house, I had to admit that there was no way I could break into the place without rousing everyone inside.

So I retreated to a stand of nearby trees where I had a clear view of two sides of the house. Here I would wait for the first signs of renewed life within the old farmhouse. I dry-swallowed another of Doc Rogers's stay-awake pills, set the Ingram on its single-shot action, and sat down with my back to a tree.

Sitting there in the dark, my blood singing with amphetamines, made for the longest night of my life. I kept wondering and worrying about what was going on in that house. I kept telling myself Maria was all right. Every few minutes or so, I'd decide that I'd have to kick in a door and rush in with the Ingram blazing. It was my only hope of getting Maria out alive. Then rational thought would reassert itself and I would settle down again for another five minutes or so.

The last thing I remember was noticing that the night sky appeared to be lightening up. Some time after that, my magic pharmaceuticals failed me. I don't even remember feeling drowsy. No warning, just a muted zap and a quick dive into the darkness. I only woke up when my precarious balance against the tree slipped. Thudding onto the ground brought me back to life, totally and instantly. I was up and on my feet in a flash, Ingram in hand. Overhead, the sun hung high in the morning sky, bathing me with its warmth. A quick look at my watch told me it was ten thirty-eight. I'd been out for hours.

Less than fifty yards away, the old farmhouse stood. Still quiet, with no sign of activity. But I wasn't fooled. I cursed my body for betraying me, cursed Doc Rogers's little white pills, cursed God. Try as I might, I couldn't get my feet to move, to walk me over to the house. All I could do for the longest time was stand there under that damn tree, muttering the word over and over again.

No.

33

The silence was overpowering. I kept wanting to scream out
Maria's name. But I didn't. I knew the unanswered call
would make the quiet all the more unbearable.

The house was waiting for me. It wanted me to bear
witness . . . to its wonders. Inside awaited the rewards of
the good life. Work hard and sacrifice and you too can share
in this slice of the American dream.

As I finally started to walk toward the house, I dropped
the Ingram on the ground. It would be too cumbersome
using it in the close quarters of the house. Then I loosened
my gun in its holster, just in case someone tried to sandbag
me. I know the odds were awfully slim against that happening. Any hope of the Donovans' being late risers was the stuff
of dreams.

The kitchen door wouldn't open. So I punched through
the screen and unhooked it from inside. As soon as I stepped
into the house, the smell hit me. It was a familiar odor. I'd
smelled it many times since the Nam. The smell of death
never changes.

Somehow the flies had beaten me in there. They were all
over the kitchen. They flitted around the three half-eaten

breakfasts that sat forlornly on the kitchen table. They buzzed about, landed on the flaccid-looking pancakes, and buzzed off again.

They also liked the body on the floor. The insects circled the large butcher knife sticking out of its back. Occasionally they dipped down to skim off some of the thick rich blood that was slowly drying around the blade. Other flies scampered across the biker's exposed hands and face.

The dead man looked like he might have been around forty. Barney? Chet? Who cared? He was a big man with a full beard and long hair, which he wore in a ponytail. He also looked like he was a dirty son of a bitch. The flies didn't seem to care.

I went to the sink and got myself a glass of water. My throat felt like a dry riverbed, cracked and parched. One glass wasn't enough. I had a second but didn't finish it.

The dining room was empty. A chair lay on its side. Another chair had a brown leather bomber jacket draped over it. The table was littered with empty beer cans and filthy paper plates. Messy but strangely inviting. So I stepped into the room. Then I saw the other biker. Well, I saw his feet. They were sticking out from behind a couch. I walked toward him. Every step revealed more of the dead man to me.

He was lying facedown. Black leather boots with straps and buckles, under faded blue denim. He wasn't wearing a gun belt. His T-shirt was soaked with blood. I could see where Maria had driven the knife deeply into him at several points. Judging from the amount of blood all over the front room, I'd say this Donovan brother just plain refused to die until long after he should have. His arms were outstretched above his blond head as if he had been reaching for something when he died.

One last step showed me what it was. Maria's throat. The angle of my approach and the biker's body had kept her hidden from view. What I saw made me feel I couldn't breathe. Her beautiful face was twisted in death. The biker's fingers had dug deeply into her soft white flesh. Her eyes were open, bloodshot. I tore my gaze away from her face, but it was too late. That image was seared into my brain forever; it would fuel my nightmares.

It was not an easy job breaking loose the biker's rigored

grip on Maria's neck. I concentrated on the hands and didn't look at her face. Then I kicked the dope dealer off her and gently carried her to the sofa. I covered her with a sheet I found in a nearby bedroom.

I sat down in a tattered easy chair and looked over at the shrouded figure that had once been my wife. Her silky blue robe trailed out from beneath the sheet. I wondered why I couldn't cry. Perhaps because I felt no sorrow. I felt nothing. Was it shock? Or had I gone beyond emotion? Somehow I knew I couldn't be that lucky. The pain would come later. The numbness, too, would pass.

The draped form that was the woman I loved just lay there, a mute testament to the loss of everything fine in the world. Maria was gone, I hoped to someplace kinder than this world, someplace where she could be happy again, someplace that would rekindle that marvelous glow that once had sparkled behind her blue eyes.

But her leaving had punched an ugly hole in the world. It was a dark pit full of all those things that should have been but never will be. Its sides were lined with all the paintings Maria would never create, all the songs she'd never play. In it slept the children she and I would never raise, a million unrealized smiles, almost as many lost kisses and caresses, a cache of secrets and joys unshared, countless troubles we would have overcome together, and a billion precious moments that had our names on them. Gone forever an entire lifetime of lost treasures. All gone . . . fading to a phantom-like zone of unreality. The flame had been extinguished, and I had slept right through it. Decades of darkness stretched out before me. Maria was gone.

It was a truth I couldn't seem to accept even though her corpse lay only a few feet away.

I pulled my .45 out and stared down into the cool beckoning darkness of its barrel. I couldn't imagine what it would be like without Maria. It wasn't supposed to end like that. She was getting better.

No, that was only a dream we had shared that last night together. A lovely dream . . . and it was over. Once a berserker, always a berserker. So unfair.

The gun was cool in my grip. I popped the clip to check the load. Six bullets in the magazine, one in the chamber. I doubted I'd need more than one. I pushed the clip back in place and cocked the hammer.

As soon as I did that, I knew I'd never be able to put the barrel in my mouth and pull the trigger. I'm not put together that way. Too much Catholic schooling. Suicide is the ultimate taboo. I let the hammer down gently and shoved the .45 back into my holster.

For the next half hour I sat with Maria. I thought about our life together. I remembered it all, good and bad. There was so much more good than I had ever realized before. I could taste the sweetness that was our life together. It should never have ended.

Finally, I said goodbye.

I found a five-gallon can of gas in the garage and carried it into the house. She had the dog lying at her feet already, just as in *Beau Geste*. Maria would appreciate a Viking funeral. I splashed the can's contents all over the living room. The only thing that didn't get doused was Maria's body. I couldn't bring myself to do that.

I poured a thin trail of gasoline out into the dining room, but the petrol ran out before I reached the kitchen. I spotted a box of large wooden matches sitting on a shelf above the stove. I remembered how Maria liked to keep an orderly kitchen. Everything always where it was supposed to be. All gone now. No more order. Chaos and the road awaited.

The flipped match ignited the petrol. I was driven back into the kitchen by an irresistible wave of heat. The flames danced a funereal ballet. The house quickly filled with smoke. I found myself out on the lawn, coughing.

I backed away from the inferno and silently watched as my life was consumed by flame. Then I did something I haven't done in over a decade. I said a prayer. I prayed for Maria's soul. I hope God is a merciful and forgiving Being. None of this was her fault.

Maria's funeral pyre would burn just fine without my tending it. The house was far enough from any woods so that I didn't have to worry about the fire spreading. It was time for me to hit the road. It was time to get lost out on the highways.

I wiped a hand across my burning eyes and headed for the patrol car.

*   *   *

A fire truck, followed by two carloads of volunteer firemen, passed me on my way into town. I didn't slow down. Their arrival didn't trouble me. The house was already too far gone for them to do anything but watch.

Maria would have found their presence amusing. A fine turnout of mourners for her wake by the good citizens of Blennum. Not bad for the pariah of Shandaken.

As I passed through Blennum, Sheriff Towner tried to flag me down. Explaining why I torched one of the houses in his fair town was more trouble than it was worth. So I drove by, pretending I didn't see him. I figured he'd come after me, so I pulled one of the Ingrams out from under the front seat, but Towner never popped up in my rearview mirror. Part of me was disappointed. A little violence would have felt good. Feeling anything would have been an improvement.

I drove. My eyes obviously saw the road even if I didn't. Farms and villages flashed by my window without registering. I was on some kind of shock-induced autopilot. The miles disappeared without notice. I was lost within the emptiness. So lost, I was almost home before I realized it. Home? What possessed me to go there? It was where the heart was, for Christ's sake. I realized my autopilot had brought me there to get my stuff. I would just pack up and beat it. Seemed I'd been making some decisions while tooling down unseen roads.

It took me a while to find the two unmatched suitcases I remembered having. They finally turned up under the bed. I quickly stuffed them with whatever clothes I thought I'd need. My shaving kit fit in with no trouble. As soon as I closed the cases, I took them out and threw them into the backseat of the crusier.

In the back room, I dug out a couple of sleeping bags, a tent, and whatever other camping gear I thought would come in handy. I transferred all this equipment to the car's trunk. It was a tight fit.

Next came the firearms and ammo. I'd amassed quite a collection of rifles and pistols over the last few years. They had to come with me. Those I didn't use I could trade on the road. A gun's the best legal tender a man can carry.

From the kitchen, I gathered up a few pots and pans, some cutlery. I filled a box with food, mostly canned goods, and chowed down on some dried meat as I packed. I wondered if I should take more along. There was no telling how tough it was going to be to get a meal where I was going. Where was I going? I didn't know. Didn't care, either. Just wanted to be away.

The only photo I took was the smiling portrait of Maria from the mantelpiece.

I tossed a few last things into the car and left. As I drove off, I didn't bother to lock up or look back. There was no one there to say goodbye to. Before I knew it, I was in town, cruising past the station house without stopping. I turned off at the nearest exit, to avoid hitting Main Street.

The guards at the town's fortifications passed me through without my even stopping. I turned south onto Route 28. Maybe I'd head down to the sunbelt. Florida might be a good place to visit. No winters down there. No snow. The easy life.

I drove about a quarter mile down the road and stopped before I even realized I'd made the decision. That was okay. I decided to let my impulses rule me. No more planning. No more thinking. No more . . .

I stopped for one last look at the ol' homestead before I became one with the interstates. Aside from what I could fit into the car, the only baggage I'll ever carry with me is memory.

Actually, Shandaken wasn't a bad place to live. Looking back on the peaceful little village will soften the edges of my remembrance. The people were always good to me, even if they didn't treat Maria all that swell near the end. I guess I can't blame them. Maria was death. No one wants to get too close to death. Despite everything, I will miss them. I may even forgive Mayor Hayden someday.

They'll make out fine without me. Someone will take over my job. A week from now, it will be as if I never existed. A year from now, a visitor will be hard pressed to find anyone who remembers me.

I was simply a little cog in the machinery. A new cog will take my place and everything will continue to roll along as always.

As for myself, I'm going to get lost. No more responsibility. No more duty. No more pain . . . no more caring. I'll let the days drift past without numbering them. That way I won't be bothered by what I've gained or lost when they finally run out.

Let Josh worry about tomorrow. Let him weather the crisis. He can tell the children what it was like before the berserkers came. Josh can help form the future. He still believes. He still eares. That means he's still fully alive.

Let's face it, I'm not as strong as Josh. All caring is now beyond my reach. I've no one but me to worry about now. There's no room left inside me for anyone else's problems. I've become a road person. From now on, I travel alone from one small town to the next until death catches up with me.

I'm sorry, but I can't take any more. There's too much pain. Too much loss. Too much responsibility. I don't have what it takes to fight back anymore. It's someone else's turn to play Wyatt Earp.

Storm clouds fill the sky over Shandaken. I watch the heavy Catskill winds push their dark and billowing forms over the towering mountain peaks. I feel as if I've fallen into a painting by J.W.M. Turner. I have no idea how long I stand there looking up into the sky. Finally the rain begins to fall. It feels cool and oddly forgiving on my face.

I walk back to the patrol car, turn it around, and drive back into town. Maybe I'll stay another day or so. I really hate traveling in the rain.

About the Authors

JIM STARLIN

This talented forty-year-old native son of Detroit has spent his last nineteen years in New York State, following a three and a half year hitch in the navy. Although his time in New York, most of which he spent working for the two big comic-book publishers (Marvel and D.C. Comics) was interrupted by a year and a half sojourn in California, Jim decided that California was just "a nice place to visit." During his California idyll, he did manage to find the time to work in animation for both Ralph Bakshi and the Hanna Barbera studios.

His return to the East in the year of the bicentennial marked the beginning of a serious romance with wife, illustrator and, much more recently, co-author—Daina Graziunas. Jim's professional track record has included stints at other comic publishers, as well as a *New York Times* bestselling graphic novel, *The Death of Captain Marvel*.

DAINA GRAZIUNAS

Born thirty-seven years ago in the mythic borough of Brooklyn, New York, Daina survived many years of parochial schooling with seemingly few ill effects. She followed up a short stint at Queens College with a short marriage.

Things began looking up from then on. She was graduated from the School of Visual Arts (illustration department) in 1977, a year after she and Jim became thick as thieves, and after years of trying to make pictures together they now write. (A good thing too, since his pictures were about death and violence, hers about sex. In writing they happily manage to encompass all three.)

Jim and Daina live in a small town in upstate New York in the Catskills, with a pantheon of three cats named Electra, Oedipuss, and Medusa.